The Chinese Alchemist

*Berkley Prime Crime Books
by Lyn Hamilton*

THE XIBALBA MURDERS
THE MALTESE GODDESS
THE MOCHE WARRIOR
THE CELTIC RIDDLE
THE AFRICAN QUEST
THE ETRUSCAN CHIMERA
THE THAI AMULET
THE MAGYAR VENUS
THE MOAI MURDERS
THE ORKNEY SCROLL
THE CHINESE ALCHEMIST

THE
Chinese
Alchemist

LYN HAMILTON

BERKLEY PRIME CRIME, NEW YORK

THE BERKELY PUBLISHING GROUP
Published by the Penguin Group
Penguin Group (USA) Inc.
375 Hudson Street, New York, New York 10014, USA
Penguin Group (Canada), 90 Eglinton Avenue East, Suite 700, Toronto, Ontario M4P 2Y3, Canada
(a division of Pearson Penguin Canada Inc.)
Penguin Books Ltd., 80 Strand, London WC2R 0RL, England
Penguin Group Ireland, 25 St. Stephen's Green, Dublin 2, Ireland (a division of Penguin Books Ltd.)
Penguin Group (Australia), 250 Camberwell Road, Camberwell, Victoria 3124, Australia
(a division of Pearson Australia Group Pty. Ltd.)
Penguin Books India Pvt. Ltd., 11 Community Centre, Panchsheel Park, New Delhi—110 017, India
Penguin Group (NZ), 67 Apollo Drive, Mairangi Bay, Auckland 1311, New Zealand
(a division of Pearson New Zealand Ltd.)
Penguin Books (South Africa) (Pty.) Ltd., 24 Sturdee Avenue, Rosebank, Johannesburg 2196,
South Africa

Penguin Books Ltd., Registered Offices: 80 Strand, London WC2R 0RL, England

This book is an original publication of The Berkley Publishing Group.

This is a work of fiction. Names, characters, places, and incidents either are the product of the author's imagination or are used fictitiously, and any resemblance to actual persons, living or dead, business establishments, events, or locales is entirely coincidental. The publisher does not have any control over and does not assume any responsibility for author or third-party websites or their content.

First edition: April 2007

Library of Congress Cataloging-in-Publication Data

Hamilton, Lyn.
    The Chinese alchemist / Lyn Hamilton. — 1st ed.
        p. cm.
    ISBN 978-0-425-21395-7
    1. Antique dealers—Fiction.   2. New York (N.Y.)—Fiction.   3. Beijing (China)—Fiction.
I.Title.

    PR9199.3.H323C48 2007
    813'.54—dc22

                                                                            2006038921

PRINTED IN THE UNITED STATES OF AMERICA

10   9   8   7   6   5   4   3   2   1

To Mary Jane Maffini,
fellow mystery writer and great friend

ACKNOWLEDGMENTS

Thank you to Yvonne Chiu for her support and for sharing her memories of her childhood in China with me, and to Dr. John Marshall for his advice on medical matters. My primary source for information on life in T'ang China was Charles Benn's *China's Golden Age: Everyday Life in the Tang Dynasty*. All errors, however, are my own.

A note on spelling of Chinese words: There are two main systems, Wade-Giles and pinyin. I confess I have blithely moved between the two, usually opting for the spelling that I think will be easier for readers.

The Chinese Alchemist

Prologue

I used to believe that brigands lurked in the bamboo forests at the edge of our garden, and that a ghost haunted the well. It was Auntie Chang who told me about the brigands. I expect she said that to frighten me, to make sure I did not stray far from home. It may be, though, that she especially didn't want me to go to that part of our property. The brigands didn't worry me. When I grew up, I planned to be a brave soldier in the service of the emperor, just like Number Two Brother. Brigands would have cause to fear me.

The ghost was a different matter. She was an ugly woman with disheveled hair and eyes that burned through you. I knew that because Auntie Chang had seen the ghost, and was very frightened. She said it is someone whose hun *had escaped the body, and that the ghost could not rest until the proper rites were performed, and the corpse's mouth sealed with jade so the hun could not escape.*

Sometimes I dreamed that Number One Sister had joined the

brigands in the bamboo, that the eerie knocking sound bamboo makes as the wind blows through it was Number One Sister sending me a message. Number One Sister, you see, had simply vanished from my life. One day she was there, the next morning she was gone.

If Number One Sister was not with the brigands, then she had run away to the Gay Quarter to become a dancer. I thought that would be exciting, too. I decided that when I was older and able to make my way about the city as I pleased, I'd look for her there. She would be wearing gowns of the finest silk in the latest fashion, with jade and pearls and kingfisher feathers, and all the men would cheer as she danced and sang. She sang and danced very well; that I knew, having watched her when she thought she was alone. When I found her, I would cheer, too.

I missed my sister. She was the only one who would play in the gardens with me, and she also let me watch while she put her hair up in elaborate tall bindings. Her favorite styles were flower bindings, where she wove most favored peonies into her hair. When she was married, she told me, she would be able to go into the streets with her hair made up so. She was also the only member of the family who would play with me in the snow, the rest of them preferring to huddle behind screens to cut the drafts or hold their hands to braziers for warmth. I was grateful for these moments with my sister. Number One Brother was too busy studying for his civil service examinations to pay any attention to me. He was angry when I interrupted him. He told me his future depended on success in the examinations. I didn't know why he would say that when he could be a brigand instead. Number Two Brother simply ignored me.

The drums of the Imperial Palace are now sounding. Soon the drums of the city will do the same, and the doors of the wards will shut for the night. It was on one such night that Number One Sister *did not return until dawn. Our father waited by the gates all the night long, afraid that she would be found outside and beaten by the Gold Bird Guard, twenty blows of the rod for remaining outside our ward during the night.*

It was shortly after that event that Number One Sister disappeared for good. I did not understand why she didn't say good-bye.

One

THE FIRST SIGN THAT THERE WAS SOMETHING amiss came in the form of a phone call from someone suggesting he was ready to install fire detection equipment in my home. I said there must be some mistake, even though he had quite correctly asked for Lara McClintoch. He disagreed. He had my name, address, and phone number. I said I already had smoke detectors, thank you very much. The next day, another man called to say he wanted to book a time to pour the new concrete in my basement. I have rather lovely Mexican tiles, all in good repair, in my basement. Both men spoke with a foreign accent I couldn't pinpoint, and sounded as if they had socks in their mouths. Within a few hours of casually, or perhaps not so casually, mentioning these calls to my partner, Rob Luczka, a sergeant in the Royal Canadian Mounted Police, I found myself living in a hotel.

It seems that Rob, of whom I am inordinately fond, had seriously annoyed members of a gang that was terrorizing the merchants of Chinatown. These thugs called themselves Golden Lotus, which just goes to prove you should never judge an organization by its name. I suppose that is his job, annoying bad guys. Still, I had never thought it would have much to do with me, other than the fact that I occasionally worry myself sick about him when he's off on some assignment.

"Why exactly am I here?" I said in a tone I seem to acquire when I'm unnerved. I was finding it a tad stressful, all that slapping stuff into a suitcase and running around the house to see that everything was turned off so that my smoke detectors would not have to be put to good use through some fault of my own, as opposed to malfeasance on the part of men with socks in their mouths.

"You are here because some very nasty people have figured out that you are a person of some importance to me," he said. "They probably know that because I live right next door and spend a lot of time going out my gate and in yours for sleepovers. Now if you'd let me knock down the wall between our two houses so I would not have to brave rain, snow, sleet, and hostile neighborhood dogs to pay a visit, they might not have known that."

"If this is a ploy to get me to move in with you, it isn't exactly working."

"No? They were trying to tell you they are going to burn your house down with you in it. Either that or kill you by some other means and bury you in your own basement."

"Burn my house down!" I said. "They can't do that. Our

cottages were built in 1887 and are protected under the Ontario Heritage Act!"

"The Heritage Act! I wonder why the brains at headquarters didn't think of that. These lowlifes extort, rob, and kill on a whim, and so far we haven't been able to stop them. But then, just like that, you come up with the Heritage Act."

I looked at him for a moment. Rob, unlike me, is hardly ever sarcastic. "You're really worried about this, aren't you?" I said.

"I wouldn't want you to think I cared," he said, looking away.

"I'd never think that. Jennifer is safe, isn't she?"

"I don't think these guys from Golden Lotus would go to Taiwan to find her, no. That at least is working in our favor." Jennifer, Rob's daughter, was teaching English in Taiwan for a year. We worried about her, of course, but right now Taiwan sounded better than Toronto where her personal safety was concerned.

"Good. Everything will be fine. Now, what's my name again?"

"Charlyn Krahn," he said. "We're Herb and Charlyn Krahn. Please try to remember to sign all chits that way."

"Are the Krahns paying for this?" I said.

"They are, indeed. Nice of them. I even have a credit card with Herb's name on it, compliments of my employer."

"So what happens now? This is a short version of the witness protection program, right? Which is to say, how long do we get to lounge about in this hotel? I can go to work, even if you can't?"

"It is the considered opinion of my superiors that, no, as an undercover officer I am to stay out of sight, and yes, you can go into the shop. Someone will be keeping an eye on the place and if there's any sign of trouble, then we'll reassess. I know you don't want to leave the redoubtable Clive in charge for too long."

Clive Swain is my ex-husband and my partner in an antiques business called McClintoch & Swain. And no, I don't like to leave Clive alone in the shop for too long. I usually return from my buying trips to find the store completely rearranged, and not always, which is to say almost never, to my liking. "As for how long, it shouldn't take long. My brothers in the force will take care of these people," Rob said.

"What does 'take care of these people' mean?"

"Whatever it takes," he said. "In the meantime, we're having an all-expenses-paid holiday. Now let's see what's on the room service menu."

As pleasant as an all-expenses-paid stay in a pretty nice hotel sounds, with someone cooking and cleaning and even making the bed every day, I can tell you it is amusing for about forty-eight hours. After that it gets a little claustrophobic, the room service fare starts to taste like prison food, assuming prison food tastes the way I think it does, and generally your roommate begins to get tiresome. I believe the feeling was mutual. If we ever move in together, the place will have to be very large, something on the scale of, say, Versailles.

So it was that what I consider to be my acutely sensitive nose for dissimilitude was not working as it should, so eager was I to get out of the place. What I saw as a godsend, but was really a trap—which if not set for me, certainly caught me in its snare—came in the form of a call to the shop on a fine autumn day from one Dorothy Matthews, known to her friends as Dory.

"I have a favor to ask," she began.

"Ask away," I said.

"It's more of a proposal than a favor, although I would be exceedingly grateful if you would undertake it for me. I suppose I'm actually asking two favors. Would you consider having lunch with me at my home? I need to show you something, and my arthritis is acting up today. Taking it to you at McClintoch and Swain, no matter how much I might enjoy it once I got there, would be difficult. Would one o'clock work for you?"

"I'll be there," I said.

The maid was setting out a plate of sandwiches and some fruit when I arrived shortly after one. Dory was in an arm-chair, a cane at her side, and she greeted me warmly. I first met Dory when I was researching Chinese bronzes for a client of McClintoch & Swain. At that time, Dory was the curator of the Cottingham Museum's Asian galleries, hav-ing been lured there from her position at one of Canada's most prestigious galleries by Major Cottingham when he first opened the museum to house his private collection. Within five years, the Cottingham's Asian galleries had not only expanded, but had earned an international reputation, all thanks to Dory. Everything I know about Chinese art and antiquities, I learned from Dory Matthews.

People who knew Dory by reputation only, as a preemi-nent scholar of Chinese history and art, were surprised to meet her in person, not expecting the Asian woman in front of them. She got Dory from her English mother, and Matthews from her husband, the industrialist George Norfolk Matthews. Born Dorothy Zhang, or more accurately Zhang Dorothy in 1944 in Beijing, she was taken to England by her mother in 1949 as the Communists took power, eventually settling in Canada. It was a harrowing experience, she told me, getting out of China. In the chaos of that time, with so many people trying to leave the country before the Communist forces of Mao Zedong took over, she and her mother became separated from her father. She never saw him again. She was led to believe that her father had survived, but had never joined them, choosing instead to become a part of the People's Republic of China. She believed that at one time, at least, he held a senior position in the government of Mao's Communist China, having been a loyal supporter of Mao, most notably having accompanied Mao on the Long March in 1934. This was one of the most famous strategic retreats in history, a five-thousand-mile march that took just over a year, but which enabled Mao to break through the Koumintang lines and eventually push the Koumintang, and their leader, Chiang Kai-Shek, off the Chinese mainland to Taiwan, then called Formosa. Dory thought she might even have had other siblings in China, a half-brother or sister, although she never tried to find them. Dory's mother remarried, whether or not exactly legally, neither I nor perhaps Dory was ever entirely sure. I think she probably just said her Chinese union wasn't legal, and carried on.

Once we were alone, and I was tucking into my lunch—I noticed she wasn't eating—she began to talk. "You are aware, I'm sure, that it is not really ethical for a curator to personally collect in the area in which he or she works. My husband has collected for some years, and I gave him advice as often as I could, but never when the object he wanted could be considered Asian art. But now that I am under no such restriction, I feel that I can get into the market, if I wish to do so. Would you agree?"

"Sure," I said. "Why not?"

"Good," she said. "I was worried what you would think about that."

"Why would you? I'm assuming you're not trying to smuggle antiquities out of some country, or buy on the black market."

She was silent for a moment. "Do you know how my stepfather made his fortune?" she said at last.

I decided I'd better stop stuffing my face with her lovely homemade sandwiches—such a nice change from hotel fare—and pay attention, as this conversation did not seem to be following a nicely logical path, and there were some undercurrents, possibly disturbing ones. "Didn't you tell me he imported china and porcelain, some of it from Occupied Japan after the war? Or was it Hong Kong?"

"Both," she said. "That's how he made his living. He made his fortune by importing very high-end Chinese antiquities, by which I mean very old imperial treasures, sometimes even older than that, a lot of them smuggled out of China and into Hong Kong, where they joined his regular shipments. He used a contact of my mother's to do so, a high party official in Mao's regime, someone I have come to believe was my father. If so, my father had no compunction feathering his nest by selling whatever he could get his hands on, and in his position that was quite a bit, and my stepfather had no compunction expediting its passage out of the country, and making a good deal of money for himself as well."

"I can understand why this would bother you for any number of reasons," I said carefully. "I'm not sure, though, what you mean by 'smuggled.' It really depends when the objects came out of China, as you know only too well. There was a period when a lot of antiques and antiquities were considered decadent imperialist trappings by the Communist Party, and nobody cared if they were taken out of the country or even destroyed."

"It may have been legally acceptable, but it was never morally acceptable," Dory said. "So is what I am about to ask you to do legal? Of course it is. Ethical? I suppose that depends on what I propose to do with what you get for me—if, that is, you agree to do it. I promised to show you something. Would you mind going over to the walnut cabinet? On the lower left side there is something wrapped in cloth. I want you to bring it here so that we can look at it together."

"It" was an exquisite rectangular silver box with a hinged and rounded lid, of a shape sometimes referred to as a casket. Incised on the top was a bird, and a scene showing a number of women together in a garden wrapped around the four sides. "May I open it?" I asked. I believe I was whispering.

Dory nodded. Inside, along the sides and bottom, were Chinese characters. I couldn't read them, but I thought perhaps Dory could. I closed it carefully.

"Beautiful," I said. "Very old." I waited for her to say something.

"T'ang dynasty," she said. "You know when that was, of course."

"Don't tell me," I said. "I'll remember. T'ang dynasty is, just a minute, 618 to 907. Capital was Chang'an, essentially where the city of Xi'an is now. It was preceded by the Sui dynasty, and followed by the Five Dynasties Era and then the Song, Yuan, Ming, and Qing dynasties in that order. How am I doing?"

Dory smiled. "For a time I thought you would never learn! I know you regarded me as a stubborn old bat for making you memorize all the dynasties, but really, if you don't know your dynasties, you don't know your Chinese history, and for sure you don't know your Chinese antiques."

"Not so. I never thought you were a stubborn old bat, and furthermore, I like to think I'm your most accomplished student," I said, and she actually laughed, something I hadn't heard her do much lately.

"I think you may well be," she said.

I looked at it a little longer. "Beautiful workmanship," I said. "I've never seen anything remotely like it. But what is it exactly you want me to do, Dory?"

Rather than answering me directly, she slowly and painfully reached for something in a magazine rack to one side of her chair, and set in front of me the catalog for the annual Oriental auction at Molesworth & Cox in New York. A yellow sticky marked a page on which was shown another silver box.

"You're selling it," I said. "No, just a minute." I eyed the box in front of me. It was about six inches long, four inches wide, and maybe six or seven inches high measured to the top of the domed lid. "The one for.sale looks very similar, but I think it's slightly smaller all'round."

"Very observant," Dory said. "And you are quite right. They are almost identical, although I believe the text inside is different, the scene depicted on the outside is as well, and mine is larger. I think there is a series of boxes designed to fit inside each other, like those Russian dolls. There will be a third in silver even bigger than this one, and possibly a fourth box in wood rather than silver—the largest, at least that is what my stepfather said—but of course the wood is unlikely to have survived. The silver, in the proper circumstances, would have."

"You want me to go to New York next week to bid on this box for you," I said. My heart soared. I'd still be staying in a hotel, of course, but it would be a different hotel. Even better, I wouldn't have to look over my shoulder for gangsters every time I left it, nor would I trip over Rob's feet every time I turned around.

"Would you consider doing just that? I would pay your expenses of course, plus something for your time, and I would pay you a commission if we get it."

"Sure," I said. "I'll see if Alex will come into the shop to help Clive out for a few days. I'd like to go early and get a good look at this at the preview to make sure it's authentic before we buy it."

"You should go right away," Dory said. "But is it authentic? Almost certainly. You see, this silver box in front of us is one of three that my stepfather smuggled to Hong Kong, and thence to North America where they were auctioned off one at a time in the mid–nineteen seventies. I expect my stepfather believed that he could get a better price if he sold them separately, although I'm not so sure he was right. George, my husband, bought it at auction about ten years ago. Have I ever showed you his collection? Please, have a look in the next room."

The room was lined with built-in shelving divided into twelve-inch squares and fronted by glass doors. In each of the squares was a single object, lit from above. On one wall, which was dark, the objects were in sealed display cases, and the humidity and temperature in each was being monitored. "May I turn on the light on the end wall?" I called out to Dory, and did so when she agreed. These objects were really, really old, some old silver bowls, a couple of gold boxes, and a number of puzzling objects I couldn't identify. It took me several minutes to figure out what this collection was all about. "Medical equipment of some kind," I said finally.

"Correct," Dory said from the next room. "My husband, as you know, is head of an international pharmaceutical company, and he collects objects related to that business. There are molds for pills, very old syringes, beakers, and boxes that would have been used for medicinal herbs. It is quite an extensive and unusual collection. Some of the objects there are over two thousand years old."

"Maybe these should be in a museum," I said.

"George has finally agreed that when he dies they will, indeed, go to a museum."

"I hope you have a good security system."

"Oh, yes. I turned it off just for you to see the collection. The door here is usually closed and locked."

"So does this box have something to do with medicine,

or did it just come in a lot with something your husband wanted?"

"Inside the box is a process for making something," Dory said. "It tells you to heat the ingredients, unspecified, in a sealed container for thirty-six hours, and then to partake of the resulting substance for seven days. George interpreted it as a process for making drugs, and that is why he acquired it. It's Chinese, so he didn't discuss it with me for reasons I have already explained. I recognized it as soon as I set eyes on it, however. I saw the three boxes when my stepfather got them. I fell in love with them, but he sold them, over my protests. George found this one, a second has turned up in New York that I plan through you to purchase, and I hope to find the third before I die. George and I may be the only people, along with you now, who know that this is part of a nesting set. When I find all three of them, I plan to give them to the Shaanxi History Museum in Xi'an, China. I want them to go home."

"That is very generous of you. This will not come cheap. You have to think about how much you'll pay for it. We'll get you registered as an absentee bidder and establish your credit worthiness through Molesworth and Cox here, and I'll also arrange to be on the telephone with you for the bidding. I'll book my flight as soon as I get back to the shop."

She nodded. "Thank you, but I don't want to register as a bidder, absentee or otherwise. I am going to transfer a great deal of money to your account, and you are going to be the bidder. I don't want anyone to know I am attempting to purchase this."

"I could head for Brazil with your money," I said.

"You could, but I know that you won't. It is possible, by the way, that Burton Haldimand, representing the Cottingham Museum, may be after this as well. I hope to outbid them. I would most particularly not want Dr. Haldimand to know of my involvement in this."

I opened my mouth to say something, but then decided against it. What I wanted to ask was if this last stipulation was what her request was really about. You see, when Major Cottingham died and control of the board of directors went to his trophy wife, Courtney, a decision was made that new blood was required at the museum. In the case of Dory's job as curator of the Asian galleries, that new blood came in the form of Burton Haldimand. It was all done rather lavishly, of course, in true Cottingham style, with an elaborate farewell dinner for Dory, and the gift of a watercolor by one of China's leading nineteenth-century artists. There were hosts of speeches, including a very gracious one by Dory welcoming Burton to the position she was leaving. Only those of us who knew her well were aware that Dory was devastated. To her credit, none of us had ever heard her criticize the museum, or for that matter, Burton Haldimand for getting her job.

It took her awhile to get her equilibrium back, if she really ever did. At first, she would come and just sit in a chair at McClintoch & Swain, chatting away to my neighbor and sometimes employee Alex Stewart, who is getting along in years himself. Clive and I were glad to have their company, and it certainly didn't bother the customers. In fact, the only member of the McClintoch & Swain team who seemed less than enthusiastic about Dory was Diesel, the orange cat who guards the store for us. That was undoubtedly because Dory insisted upon making a fuss over Diesel and kept trying to pet him, something this particular cat abhors. The minute Dory came through the door, Diesel would turn his full attention and his considerable talent for spotting shoplifters to the back room.

I don't know whether the shock of being replaced had anything to do with it, but Dory's arthritis, well under control while she worked, had been steadily getting worse through her forced retirement, and soon she had to abandon even those outings. It was a shame, really, not the least because I didn't think Burton could hold a candle to Dory. It would be my pleasure to help outbid him.

It was unseasonably warm in New York when I got there. The Molesworth & Cox Oriental auction was the first of the season and had attracted a lot of attention. There were some wonderful objects in the show, and the people at the auction house were justifiably proud, managing to get some play in the *New York Times*. Unhappily, the silver box was one of the objects featured, almost certainly ensuring I would have more competition for it.

Consequently, there were a lot of people interested in the sale, some of them with major museums, and the usual suspects in terms of collectors. At the preview, the first person I saw was a curator from the Smithsonian. The second person I saw was Dr. Burton Haldimand.

Mention the name Burton Haldimand in certain circles, and you're almost certain to be subjected to a wide range of opinion. To wit: Haldimand is exceptionally talented, perhaps even a genius, and he should be forgiven a few eccentricities. Or: Haldimand may be talented, but he is also the most ruthlessly ambitious person in the whole field of museology, and woe betide anyone who gets in his way. And finally: Haldimand is not so much eccentric as seriously disturbed.

All of these things were true. Haldimand came to the Cottingham with a reputation as an expert in Chinese antiquities, and I'd never heard anyone say he wasn't as represented. I'd had few dealings with him, but I was certainly prepared to acknowledge that he was good at his job. There was no question he was ambitious. No sooner had he taken over responsibility for the Chinese galleries than he set his sights on the furniture galleries as well. So far the targeted curator had managed to fend him off, but I wasn't sure for how long. Burton seemed to have a way of insinuating himself into good standing with the powers that be anywhere he worked, and generally got what he wanted.

More than anything else, though, few could deny that Haldimand was very odd. Haldimand, you see, had a thing about germs. Even in the warmest weather—and that day in New York was no exception—he wore a scarf, almost always an azure color, and gloves. True, museologists often wear gloves to protect the objects they are handling. This is not what I am talking about here. Haldimand wore gloves all the time, those plastic surgical gloves which he removed the way surgeons do, wiggling their way out of them so that they never actually touch the outside of them with their bare fingers. He wore them under winter mittens. He also, if Cottingham Museum staff were to be believed, sprayed his desk and all objects on it, including the phone, with disinfectant every evening when he left, and then again in the morning when he arrived. I have no idea why, other than he thought the cleaning staff must be running a business out of his office at night.

If you went to a meeting in his office—which wasn't often given that you could hardly hear yourself think over the drone of the huge air filter he had there—he probably sprayed your chair after you left. He was always dosing himself with some remedy or prophylactic. His assistant, one Marla Chappell, said he had a cupboard full of medicines of all sorts, homeopathic and otherwise. She also maintained that he never used the toilets, either staff or public, at the Cottingham. Fortunately he lived close enough, and apparently had a strong enough bladder to wait until he went home at lunchtime, and then again after work. It probably explained why he was never seen with a cup of coffee in his hand.

In flu season, he augmented his scarf with a surgical mask. When Toronto was hit with the horrible SARS outbreak, he called in sick, holed himself up in his Victorian townhouse in the Annex neighborhood, and didn't come out until the all clear had been sounded. Mind you, the all clear was sounded a little prematurely, which probably brought Burton to the brink of mental collapse, given that he'd ventured abroad too soon. Somehow he survived. We all speculated that he must have had quite the supply of food stashed away to outlast the germs. He most certainly wouldn't have been calling for pizza delivery.

Despite this, or possibly because of it, Burton seemed to be sick more often than average. He always seemed to have a cough or the sniffles, a headache or some tummy upset.

Sick or well, though, Burton knew his stuff. He was intent upon building up the T'ang dynasty collection at the Cottingham, and while Dory had had to tell me the silver box was T'ang, Burton headed straight for it. There was none of the pretend-I'm-not-interested approach of many buyers at auction previews. Under the watchful eye of a Molesworth & Cox staff person, Burton picked it up—he was allowed to do that given he was wearing gloves—and scarcely concealed his glee. It was not until he had examined it in minute detail through a magnifying glass, as I had done a few minutes earlier, that he noticed me.

"Lara!" he said. "What a pleasure." For once, Burton looked to be in better shape than I was, the picture of health, in fact: just the right amount of tan for the fall that said he got enough sun, but not too much, and a general spring in his step. I, on the other hand, was nursing a cold, and had been for a couple of weeks. It was more nuisance than anything else at this stage, and something I attributed to stale hotel air, but I couldn't shake it, and continued to blow my nose at regular intervals. Feeling this way also made me grumpy, and seeing someone I was not fond of in such glowing health was something of an annoyance.

Needless to say, Burton did not extend his hand for a polite handshake, my having managed to sneeze twice since I entered the room. He may have had gloves on, but I didn't. He spoke a bit loudly, as he had the habit of standing well away from those to whom he spoke. Someone must have told him that germs could travel no more than six feet because that was about how far away from me he'd placed himself. He would have had a rather trying time at those cocktail receptions the Cottingham threw for high-end donors.

"Something special you're looking at?" he went on.

"The same thing you are, I expect," I said.

"The cloisonné vase, you mean?" he said, coyly.

"Exactly," I said.

"Oh, ho," he said in a jovial tone. "McClintoch and Swain are aiming for a wealthier clientele, are they? I hate to tell you, but this one starts well into six figures."

"The cloisonné vase?" I said. "That would be a little high, wouldn't it?" I had him there. He was tripping over his own lies.

"I know you're after the silver *coffret à bijoux*," he said. If there is a fancy term for anything, in this case French for "jewelry case," Burton was almost certain to use it. "You can't fool me. And you can't afford it either."

"Quite right, Burton. Under normal circumstances I couldn't, but I'm buying for a client, I'm happy to say. It's somebody else's money, so it's no problem." In fact I had half a million dollars of Dory's money in a trust account, although I promised her I'd spend as little of it as I could.

"I see," he said. "Still, I rather suspect that you won't have the resources of the Cottingham estate. I hope you won't be too disappointed if I get it. It's better that way in any event. It's a public institution and far more people will have the opportunity to enjoy it. It will be the anchor piece of our Asian galleries. You know that is what the Cottingham tries to do, to have at least one piece of international importance in each of its galleries. Now we'll have Lingfei."

I knew about anchor pieces all right. I'd nearly been

killed over one of the museum's so-called anchor pieces, a twenty-something-thousand-year-old mammoth ivory carving called The Magyar Venus, although what this Lingfei business was about I had no idea. "My client plans to donate it to a worthy museum," I said. It is possible I put just the slightest emphasis on the word "worthy." Haldimand was starting to get up my sore nose.

"I don't suppose you'd tell me the name of your client," he said, seemingly oblivious to my slight.

"No, I don't suppose I would," I said.

"The rules applying to auction houses with regard to revealing that information would not really apply to you, you know," he said.

"How exactly is that relevant here, Burton?" I replied. "My client wishes to remain anonymous, and I'm not going to tell you."

"Well then, may the best man win," he said. He sounded supremely confident. In retaliation, I took two germ-ridden steps toward him and stuck out my hand. He blanched, sort of waved in my general direction, flung his azure scarf over his shoulder and hurried away. "See you Thursday evening," he called out from a safe distance. "I hope you're feeling better. You should do something about that cold, you know. I'd suggest ginseng tea. You need to bolster your immune system."

"I've been taking echinacea," I said. Actually, my favorite cold remedy is a warm whiskey with honey and lemon at bedtime, but I didn't think Burton would be impressed.

He was not impressed by echinacea either, waving his hand in a disparaging gesture. "Too late for that, I'm afraid.

If you were familiar with the medical classic of the Yellow Emperor, you would know that your illness results from a disharmony of *qi*. You don't treat a formed illness. Rather you treat the unformed illness. In other words, you work to prevent illness, not treat it after you're sick. You have to say yes to good health."

"I'm sure you're right, Burton," I said. Personally I thought that what I needed was to be the successful bidder for the silver box. I might still have a cold, but I wouldn't care, and I would certainly feel better than he did, no matter how harmonious his qi. That and being able to move back home safely would add years to my life.

"Then farewell, my concubine," he said, blowing a kiss in my general direction.

"In your dreams, Burton," I replied, and heard his chuckle. It was difficult to think of Burton with a close companion. All those germs!

"Do you have any idea who that Yellow Emperor is?" I said to the representative of Molesworth & Cox, a young man by the name of Justin who was accompanying me while I assessed the merchandise.

"Absolutely no clue," Justin replied. "But if you're interested in immortality, perhaps I can help you."

I gave him a baleful glance. "A little joke, there," he said. "There's actually a formula for the elixir of immortality written in this box. You need a magnifying glass to read it, assuming you even know how to read Chinese. Let me go and get you the translation, just for fun."

He did just that, giving me a copy for my records. It did indeed contain a recipe. Apparently the elixir of immortality contains potable gold, realgar, cinnabar, salt, and powdered oyster shells.

"I'm sorry to say there are no details on the proportions of the ingredients, or instructions as to how to take it," Justin chuckled. I could have told him: you heat it in a sealed container for thirty-six hours and then take it for seven days. That information, according to Dory, was to be found in the box in her husband George's collection. This was indeed a very interesting collection of boxes. "Don't know about the potable gold. It seems too bad to drink it when you could wear it instead," he added, pulling up his shirt cuff to reveal a very impressive gold watch.

"Cinnabar," I said. "I know what that is. Lovely red color, but when you heat it you get some form of mercury."

"And realgar is arsenic," Justin said. "I asked."

"So I guess if you actually mix this up and take it for any length of time you're almost assured of immortality, although perhaps not in the form the person who wrote this had in mind."

"Perhaps not. Let me tell you about this box, though. It dates to T'ang China, specifically, we believe, to the reign of Emperor Xuanzong, known to us as Illustrious August. He's named in the text inside. He reigned from 712 to 756. Furthermore, apparently we know the box belonged to someone by the name of Lingfei who was probably a person of some importance in the court of Illustrious August."

This was all very interesting, not least because you have to love a guy who names himself Illustrious August. It was also considerably more information than Dory had given me, and explained Burton's reference to Lingfei. Regardless of its history, this box was a beauty, too. On the top was incised a bird, a magical crane, a symbol of immortality for the T'ang—at least, that's what Justin said. On the sides were depicted a woman of high standing, according to the write-up, and her maid servants, some of whom were playing instruments. If anything, it was even more beautiful than the one I'd seen at Dory's, perhaps because it was smaller, and the workmanship therefore more precise. In other words, the box was priceless. Still, someone had it, and wanted to sell it. The reserve bid was $200,000 as Dory and I both already knew, and the presale estimate was $300,000. And Burton and I were not the only people interested in it.

A young man of maybe thirty, Asian with stylish spiky black hair, was showing an inordinate interest, moving steadily closer as Justin talked to me about the box. He was dressed very fashionably, Hugo Boss, I'd say, except I was certain even from a distance of a few yards that it was knockoff Hugo Boss and not the real deal. Quality does tell, and I can usually spot a fake a mile off. China being the source of so many of the world's knockoffs, from Rolexes to Nikes, fakes are definitely a distinct possibility. But if you can't afford the real thing, then Molesworth & Cox's annual Oriental auction is not the place for you, unless, like me, you have a patron of considerable means.

Mr. Knockoff was trying to give the impression he was interested in something else, in this case the gorgeous cloisonné vase that Burton had pretended to want, Qing, pronounced "Ching," dynasty, which is to say 1644–1912. Dory would be proud of me. He wasn't any better at faking his interest in the vase than he was in faking his suit. He was definitely interested in the T'ang silver box. I didn't think he stood a chance.

Thursday evening I was in my favorite position at the back of the room, waiting for the silver box to come up. I had my paddle, and was ready to raise it as required. I was also calling up my killer instincts, something that was easy enough for me to do. I just thought of those thugs who were planning to firebomb my heritage cottage with me in it.

Burton was also at the back, but over to one side where perhaps he couldn't see very well, but where there were some empty seats on either side of him, providing a little buffer from the germs. He also had his cell phone out, but I didn't think he had to consult Courtney Cottingham about how much to pay. He would know very well how much he had to spend. Although it pained me to think so, it might even be more than Dory, for all her stepfather's and her husband's resources, could afford.

Mr. Knockoff, the Asian man with spiky hair and fake Hugo Boss was there, and he had a paddle. That would indicate that he was indeed interested in bidding on something, presumably, given his interest, the silver box, even if he didn't look to me as if he could afford it. Perhaps I should have tried to get a closer look at his suit, or perhaps my instinct for fakes only applied to furniture and not clothing. Or maybe the fake suit was designed to put people like me off their guard.

The T'ang box was to be auctioned relatively late in the evening, but both Burton and I were there right from the opening bid on the first object, a beautiful, and highly collectible, bronze *jia*, a three-legged vessel for heating wine, dating to the Shang period, or, as Dory had made me memorize, the eighteenth to the twelfth century BCE.

I called Dory, at home in her armchair, to tell her the auction was about to begin, being very careful not to call her by name in case Burton was eavesdropping. "Have you ascertained who might be bidding for the silver box?" she asked.

"The Cottingham Museum in Toronto," I said carefully. Burton was no doubt straining to hear, and I didn't want him to think it would be anyone familiar with his name. "There was also a young man at the preview who was interested. He's here but he doesn't look as if he can afford it."

"Young?"

"I don't know. Maybe thirty? And there's a telephone bidder. I was told that when I arrived. I have no idea who that is."

"Telephone," she repeated. "Are there any Asian people there who might be bidding?"

"Only one, the young man I've already mentioned, who does not look as if he is in the right league," I said.

"I see," she said. She then started to cough, almost as if she were choking. "Excuse me, will you? I'm going to have to get myself a glass of water," she gasped. "Call me when the bidding is about to start."

"Don't worry, I will," I said.

It was after a break in the proceedings, about midway through the auction, that the situation changed significantly. The announcement came from the auctioneer, Gerald Cox, the Cox of Molesworth & Cox, who told us that an object had been withdrawn. Next to me, Burton was shuffling papers nervously, unwrapping something, most likely a cough drop, as he had been making little throat-clearing sounds all evening in a most irritating manner. Perhaps he had forgotten to say yes to good health that day. The rustling stopped, however, as Cox spoke.

"I'm afraid the timing of this is highly unusual," Cox said. "Item eighty-three, a silver coffret dating to the reign of T'ang Emperor Xuanzong has just been withdrawn by its owner." In the booth next to me, Burton dropped his pen, which rolled in front of me. Mr. Knockoff, who had been leaning against the wall on one side of the room, slammed his paddle against the wall in frustration.

I took a deep breath and phoned the news to Dory, hearing her sharp intake of breath. "I'm sorry," I said. I could feel her disappointment across the phone line.

"It's not for you to apologize," she said quietly. "There'll be another time."

There wasn't another time for Dory, though, because ten days later she was dead.

Two

Life does not always unfold as we hope, of course, particularly when we make our plans without understanding the course of action others intend for us. I was not to become a soldier like my brother, nor a civil servant scurrying about the corridors of the August Enceinte where, Number One Brother informed me, the important business of managing the empire took place. Both my brothers were successful at their careers, none more so than Number Two Brother who, posted to the northern frontier, spent his idle hours trading with the caravans on the Silk Route, or perhaps, given his ne'er-do-well attitude, robbing them, thereby amassing a considerable fortune. The money he sent for the family was well regarded by all, irrespective of the manner in which it was acquired. My father was addicted to the gaming tiles, and regularly gambled much of the family income away. We lived, I suppose, in a state of decaying gentility.

No, my destiny had been decided long before I was born. My family, it seems, had a long tradition of service to the Imperial Court. I was to be adopted by Wu Peng, a very important personage in the court. Wu was a eunuch in the imperial household. I was to be a eunuch, too.

I did not understand when I was sent to Wu Peng on my tenth birthday what a eunuch was. I was soon to find out. Number One Brother, who by now had a wife and two concubines, told me to take it like a man, which was, I suppose, his idea of humor. My mother and father told me to be brave, that it was a tremendous honor. Brave about what? An honor for what? I was told that the Son of Heaven's closest advisor and confidant was a eunuch, someone so powerful that he walked the chambers of the Son of Heaven. I was told that the workings of the Imperial Palace depended upon the skill of eunuchs as much as on the ministrations of the most senior mandarins, a position to which Number One Brother aspired. I did not understand any of this. I did know that my mother cried herself to sleep for several nights before I left.

Perhaps that is what they told Number One Sister, too, that it was an honor to serve the emperor. And it was.

Dory suffered a massive heart attack and died on the spot, seated in her favorite armchair. She'd had a heart condition for a few years, something she'd neglected to mention to me. Her maid found her when she returned to the house with the groceries. Her husband was at his club at the time. Dory died alone. In fact, it didn't matter that neither George nor the maid was on hand. The doctors said there was nothing that could have been done. It was a shock. Dory had looked younger than her years, but even so, she was taken way too soon. More than anything else I blamed the Cottingham, convinced Dory would still be alive if they'd let her work as long as she wanted to, or at least for a few more years until she turned sixty-five. Rob, Clive, Alex Stewart, and I all went to the funeral. I saw no one that I knew from the Cottingham, and certainly not Burton Haldimand.

I also blamed whoever it was who had changed his or her mind about selling the T'ang box. The auction house wasn't revealing any names, which would be standard procedure, so this person was both nameless and faceless. That didn't stop me from being mad at them. Dory had been so excited about that box, the idea that she would have two of the three boxes her stepfather had, in her mind, stolen from China. Maybe if I'd been able to get it for her . . .

It was at the funeral that I saw Dory's husband, George Norfolk Matthews, for the first time. He looked to be older than Dory by maybe ten years, and he seemed to be a very sad man, not just because of Dory but because of life. I have no idea why I thought that. He had plenty of money, and Dory had always spoken of him with affection. She had many photos of the two of them in her former office at the Cottingham, and of course at her home. Their daughter Amy, a doctor, came from Florida. It was the first time I'd seen her in person, too. She looked like her father, not Dory, and I knew that she was divorced. With her was a young man whom I recognized from photos I'd seen at Dory's as her much-loved grandson, George, named for his grandfather, but better known as Geordie. Geordie looked like Dory's side of the family, which is to say more Asian. He was an extremely attractive young man, the sort who would have the girls swooning. There was also a half brother of Dory's by the name of Martin Jones. I didn't get a chance to talk to any of them.

Several weeks later, long after Dory was buried, I was still playing at being Charlyn Krahn, to my displeasure. Taking care of these bad people, to use Rob's expression, was taking rather longer than either of us wanted. Rob and I had been moved to a small apartment, which was a good thing, given that we'd have killed each other after that long in a hotel room. The only positive news, at least from my stand-point, was that my lovely little cottage was still standing. One of Rob's brothers and sisters on the force went in and got my mail and checked the place from time to time. No new cement floor in the basement. No smoke in the front room. Maybe the Heritage Act was more powerful than Rob thought.

Still, I was slowly, or maybe not so slowly, going gaga. Again Dory came to the rescue, not in person, needless to say, but through the offices of one Eva Reti, barrister and solicitor, of Smith, Johnson, McDougall and Reti.

Ms. Reti was the executor of Dory's estate, she informed me, and she hoped that I might meet with her at her offices downtown on a matter that she was sure would be of interest to me. She was a little brusque of tone, and she kept me waiting for several minutes before I got in to see her. With her was George Norfolk Matthews. He was holding a box that was about eight inches long covered in grey silk. After the usual introductions and pleasantries, he handed it to me. "Dory wanted you to have these," he said. "They belonged to her mother."

I opened the box to find a long strand of some of the most beautiful pearls I'd ever seen, a lovely creamy color, with a beautiful clasp. "I can't accept these," I said. "Surely your daughter would want them."

"She favors less traditional design," he said. "And she has received a great deal of jewelry from her mother. She is very happy for you to have them."

"I will treasure them," I said. "You know, I sell old jewelry, but I don't have much of it myself, and these pearls are exquisite, and all the more valuable to me because of Dory."

Ms. Reti and George smiled for the first time since I came in. Apparently my quite sincere expression of appreciation had melted the ice a little. "There is another matter arising from Dory's will that we must discuss with you," George said. "I will leave that part to Eva here."

Ms. Reti shuffled a little in her chair before getting to the point. "The T'ang silver box has come back on the market," she said. "It is to be auctioned in Beijing in two weeks."

"That's very interesting, I'm sure," I said. "But obviously Dory's original request is no longer practical, and while I thought it was extraordinary and would love to own it, I'm not really in that league."

"Mrs. Matthews has provided for its purchase, and for the purchase of a third, even larger box, should it come on the market," she said. "She believed they belonged together, as you know. Not only that, but she has provided for your expenses to go wherever they show up, and to pay you a significant commission when you acquire them for her estate."

"That's ridiculous, Ms. Reti," I said. "I mean . . ."

"Unusual, yes," Ms. Reti said. "Ridiculous, no. Please call

me Eva. May I call you Lara? Dory told me so much about you, I feel as if I know you."

I nodded. Alarm bells were clanging away in my head. This had the air of an obsession extending beyond the grave, and I wasn't entirely sure I wanted to be a part of it.

"A large sum of money was set aside in Dory's will for this purpose. I can tell you it's in the seven-figure range, with a top-up possible. Under the terms of the will, you are to consult with me on the price to be paid, but please be assured I intend to take your word for it. I know nothing about this sort of thing, and I know Dory trusted your judgment implicitly. She also wanted those boxes no matter the cost, so my role in this is peripheral only."

"George, how do you feel about this? How does your daughter feel?" I asked.

"Dory had her own money," George replied. "She inherited from her stepfather. You probably know that I don't need the money."

"Forgive me," I said. "But I don't think you answered my question."

George thought about that for a moment. He looked very tired, almost drawn, deep lines etched in his face. He seemed to be struggling to find the right words, but then he straightened up in his chair and said, "Anything Dory wanted is fine with me. Our daughter feels the same way. She's a successful doctor, and like her father can afford to indulge her mother's wishes. We know that the money set aside for this purpose will be tied up for some time, and if you are successful, will be used for the purpose of realizing Dory's wishes. There are no other heirs. Eva, will you give Lara the details?"

"The silver box is being auctioned in Beijing as I've said, at an auction house called—just a minute while I consult my notes—Cherished Treasures House. That's a translation, of course. I won't even attempt the Chinese. It's a lovely name, though, don't you agree? Why don't we just call it Treasures, for the sake of simplicity. I hope you'll be able to be there, and will succeed in purchasing the box. If you are unsuccessful, you will still be paid a fee for your time that I think you will consider more than acceptable. If you do manage to acquire it, you will be paid a commission of ten percent on the price realized, which, if I understand auction terminology correctly, includes the buyer's premium."

"That's right," I said. "The price realized is the high bid, plus the buyer's premium, which might be as high as ten percent, and any applicable taxes," I said. "This would be a rather handsome commission for me. Are you sure?"

"Dory's wishes were very clear. She was absolutely certain you would get the boxes for her," Eva said, and George nodded. "Any other issues?"

"I don't speak Chinese."

"We can help with that," she said.

"There's something else bothering me, too," I said. "Dory wanted the boxes to go back to China. That box is now in China. So . . ."

"But it still may go to a private collector," Eva said. "That was not Dory's intent. My instructions are that once the three are assembled they are to go a museum in Xi'an, the, let me see, Shaanxi History Museum in Xi'an."

"I do recall her telling me that. I'm just not sure what's going on here. I mean, why was the box withdrawn from sale in New York just before it went on the auction block? I suppose there are many reasons why that might have happened. Maybe there was a legal dispute over the ownership of the box, and it couldn't be sold until that was resolved. Maybe someone was contesting ownership and got a court injunction to stop the sale or something. Maybe the owner died an hour before the auction. The auction house had no obligation to reveal what happened, and for sure they didn't." I was just thinking aloud here, but George and Eva waited patiently while I did so.

"But it wasn't money. If the seller decided from the look of the crowd or even the prices realized on earlier items that they weren't going to get what they wanted, or even if they decided they didn't like the look of those who might be bidding, they could withdraw it. But it's easy enough to guard against the money issue. You just place a reserve bid, below which you won't sell, and if the bids don't go that high, then no sale. That is exactly what they did, too. The reserve was two hundred thousand, and the presale estimate was three hundred thousand. I left my card and the lot number at the auction house and offered three hundred and fifty thousand if the seller changed his or her mind again and wanted to sell. I didn't hear from the auction house. I thought perhaps someone else had put in a similar offer higher than mine, but that can't be the case if it's on the market again. I did ask for the name of the seller, but the auction house wouldn't give it to me, and they were quite within their rights not to do so." By "someone else," I meant Burton Haldimand. He'd tried to make sure I didn't see him do it, but he'd left his card at the auction house, too, and I assume he also made an offer, although I'd be the last person he'd tell about it.

"Does this matter?" Eva asked. "It's back on the market. You get another chance at it."

"It matters if it is just going to be withdrawn again. That's a waste of Dory's money, and I've already wasted some of it."

"That was hardly your fault, was it?" George interjected. "Aren't you being a little overly conscientious about this? Not that I don't appreciate it, of course, but Dory didn't care about your expenses. She could afford it. She just wanted the box. Her will is clear."

"I suppose I'm fussing needlessly. I wonder if Burton Haldimand knows about the sale," I said.

"Burton Haldimand?" Eva asked as George frowned and lightly pounded the arm of his chair with his fist.

"He's . . . a rival for the boxes," I said.

"The fellow from the Cottingham! Then you better get moving," Eva said. "I thought it was disgraceful the way they treated Dory. From what she told me about how her so-called retirement was handled, I believe them to have been a little light in the due-process department. I told her she should sue, and I'd be only too happy to represent her, but she wouldn't. She said if they didn't want her, then she should just leave. True, she was pushing sixty at the time, but they still had to handle it properly. I told her she could at least get a better settlement. She said she didn't need the money, which of course she didn't. But let's just make sure the Cottingham doesn't get our Dory's box.

"Now, as to how we can help here: Our firm has an office

in Beijing, run by one of our senior partners, who has been in Beijing for five years now. Her name is Mira Tetford. She works with North American corporations that want to do business in China, and just about everybody does. Sign of the times. Here are her coordinates. She'll arrange for someone to meet you at the airport if you let her know when you're arriving, and she'll arrange for your accommodation. She'll also make sure the money is there for you, and provide a translator. Dory wanted you to fly business class by the way. Let us know when you want to go, and we'll make the arrangements. You'll do it?"

"Please," George said. "I would be very grateful."

"I'll do it, yes," I said.

"How about we get out of town?" I said to Rob about an hour later. "You know, go back to being our real selves for a few days, far away from the bad guys?"

"Okay," he said. His enthusiasm was distinctly underwhelming.

"I have to go to Beijing." I told him about Dory's project.

"Beijing," he said. "Do I want to go to Beijing?"

"Probably not," I said. "But you do want to fly to Taiwan."

"Jennifer!" he said, his face brightening for the first time in about a month. "Brilliant idea! She'd like to see you, too, though."

"And she will, once I get my work done in Beijing. But wouldn't it be nice for the two of you to have some time to yourselves, just father and daughter?" By which I meant, of course, that Rob and I had been spending way too much time in the same room, and for all his talk about the two of us getting married, all this togetherness was putting a strain on our relationship. Not that this was a fair test exactly, given that under normal circumstances he'd be at work every day, not sitting around a tiny apartment that wasn't even ours, getting more depressed by the minute. Still, we would definitely benefit from some time apart. I said none of this.

There isn't much that gets past Rob, however. "You're getting a little tired of life with the less-than-cheerful Herb Krahn," he said. "You're thinking it's like living with a caged lion."

"I won't comment," I said. "As long as you promise not to point out that Charlyn Krahn has not been the poster child for the perfect roomie herself."

"Deal," he laughed. It was good to hear him do that.

The next ten days were a flurry of activity. There were visas to be obtained, packing to be done, and shopping, too, given we couldn't go back home to get what we needed. Fortunately we'd both taken our passports. It was not until the night before I left that it all caught up with me, the enormity of what I was undertaking. I sort of slumped on the bed beside my suitcase. "I don't know about this," I said.

"What's bothering you?" Rob said.

"I don't know."

"Sure you do. I know we haven't been talking much, even though we've been spending way more time together than usual, but let's give it a try. You haven't been sleeping well, and you've been a little cranky. It's not like you. Usually you look forward to trips. Talk to me."

"I am unsure about going back to China. I was there twenty years ago. I loved the people, I loved the sights, but I got out into the countryside and I saw how poor and oppressed the people were. I saw the ravages of the Cultural Revolution still affecting people years later, and I was upset, afterwards, about the massacre at Tian'anmen Square. I wondered if some of the young people I met had been injured or killed."

"I expect things have changed a lot since then. You need to go and reassess."

"True. I'm apprehensive about everything, though. I don't know how to handle auctions in Beijing, particularly in Chinese."

"I can certainly understand that. But they're going to get you help with the language, aren't they? The lawyer in Beijing?"

"Yes. I won't know my way around, though, after all these years."

"There will be maps, and you'll have help. What else?"

"I don't know," I said.

"You'll have to do better than that."

"I really don't know. I just feel anxious about the whole thing. There is something wrong about this, an obsession of a dead woman. Yes, Dory was right in wanting to return the box to China, but if the Chinese government wants it to stay there, they can purchase it. George isn't entirely comfortable with this, either. I can tell, even if I don't know him at all well. He should just send the box he already owns, tell them about the other one on auction, and suggest there might be a third. Case closed."

"They were married a long time, did you not tell me, thirty-five years or something like that? It would be difficult not to respect the wishes of a partner of thirty-odd years, and a dead one at that, even if you thought the idea was completely ridiculous. Relax. You'll do fine. Everything will work out as it should," he replied. "I'm anxious, too, you know."

"Why?"

"I don't know how I'll manage without having you underfoot constantly."

That's one of the best things about Rob, the way he can make me laugh. The next morning we were on our way, Rob to Taiwan, and I settling down in business class en route to Beijing.

Despite my misgivings, I was looking forward to the flight, a little pampering in business class that I don't normally enjoy, and a full day of no phones and no Clive. What more could I ask? Well, I could ask that Burton Haldimand be on another flight. Unfortunately, I heard his voice almost immediately upon boarding. He was asking for a blanket that had been sealed in plastic and some fresh orange juice.

"Hello, Burton," I said as I walked past his seat to mine. He had already put a little sign up on the top of his seat to indicate he didn't want to be interrupted for anything during the flight. Personally, I thought that would be a shame, missing the champagne.

"Lara! A pleasure to see you again. How are you feeling today? Over that cold?"

"Quite over it, thank you, Burton." I had looked up the Yellow Emperor, not prepared to let Burton tease me about it again. The Medical Classic of the Yellow Emperor, or *Huang Di Nei Jing*, is the theoretical basis for traditional Chinese medicine, and is supposed to have been compiled something like two thousand years ago. The Yellow Emperor is one of the mythical founders of China, and the book expounds on medicine through a conversation between this mythical emperor and some wise men and doctors. Just so you know.

"That's good. Now you can begin to work on good health." That was no doubt true, but Burton himself wasn't looking quite as perky as he had been the last time I saw him. Too bad the auction wasn't the day after we arrived, because I would be in better form than he.

"I plan to rest for the flight," he said, indicating the sign at his seat. "But I look forward to seeing you in Beijing. Perhaps we're going to the same place?"

"Perhaps we are," I said.

"Your first visit to China, is it?" he said, sticking one earplug in, but holding the other for my reply.

"No, it isn't," I said. "Although it has been a number of years since I've been there."

"You'll find it changed," he said.

It had changed all right. The truth of the matter is, if I hadn't been told Beijing was the destination of my flight, I could safely have assumed, except for the racial homogeneity of the people, that I was in a large city almost anywhere. When I'd been there two decades previous, no one except high Communist Party officials were allowed to have cars, people all wore the same uniform, the so-called Mao jacket in either grey or navy, and while there were some high-rises to be seen, Beijing was still a city of little neighborhoods and thousands upon thousands of bicycles. I'd heard about China's headlong rush to modernize, of course. Who hadn't? But nothing prepared me for what I saw. Office towers loomed over expressways and wide avenues. The whole city seemed to be one large construction site. I kept looking for the neighborhoods, the *hutongs* or lanes, and the street markets that I had loved. I couldn't see them.

And the cars! I had never seen anything like it anywhere in the world. I suppose, given that cars had only been allowed a few years before, that I was looking at an entire nation of new drivers. It was one of the scariest experiences I have ever had.

Burton hadn't arranged for a limo and driver at the airport. We were, it seemed, staying at the same hotel, chosen I suppose for its proximity to the auction house, which made it difficult for me not to offer him a lift in the car Mira Tetford had sent for me. I was beginning to realize I was destined to spend way too much time with Burton, a thought only slightly less terrifying than the traffic.

Burton might worry excessively about his health, but the traffic didn't seem to bother him. He chatted away amiably to a young woman by the name of Ruby who had accompanied the driver, and who introduced herself as Mira's assistant. It was only as the Mercedes hurtled through a red light, narrowly missing a woman pedaling a three-wheeled cart loaded with persimmons across what was clearly a deadly intersection, and coming inches away from being t-boned by a bus that was making an illegal left turn, that

Burton reacted. "One has to wonder if they have to take a drivers' test here or if they just buy a car and drive it off the lot," he said in a disapproving tone.

"Of course we do," Ruby said, giggling into her hand. "You are not the first foreign visitor to mention the driving. You will get used to it soon enough."

"I don't want to get used to it," Burton said. "I just want to survive it. You'll be happy to hear, Lara, that except under rather limited circumstances, foreigners are not allowed to drive in China." I guess he thought I might still have germs, because he tried not to look at me even though he was addressing me. "A good thing, don't you agree? Those of us who think traffic lights, turn signals, and lanes are a useful concept would be squashed like bugs within minutes of venturing forth."

If the driving wasn't to my liking, the hotel room certainly was. It was not all that large, but it had an absolutely spectacular view over the golden roofs of the Forbidden City, wave after wave of them, now glowing in the late afternoon sun. If I stood on tiptoe I could see the large plazas that separated the various palaces in the huge complex, and even pretend that the tourists flocking along the streets on either side or crossing Tian'anmen Square to the south were servants of the emperor, or perhaps foreign delegations paying their respects. It had been home to emperors, "forbidden" to almost everyone else. From this viewpoint, Beijing was absolutely enchanting.

Mira's office was atop another tower, this one just a little east of the hotel, in the foreign embassy section of Beijing. After the usual pleasantries and a cup or two of Chinese tea the next day, we got down to business. Mira was maybe forty, and struck me as very competent in a quiet, unassuming way. She appeared to be fluent in Mandarin, although I was no judge on that subject, and she clearly knew what she was talking about. Joining us was her assistant Ruby, the young woman who had met me at the airport the previous day.

"I've done some research on the art auction scene here with Ruby's help," Mira began. "Let me digress a little to say how much I'm enjoying this. For some reason I'm finding it more interesting than yet another joint venture between Chinese and North American companies wanting to manufacture plastic widgets here. To summarize my findings: One, art auction houses are a new concept here in China. We don't have the experience of, say, Hong Kong.

"Two: auction houses are supposed to be licensed by the Cultural Relics Bureau of China. My conclusion is that most are not. In other words, there are many more auction houses than licenses. Three: if you asked four people the number of licensed facilities here, you'd get four different answers, meaning it is difficult to tell which are licensed, and which are not. Four: this may be because Beijing Municipality also licenses auction houses. Its standards are reputedly lower than that of the CRB. Five: even licensed auction houses have, because of the infancy of the profession, no prior experience in art auctions. Six: there are probably only five auction houses in Beijing that are truly licensed by the Cultural Relics Bureau to conduct auctions, and seven: Cherished Treasures House is not one of them. So, in conclusion . . ."

"Caveat emptor," I said.

"Caveat emptor, 'buyer beware,' in spades," she said. "The art market here on the Chinese mainland is pretty much unregulated. Under those circumstances, you cannot assume any appraisal is accurate. . . ."

"Tell me how this is different from anywhere else. You can't assume that at home, either. All kinds of stuff is labeled 'as found.' In other words, no guarantees."

"Of course. But at home you have reputable auction houses with expert staff. . . ."

"That still doesn't guarantee anything, I can assure you. Some top auction houses have been implicated in various scandals rocking the art and antiquities market. I'm not comparing established European and North American auction houses with the ones here, because I wouldn't know, but I am saying that you should be careful anywhere."

"I doubt you've seen anything like this. One quite reputable auction house here has been rocked by an allegation that it has been selling stolen paintings. They are contemporary paintings, and as it turns out, the artist is still very much alive and has accused the auction house of selling stolen work. Now, who knows what the real story is. I mean we don't know who actually put the paintings up for auction because in China, as elsewhere, the auction house is obliged to protect the name of the seller and buyer if requested. But it does not inspire great confidence.

"As for Cherished Treasures House, it's new in the field. In a sense, it came out of nowhere. I tried to find out who owns it and got the name of another corporation that I didn't know either. Cherished Treasures House did, however, have an amazing inaugural auction a few months ago.

There was a small drawing by a Ming emperor for which they managed to fetch a rather breathtaking price, so it has established itself quite quickly. As for the T'ang silver box, I've been told by my partner Eva Reti that you know what it looks like, and that you should be able to identify a forgery if indeed that is what we have here."

"I know what it looks like. I went over it with a fine tooth comb in New York. I have the photograph from the Molesworth and Cox catalog, and I also have very good photographs from all angles of the box already in Dory's possession, or her estate's, that is. I think I'll be okay on that score. I'm worried about language, however."

"Both Ruby and I will be there with you to translate."

"You may have to translate fast," I said. "These things can really move along if there's a lot of bidding."

"We'll manage," she said. "We've translated for some pretty big deals here. We know what's at stake. I'm fairly fluent, but I can't read Chinese. Ruby, of course, can. So she'll help with any text we need to deal with, and she's faster than I am on the numbers. Now, once you get the box, in the happy event that you do, we will take it from there. We'll see it is properly presented to the museum in Xi'an. You can't take it out of the country, anyway, given that it's much older than what's allowable. You probably know that China is clamping down on exports of antiquities."

"I'm wondering why someone who already had an object legally out of China would bring it back to sell it," I said.

"Because of the prices they're getting? There is a lot of money here now, in certain circles, and people want the best. I mentioned the Ming drawing. It fetched in the range of four million yuan. Right now you get about eight yuan to the U.S. dollar. I'm told that is more than it would have sold for outside of China."

"I suppose that might also explain why the person who owned the box withdrew it at the last minute in New York."

"I suppose it might. The preview is tomorrow afternoon. Are you up for it?"

"I am," I said.

"Good. Both Ruby and I will be there."

To reach Cherished Treasures House, you enter a rather sterile office tower just off Jianguomenwai Dajie, or what we would call Jianguomen Street. "Dajie" is a term for a street or avenue. The "wai" part of the name indicates that this street would have been outside the original city walls that enclosed the ancient city. Jianguomenwai Dajie is essentially a section of the major east-west axis of Beijing, often referred to as Chang'an Avenue, although it changes its name a few times, which runs right in front of the Forbidden City, between it and Tian'anmen Square. The north-south axis of ancient Beijing was, and still is, the Forbidden City itself, which is oriented north-south.

Cherished Treasures House was on the second floor, reached by a long escalator to the left of the building entrance. The glass doors to the room were open. There was a desk just inside the door, at which sat a man in a blazer with the auction house logo on the pocket, who was peering at a computer and generally ignoring us. The room was empty of other visitors with the exception of two. I was disappointed, if not surprised, to see that Burton Haldimand was one of them. He was conversing in what sounded to my ears to be fluent Chinese to a rather attractive young man. I don't know why I would be surprised that Burton spoke Chinese. After all, this was his field. Why wouldn't he learn the language? But it made me feel at a disadvantage for the coming bidding war. "We meet again, Burton," I said, by way of warning my fellow visitors that the enemy was very near. Mira nodded very slightly to indicate my message had been received, and gently nudged Ruby in the ribs.

"Indeed, we do," he said. "This is perhaps your client?" he said, indicating Mira.

"No," I said. "Mira, meet Burton Haldimand of the Cottingham Museum. Burton, this is Mira Tetford. She's helping me with the purchase." I decided that was all Burton needed to know. "And this is Ruby, Mira's assistant."

"How do you do, ladies," Burton said. "And may I introduce Liu Da Wei. He is assisting me while I'm in Beijing."

"Please call me David," he said, shaking hands all 'round.

Da Wei, David, I thought. I suppose that's how they choose their English names, something close to their Chinese one. David and Ruby obviously knew each other, and I thought that might be a subject for some discussion when Mira and I were alone, just to size up the opposition, as it were.

The formalities dispensed with, I decided to have a look around. There were a number of contemporary paintings, rather attractive ones, up for sale, as well as much older pieces. There were several folios for sale. I didn't have a clue what they were, but they were attractive. I didn't stand a chance of understanding the catalog, so Ruby explained that one of the folios was by a renowned seventeenth century poet and scholar.

It was all very informal. People just came and went. The man at the desk carried on peering at his computer. He didn't even look up when I was a few feet away. That was because he was playing a game on his computer. It was as if we weren't there. The silver box was there, however. It looked okay to me.

Burton was taking a cursory look, as I was, at everything else in the room, and sidled up to me when I found myself alone for a minute. "Will you tell me who your client is this time?" he asked.

"No," I said. "You're getting tiresome on this subject."

"I wonder who was on the telephone that night," Burton chattered on. "Now, it could have been one of the Matthews. Or it could have been Xie Jinghe."

"Who is Xie Jinghe?" I said. I knew perfectly well, but I can never resist the temptation to tweak Burton's nose, metaphorically speaking. He'd be annoyed I didn't appreciate the fact he knew Xie Jinghe. While I'd never met the man, I did know Xie was wealthy and a philanthropist, having donated a quite spectacular collection of Shang bronzes to the Cottingham. He had a fabulous home in Vancouver, featured in a design magazine I tend to favor, and an Asian art collection that was regularly referred to in magazines on that subject.

Burton looked pained and began to explain, just as, in true speak-of-the-devil fashion, a tall, thin man entered the room. Burton looked startled for a moment, but regained his composure, and went over to talk to this new visitor. He even shook his hand. A minute or two later, Burton beckoned me over as well, although he looked reluctant to do so.

"Lara, Xie Jinghe would like to meet you," he said. "Dr. Xie is head of Xie Homeopathic, as I'm sure you know. I use his company's products on a regular basis. He is a great scholar and arts patron as well. You will find him a delight to talk to. Lara McClintoch is an antique dealer from Toronto, Dr. Xie."

While I knew of Dr. Xie, I didn't know much about Xie Homeopathic, but then I didn't spend as much time on my health as Burton did. What I did know was that Burton's fawning introduction of Xie was making me nauseous. Perhaps it was making my qi disharmonious again. I wondered how Dr. Xie himself felt about it. I was soon to find out. "Burton had no luck convincing George Matthews and his firm to sponsor his soon-to-be restored Asian galleries," Xie said. "He has therefore turned his attention to me, as you have no doubt already surmised, Ms. McClintoch." I tried not to smile. "I believe you knew my late friend, Dory Matthews."

"I did," I said. "I miss her."

"As do I," he said. Burton looked really uncomfortable. He couldn't possibly have been surprised that George Matthews wouldn't donate to the Cottingham, given their treatment of his wife. Perhaps, though, Burton was unaware of Xie's friendship with Dory. That comment should have told him in an instant that all this sycophantic posturing of his had been for naught.

I had a pleasant chat with Dr. Xie, who, it turned out, supplied various brands of homeopathic remedies throughout the world, including North America. Dr. Xie had homes in both Beijing and Vancouver. He also had an office in Toronto. "You are surprised, perhaps, that I and George and Dory Matthews are friends. George and I are competitors of a sort, I suppose, but not really. His company and mine both manufacture products to make people well, but we take completely different approaches. He holds patents on drugs I suppose you would consider traditional, while I supply products that stem from a long tradition of Chinese medicine, treatments that *I* would call traditional. We often have heated discussions on the relative merits of our approaches, but we remain friends nonetheless."

"I don't know George well at all, but I adored Dory," I said. "She taught me everything I know about Chinese history and art."

"She was indeed very knowledgeable—George as well in the field in which he collects. Now, what do we have here?" he said, stopping in front of the silver box. It was open, and placed on a pedestal so that you could view it from all sides, which Dr. Xie did. "This contains a formula for the elixir of immortality," he said after some study. "The author of the writing in this box was almost certainly an alchemist. That is most interesting."

"Alchemist? You mean someone who tries to turn base metals into gold?"

"That was part of Chinese alchemy," he said. "Yes, people did want to produce gold, just as alchemists in Europe did. But, like alchemists everywhere, there was a more spiritual dimension to their pursuit as well. Chinese alchemists wanted to become an Immortal, and to dwell in the other-world with other Immortals. Alchemists here would have almost certainly espoused Taoism as their religion, and Taoists believe that both the *po* and the hun, the body and the spirit, remain after death. Just as a matter of interest, people went to extraordinary lengths to preserve their bodies. Some alchemists, and some Taoists, managed to more or less mummify themselves while they were still alive by eating only mica and pine gum."

I managed not to gag. Despite this rather strange interest in achieving immortality, Dr. Xie was an interesting and scholarly individual. "The pill or elixir of immortality was part of that process," he continued. "You partook of it, and you became immortal. It could happen suddenly. One minute you'd be there, and the next you'd vanish, leaving your clothes behind you."

"Given the ingredients, things like arsenic and mercury, this elixir of immortality sounds a bit dangerous."

"And it was. You do know, though, that poisonous substances are used in the treatment of disease all the time," he said. "Arsenic was, for a long time, just about the only successful treatment for syphilis, and after all, digitalis, or foxglove, is a poison that is used in the treatment of heart disorders. I could name many more. We treat allergies using tiny amounts of the substances the patient is allergic to, as well. Large amounts might result in anaphylactic shock and possibly death, but tiny amounts help you build up immunity. As for the elixir of immortality, many Chinese people, including emperors, knew the ingredients were toxic, but they took it in small doses anyway. Several Chinese emperors, possibly including the first Chinese emperor, Qin Shi

Huangdi, the man we know from the terra-cotta warriors in Xi'an, died trying to become immortal. It is possible that five of the twenty-one T'ang emperors died of poisoning in their quest for immortality."

"Was this Illustrious August mentioned here one of them?"

"No. Illustrious August was deposed in a coup, abdicating in favor of his son, and dying some time later. Not nearly so glamorous."

"You've made a study of alchemy, have you?" I asked.

"In a way, yes. I am a Taoist. Technically, in the People's Republic of China there is no religion. But now, people are not usually persecuted for their beliefs, with some notable exceptions. I am happy to say I was able to contribute funds toward the restoration of a Taoist temple close to my home that was damaged during the Cultural Revolution, and I occasionally go there for spiritual renewal, and sometimes solace. I'm interested in alchemy, I suppose, because of my business. But really, striving for immortality is not so different from believing in heaven, is it?"

"No, I guess it isn't. Are you thinking of bidding on the T'ang box, Dr. Xie?"

"I don't believe so. It would be interesting to own, of course, but unlike George Matthews, I don't collect in my area of business. I am very interested, however, in the folio of the seventeenth-century poet over there. It is that I have come to see. And you?"

"I'm interested in the T'ang box," I said.

"For yourself?"

"For a client." It was tempting to tell the very pleasant

Dr. Xie, who claimed to be friend to both George and Dory Matthews, who that client might be, but I'd made a promise and I was going to keep it.

"I expect you will find Burton a formidable opponent."

"I expect I will. I plan to emerge victorious."

"I wish you the best of luck," he said. "I will enjoy the encounter, especially if you are the top bidder. Dr. Haldimand may be a good customer of Xie Homeopathic, as he is wont to tell me at great length and often, but I will be in your corner in this endeavor."

"Thank you," I said.

"Now if you will excuse me, I am going to take a look at that folio. Perhaps you and I will have a celebratory glass of champagne after the auction."

"I would like that very much."

"Excellent. I will look forward to seeing you then."

Ruby, who was looking very smart in her fake Prada shoes and handbag, headed my way when she saw that I was alone. "I am wondering if you have done something to offend Dr. Haldimand? He looks at you with some annoyance."

"That is because I have been having a lovely chat with someone he was hoping to impress," I replied.

"Xie Jinghe is a very important man," Ruby agreed.

"Yes, and I hope to annoy Dr. Haldimand even more on Thursday when I purchase the silver box that he wants." Ruby giggled. I left her to take another look at the art on offer.

I would have cause to think long and often about what transpired next. Burton was looking at a lovely watercolor on the far side of the room. Dr. Xie was chatting with Mira near the folio he wanted to purchase. They seemed to be conferring on some subject of importance, as opposed to just small talk. Ruby and David were sharing a joke of some kind. I was just standing there, trying to get a feel for the place and what I thought the prices might be like, how the room might be set for the auction—anything, really, that would make me feel more comfortable about what I had to do. I suppose I sensed rather than saw someone enter the room, and turned to see that another person had joined us.

He was dressed very fashionably in a black turtleneck and slacks and Gucci loafers. Real Gucci loafers. He looked as if he could afford to be there. He surveyed the room from the door, glanced briefly at the young man at his computer game, and then came and stood in front of a painting, studying it from a distance. Then another man, equally well dressed, came in. I couldn't see his face, but he had spiky hair, and there was something in his stance that made me recognize him as the third bidder in New York, the man in fake Hugo Boss, the person I called Mr. Knockoff. This time the man was wearing ersatz Armani.

As I watched in dismay, Mr. Knockoff took several swift steps farther into the room, grabbed the silver box, and headed for the door. I yelped, and all of us turned, including the man at the desk who finally stood up. Dr. Xie, who was closest, made an attempt to stop the man by tripping him with his cane, but to no avail. David, who was a lot faster than the rest of us, sprinted toward the doors, with the man in black right behind him. Mr. Knockoff ran down the escalator, David in hot pursuit.

Near the front door of the building, Mr. Knockoff stumbled slightly, and David, who had been steadily gaining on the thief, reached out to grab him. The man in black shouted something. The doorman rushed over and grabbed, not the thief, but David. The man in black shouted again, the doorman released David, but it was too late. Mr. Knockoff and the silver box had both disappeared.

Three

Wu Peng, the eunuch to whom I was sent, held a position of some importance in the Service for Palace Attendants. It was quickly apparent to me that this position was not due to his abilities—the man could neither read nor write, nor did he demonstrate any particular affinity for leadership. No, his position was due almost entirely to the fact that he was a distant cousin of the powerful Wu family in the palace, a clan that had produced numerous royal consorts, and most extraordinarily, an empress, Wu Zetian, ruler in her own right rather than just by virtue of marriage to an emperor. Wu Peng may not have been able to read and write, but he had amassed a fortune in a manner he would later explain to me. He had a rather lavish home outside the palace, a wife, in name only obviously, and two adopted sons. I too was adopted by Wu Peng and his wife, and took his surname, becoming known as Wu Yuan. I did

not reside with Wu and his family, however. My place was in the Imperial Palace, serving the Son of Heaven.

Once the pain and trauma of the procedure that determined my life's course as a eunuch had abated, I was brought to the Imperial Palace. That I, the son of a low-level mandarin, although certainly a mandarin with aspirations, should find himself in such a place never failed to amaze me. The beauty of the palace was simply astonishing. One could wander the passageways and courtyards, gardens and residences forever, it was so large, and every detail was exquisite. There were arches of jade and pearl, carpets of the finest silk, and furnishings of a noble craftsmanship of which I had seen no equal. There were parks of unparalleled beauty, gardens bursting with glorious scent both night and day, forests filled with animals, glorious pavilions, polo fields, archery ranges, many lakes stocked with fish, still other ponds where people of the court could drift in elegant boats, orchards of pears and plums and peaches. It was heady indeed for the boy that I was.

We eunuchs essentially have the run of the Imperial Palace. Not the inner chambers, to be sure, with a few exceptions, but in the course of our duties we see and hear much of what is going on. And we do like to gossip. As a newcomer I merely listened, but I learned much. At first, I was given many menial tasks, being sent to the markets to choose birdcages or musical instruments for the royal concubines, or to the silk market for special bolts of fabric for these same women. I was allowed to walk among the emperor's women at will, given there was no opportunity for my seed to mingle with that of the emperor's chosen ones.

It was on these errands in the city that I began to look for Number One Sister. I was particularly happy when sent to the Western

Market, which, while not as sumptuous as the Eastern Market, located as it is in the wealthier part of Chang'an, had the distinct advantage from my perspective of being adjacent to the Northern Hamlet where famous courtesans, of whom I had become convinced my sister was one, having as a more mature person discarded the brigand theory, plied their trade. Men laughed when I, a young eunuch, walked the streets and lanes of that quarter. They knew from my voice and appearance that I would never know the love of a woman. I ignored them. I was a eunuch in the Imperial Palace, and not just any eunuch but a pure one, who unlike some had never, and would never, be intimate with a woman. I considered these men who frequented the North Hamlet to be my inferiors.

Soon it was discovered that I could read and write, a skill my father had insisted upon my acquiring, and I was assigned to teach some of the young women of the harem to do the same. I was told I was a comely young man, and soon became a favorite of many of the women, a favorite and perhaps a confidant. I had been afraid that my new responsibilities would not afford me the same opportunity to scour the lanes of the great city of Chang'an, looking for my sister, but I soon found I had even more latitude in my quest, as I both penned and delivered secret letters to the rapid relay stations for these lovely ladies. They had, by and large, a great deal of time on their hands, given the impressive size of the harem. Even those who ascended to the top ranks would spend a night with the Son of Heaven once every few months, and perhaps not even that often, unless they rose to the status of imperial favorites, or were found to be unusually proficient at producing sons.

Sometimes I would see the carriages of the courtesans, watch them climbing down to choose bolts of silk or whatever pleased them. I did not see Number One Sister. But I did not give up hope.

*   *   *

"Blue Toyota, no plates," David said, as he came back into the building, casting a baleful eye on the doorman in the process. "I almost had him."

Dr. Xie was engaged in what sounded like a heated discussion with the young man from the auction house, who looked to be in the throws of a full-blown panic attack. "Scandalous security," he said to us, leaving the man wringing his hands. "How can they expect people to place items for sale under these kinds of circumstances? We will have to wait for the Beijing Public Security Bureau, I'm afraid."

The man in black said something, which Dr. Xie translated. "He's saying that the doorman is an idiot, grabbing the wrong person." I was inclined to agree.

It took the police only a few minutes to get there, but already Burton was pacing up and down in a most annoying way. The instant the police arrived, the man in black pulled them aside. The conversation was in Chinese, so I couldn't understand a word, but I noticed Burton had his head cocked in their direction, a rather bemused expression on his face. Whatever the discussion, it was brief and resulted in the man in black leaving immediately after it concluded. The rest of us were kept there considerably longer. We were all asked what we had seen, details of our passports and visas were taken, and then we were told we could leave as well. "How did that other guy get out of here so fast?" I said.

"Army," Dr. Xie said. "He's high up in the Chinese army."

"So what?"

"This is China," Dr. Xie said in a warning tone. "It is not your home. Things are different here."

"Well, that's it, Lara," Burton said, coming over to say good-bye. As usual, he didn't offer to shake hands. "It's been a blast. Might as well pack our bags and go home. See you there I hope."

It didn't work out like that.

My first order of business was to call George Matthews and deliver the bad news. I'd told Mira that she could deal with Eva Reti at the law firm, but that I should be the one to talk to George. He took it better than I thought he would, so much so that his reaction surprised me a little. "So that's it, then," he said. He sounded almost relieved. I didn't figure it was the money, which would probably stay tied up for a period of time just in case the silver box showed up again. Maybe, as Rob had already pointed out to me, George knew this wish of his wife's was a bit strange, even if he felt duty-bound to support it, and was glad to have it out of the way. "You were there when it was stolen?"

"Yes. It was an unbelievably bold heist. There were several of us there, but the thief was fast, and he had a car waiting right outside for him. No license plates on the car, either. Somebody really wanted that box very badly."

"I expect someone really did," George replied. "And now you should come home."

I told George I was off to Taiwan as soon as I could get a flight, and this adventure, such as it was, was over. However, I tried to change my booking for Taiwan and couldn't. I could have managed it for the following day, but that was devoted to a command performance at the auction house, this time to view the videotapes in the presence of three policemen. When I got there, Burton was on his mobile, also trying to book an earlier flight home. At least that was what I thought he was doing. He was speaking Chinese, and he said that was what he was attempting. I saw no reason to doubt him. That would come later.

Unfortunately, our arrival also coincided with a quiet but public dressing-down of the young auction house employee who had proven himself hopelessly inept as a custodian of the merchandise. The young man stood, head bowed, his back to us, and hands behind his back, one hand clasping a delicate wrist. Another man was speaking quietly, but there was no mistaking the tone. At the end of it, the boy let out a howl, took off his Cherished Treasures House jacket, threw it on the ground, and ran out of the place. It seemed pretty clear he'd been sacked.

"I believe everyone is here. We are ready to begin," the person who looked to be in charge, someone by the name of Chen Maohong, said. His English was very good.

"No, I think we're still missing one person," I said.

"Everyone is here," Chen said in a firm tone. I looked at Xie who very subtly shook his head. "We will now review the videotape."

The videotape showed someone walk in, hesitate for only a moment, proceed directly to the silver box, grab it, and leave in haste. The cameras also showed the rest of us: David moving very fast, followed by the man in black, and Burton and I standing stock still in amazement for a few seconds before hurtling after them. Dr. Xie had followed at a much slower pace. What the videotape didn't reveal was the thief's face, which he kept averted from the cameras, thus proving that he knew exactly where they were.

There was no question that it was the T'ang silver box, and only the silver box, that the thief wanted. Now, it's possible it was the easiest to grab, in terms of size and the fact that it was just sitting all by itself on a pedestal, but I didn't think so. I had more than one reason for thinking that, not only the actions of the thief, but also because even though I couldn't see his face, I had become almost certain it was the young man who had seemed to be ready to bid on the silver box when it was up for auction at Molesworth & Cox in New York, the man I'd come to think of as Mr. Knockoff. I mentioned this aloud.

"You remember him, Burton," I said.

"I don't believe I do," he replied.

"He was at the preview the same time you and I were," I said. "Fake Hugo Boss suit. This time it was fake Armani. And he was definitely planning to bid that night. He was standing off to one side looking bored until Cox announced that the silver box had been withdrawn from the sale. He slapped his paddle against the wall, as good an indication as any that he was as displeased by that development as we were."

"I'm sorry. I guess I was so focused on the upcoming bidding that I didn't notice," Burton said. "I knew you were there, of course, and that there was a bidder on the telephone, but I don't recall anyone else who looked particularly interested in the box."

"To have a paddle, which is to say to be able to bid on something as expensive as that, the man must have established some kind of credit with Molesworth and Cox. If you get in touch with them," I said to Chen, "they would almost certainly have a record, and you know, they might tell you who he was, given this is a criminal investigation."

"They're never going to find it," Burton said as we were about to leave. "For one thing, by the time the people at Molesworth and Cox respond to the enquiry from the police here, it will be long gone. They'll go on and on about protecting their clients' identities, and will only give up the name if they are legally required to do so. I am going to have to find a new signature piece for the T'ang gallery. The box will disappear into the black market. What a crashing waste of time! The only happy note I can think of is that it serves the seller right for withdrawing it in New York at the last minute like that. I hope for their sake it was insured."

I, too, was feeling similarly irked. "It's all a little odd, isn't it?" I said. "First it's withdrawn, then it's put up for sale halfway around the world, and then it's stolen. I know it's special, but still, this is a bit much."

"A bit much is right. I've spent thousands following it around for nothing. Yes, my travel budget at the Cottingham is generous, but who can afford something as useless as this? I'm going home tomorrow, I hope. I'm wait-listed for tomorrow, and have a confirmed booking for Wednesday. I planned to be going home with the silver box, but I guess that's not going to happen. It will not be my most triumphant return, I must say."

"Nor mine. I don't know what is worse, wasting someone else's money or your own. Now that you mention it though, how were you planning to get the box out of the country?" I said. "China is clamping down on exports, as Mira Tetford has pointed out to me."

"The auction house assured me that the requisite papers would be provided, because the piece was legally out of the country before it was put up for auction here. Anyway, it's always possible, isn't it." It was a statement, not a question. "Palms can be greased, customs agents either too ignorant to know what they're looking at, or persuaded to look the other way. But you should know that if you were planning to be the successful bidder. Does that mean you weren't planning to take it out of the country? Interesting idea," he said.

Oops, I thought. "That's a cynical attitude, Burton," I said.

"Cynical? I call it realistic. I was shopping on the antique street, Liulichang Dajie, a couple of days ago and went into a government-owned shop. At least, it was supposed to be a government-owned shop. It had the plaque outside the door proclaiming it as such. I was offered T'ang ceramics. I should probably say I was offered fake T'ang ceramics. Quite lovely, though. Pretending I didn't know they were fake, I pointed out that they were way too old for export. They promised me that would not be a problem. Now given that they were fake, obviously it shouldn't be a problem, but it does call the whole system into some question, does it not?"

"Maybe there was a language problem," I said. "Maybe they were trying to tell you they were reproductions."

"I speak Chinese, Lara. Surely you've noticed. Not well, perhaps, but well enough. Now, what are your plans?"

"I'm joining my partner Rob in Taiwan for a visit with his daughter," I said.

"You have a client in Taiwan?" he said. "How would you manage that?"

"You know perfectly well I'm not going to fall for that," I said. "You're getting a little irritating on the subject of my client. But you are jumping to conclusions. Really, I am going to visit my sort-of stepdaughter. She is teaching English there, and I miss her a lot."

"I see," he said. I could tell he didn't know whether to believe me or not, which in my opinion said more about him than about me. "Why don't you join me this evening for a drink at the bar in the hotel?"

"Good idea," I said, although I wasn't sure it was. "What time?"

"Six? Maybe we can go out for a bite after."

It seemed churlish to refuse, but the evening began even more badly than I'd feared. He couldn't wait even two minutes to start at me again on the subject of my mystery client. "I confess that in New York I thought your client might be Dory Matthews, but I guess that would hardly be the case now. Too bad about Dory. I know you were fond of her."

"Yes, I was, and still am."

"I suppose it could still be George Matthews. Or his company Norfolk Matthews Pharmaceuticals, but he wouldn't normally use you to get what he wanted." I said nothing, but Burton, as usual, rattled on, oblivious to my discomfort. "It's a bit peripheral for him. He collects medical equipment, and I'm not sure a box with a recipe for the elixir of immortality would qualify, as tantalizing as it might be for the rest of us. And anyway, it's too soon after Dory's death for him to be arranging for a purchase in Beijing, I'd think. Am I right?"

"Burton!" I said in a warning tone. "I think we should change the subject."

"There's something I've wanted to say to you for some time, Lara. Please hear me out. I know you were very fond of Dory. I was, too. It wasn't my fault she got edged out at the Cottingham. The museum approached me. I didn't know what the situation was. They told me she was retiring. Why would I think otherwise? I found out later she was pushed out against her will, but I honestly did not know that at the time, and even if I had, it wasn't up to me. They asked me for an expression of interest, and who wouldn't be interested, given the budget that museum has? I was keen, I sent my CV, and got an interview, then another, then the job. By the time I got there, she was gone."

"You're quite right, Burton. It wasn't your fault that the Cottingham decided Dory had to go. But Courtney Cottingham told me you'd approached them first, and that it was too much of an opportunity to pass up, given that you are the hot item in this field." Courtney had shared this annoying little confidence with me at Dory's retirement bash. A lot of people knew that edging Dory out would be unpopular with certain people, my being one of them. I didn't figure Courtney actually cared what I thought, nor did I think Burton did either, but both seemed to feel they had to say something to me. It's just that Burton was lying, or at the very least stretching the truth, and I wasn't prepared to let him get away with it.

Burton got just a little defensive. "I didn't apply for the job, Lara. I simply met Courtney Cottingham and her husband at a soiree in Washington, and I told her if the job were ever open, I hoped she would consider me a candidate. I know you really, really liked Dory, and clearly you're determined to think the worst of me, but what I'm saying is true. Several months after Courtney and I had this conversation, she got in touch with me. She told me Dory was retiring. If my casual remark sparked Dory's departure, I feel bad about it, but I don't think it would have changed anything. Courtney thought Dory was past it, and maybe she was. Her arthritis had slowed her down, and she wasn't open to new ideas for the galleries."

"Burton . . . ," I began, but stopped. There was no use in arguing this point with him. "Look, I know you're doing great things for the Cottingham, just as you did for that private museum in Boston. I'm sure the Cottingham is lucky to have you no matter what the circumstances. It's too late for Dory, so let's just talk about something else." It was the best I could do.

"Thank you," he said. "Dory was certainly very nice when I went to visit her a couple of weeks before she died. It was just before you and I headed for New York for our first futile attempts to get the box. She served me tea and cookies, and we had a lovely chat. She even sent me home with a care package, a box of homemade cookies and some of her own blend of tea. She used it to treat her arthritis, but she said it was good for almost all that ails you. I went to personally invite her to a reception we were having for donors. If she blamed me, she gave me no such indication, but I suppose she might say something to you and not to me."

"She never said a bad word about you to me, Burton." That was indeed true. "I doubt she said a bad word about you to anyone. She was not the sort of person to do that. She was a classy lady."

"She was," he agreed. "Now as you've already requested, let's talk about something else. I got a seat on the plane tomorrow, so this is my last evening here. I know this place that serves fabulous food. Let's go eat."

I'd had enough of Burton for one day, but there didn't seem to be a polite way to get out of it. I could hardly say I had other things to do, when clearly I didn't. Reluctantly, I went with him. He ordered, not even bothering to ask me if there was anything I wanted. However, he knew Chinese food as well as he knew Chinese art. Platter after platter of food arrived in front of us, all really delicious. Over the course of the meal, I discovered that Burton could be quite amusing when he tried. I may have even found myself warming to him just the tiniest bit. He had the good grace to make fun of his health fetish, which he had to, really, when I asked him what on Earth he was doing as he proceeded to wipe down the chopsticks. In some cases, cleaning the chopsticks might be a good idea, but these had come in sealed packages, the kind you actually have to tear open to use. I tried more or less unsuccessfully not to laugh. Heaven knows, I try to be careful when I'm traveling. If I find myself some place that I think doesn't measure up from a sanitary standpoint, I won't eat anything that doesn't have steam rising from it. It's my number one rule. I'd sized this restaurant up pretty quickly and decided it was okay. Burton, however, was taking no chances. When he put disinfectant drops on the spotless serving spoons, though, I got the giggles. Even he started to laugh.

When I'd managed to get my hilarity under control, I got around to a question I was determined to ask. "You speak Chinese, don't you? Mandarin?" I asked when I'd eaten as much as I possibly could.

"Yes," he said. "Also a little Cantonese."

"So what did that guy in black, the one who has enough pull that he avoids spending time looking at videotapes and being questioned with the rest of us, say to the doorman?"

"The guy with the expensive shoes? He said something along the lines of 'Grab the young man' or something. Why?"

"Well, what would you say under those circumstances?"

" 'Stop, thief,' I guess. I'll grant you it was a little ambiguous, but really, wouldn't you think the doorman would grab the guy with the silver box under his arm if that is indeed what the guy said?"

"I don't know. The two were about the same age—David and the thief, that is."

"Where are you going with this, Lara?"

"Promise you won't laugh? I think there is a possibility that the man in black was in on the theft."

"Whoa!" Burton said. "Chinese army. Be careful."

"You're not planning to discuss this with them, are you?"

"Of course not, but why would you think such a thing? Surely it is not because he left so soon after it happened and he didn't come back the next day like the rest of us. Perhaps his shift of duty was about to begin. I don't know, maybe they went and took his statement from him at his home or work as a professional courtesy. I don't think you can assume he is a criminal just because he dodged some of the most incredibly boring hours I've put in while here."

"It's not that at all. He was ostensibly looking at a painting. The trouble is, he was standing in the wrong place to do that. That was a detailed painting. The rest of us stood much closer to look at it. I watched the videotape very carefully: where you stood, where I stood, and indeed where everybody stood when they were looking at it, and then I went over to it myself afterward. He was standing way too far back."

"So maybe the guy doesn't know how to look at paintings properly. Why does his ineptitude in that regard matter?"

"I think he was standing in the perfect place to block the young employee's view of the silver box."

"He hardly needed to do that," Burton said. "The idiot wouldn't have taken his eyes off that computer screen for a magnitude-nine earthquake. The building would have come down around him, and he'd be found dead staring at the screen."

"Yes, but you wouldn't know that for sure would you, if you planned to grab the box? You couldn't count on the fact that there was a computer-game addict in charge that day."

"No, but you could probably count on poor security, I regret to say. They haven't yet got the hang of it here. They actually rent compartments on trains to move works of art. I mean, you've got to hope thieves don't know what they're looking at when they pry open compartment doors, or that they're interested in stealing something other than art."

"I guess. Maybe you're right and I'm just irked because the guy pulled rank and avoided two rather boring sessions with the police."

"This is China, Lara," Burton said.

"That must be the tenth time someone has said that to me."

"Remember it." Despite the fact that he lectured me, and clearly thought I was imagining things, we spent a pleasant enough evening after that, managing to avoid contentious subjects like Dory and the name of my client. We parted on good terms, Burton telling me he wouldn't see me the next day as he had to leave early for the airport, and to phone him when I got home.

I didn't expect to see Burton in Beijing again, but as I was to discover soon enough, Burton rarely did what he said he was going to do. For myself, I decided if I had to wait another couple of days, I might just as well go to the auction even if I didn't plan to bid on anything. In the meantime, I would attempt to entertain myself by seeing the sights. I started with the Forbidden City, naturally, a must-see for anyone in Beijing. I began at the south end, across from Tian'anmen Square, at the Gate of Heavenly Peace, graced as it is with an enormous portrait of Chairman Mao. If you want to see the great one himself, you can do so by filing past his remarkably well-preserved corpse in the Chairman Mao Memorial Hall. I'd done that once, however, and once was enough. In the early days of our marriage, I'd told Clive about the experience and he'd suggested that we should do an embalmed leaders world tour, Mao, then Stalin in Moscow, supplementing it where necessary with impressive mausoleums in which embalmed dictators were interred, like maybe the Perons in Argentina. The idea didn't seem nearly as amusing to me now, a much older and wiser person, but it did remind me that there had been a time when I'd enjoyed being with Clive. We never did the tour, I might add. Instead we collected watches with dead dictators on the faces, in Mao's case, a particularly impressive model with Mao waving his arm for the second hand. Clive got the watch collection in our divorce, I regret to say, something he likes to remind me about from time to time, pushing his sleeve well up and making much of looking at the time when he's wearing one of them.

The Forbidden City is called that because for much of its history as an imperial palace it was strictly off limits to almost everyone, your average person not even allowed to venture near the place. Now, however, you can wander at will, which is exactly what I did, admiring the large plazas, the brilliant red of the halls, the extraordinary carved staircases, impressive incense burners in the shape of cranes and tortoises, and of course, the throne room with the dragon throne. The further one moved north in the Forbidden City, through one vast plaza to the next, the closer one got to the emperor, known as the Son of Heaven.

I was heading for the most opulent of the imperial residences, the Palace of Heavenly Purity when I thought I saw Burton off in the distance just past a group of uniformed men—police or military, I didn't know. It was not so much that I saw Burton, but rather the flash of an azure scarf and a head of blondish hair. I started to move closer, but the group disbanded and I could see no sign of anyone remotely resembling Burton. I reminded myself that he was leaving that day for home. It was still early in the day, but the flights went out in the early afternoon, so he wouldn't have time for sightseeing. Furthermore, Burton did not hold a monopoly on azure scarves. I must have been mistaken.

Despite the grandeur of the buildings, my favorite part of the City was the garden at the north end. I browsed in the bookshop and purchased some woodcut prints that I thought might look nice framed for the shop, and generally lazed about. I felt guilty, though, as if I should be doing something. Mira had told me that my expenses would be paid until I left, but I thought I should see if I could make the trip pay for itself in some way, given that I wasn't making any commission on the purchase of the silver box, by finding more treasures to take home for the shop. If I could, then I'd tell Mira I'd pay the last few nights in the hotel. With that goal in mind, and guilt therefore assuaged, I went shopping.

Liulichang Street, which is just south and a little west of the Forbidden City, is a pleasant tree-lined street for pedestrians and scooters only, lined with old houses, or at least houses that look old. Like much of Beijing, it was flattened not that long ago, but it has been reconstructed and certainly looks authentic. It's supposed to be the premier antique street, but there are not a lot of real antiques to be found, more curios than anything else. I suppose it's a pseudoantique street with pseudoantiques, when you think about it. It's still attractive, though, most particularly the shops selling old books and calligraphic supplies, ink wells, stamp pads, and beautiful natural hair brushes in all sizes, even extraordinarily large ones, hanging in the windows of the shops. There are some interesting things to purchase, shadow puppets made of leather, for example. There are few truly old ones, but some of the new ones are beautifully done. I'd passed along my love of shadow puppets to Jennifer, and decided to bargain for two particularly lovely ones as a gift for her.

One of the best things about the area is that you get away from the high-rises, and catch a glimpse of the city that once was. There are markets, and tea houses, and ordinary little shops in addition to the tourist traps, and if you wander a little farther, which I did, given it was a clear winter day, cold but nice and sunny, you can find yourself on Dazhalan Lu, a real street with silk shops and a huge Chinese medicine store.

I was just wandering along, enjoying myself, when I saw Burton Haldimand framed, perhaps predictably, in the doorway of the medicine shop, putting on his sunglasses. Even though he was wearing a surgical mask, I was certain it was indeed Burton. I had also quite distinctly heard him say he was leaving early that day, which left me with the distinct possibility he'd lied. Perhaps because of this jaundiced view of mine, I decided that Burton was acting suspiciously. He looked carefully left and right before walking briskly in the direction from which I had just come. He was very intent on something. I followed. Fortunately the streets were crowded, which afforded me some cover. Soon we were back on Liulichang, where Burton proceeded to go into every single antique shop, and even some that looked pretty borderline in terms of antiques. Waiting for Burton would have been exceptionally tedious if he'd spent any time in the shops, but in each, no matter how big or how small, he spent only a few minutes, long enough for only a cursory look at the merchandise on offer. He had a piece of paper in his hand, which he folded each time he came out of a shop, and it didn't take me long to develop a theory as to what he was doing. Eventually, after about a dozen shops, I got bored and decided it was time to show myself.

"Lara!" Burton said with a start as he came out of a shop to find me standing there.

"Burton," I said, mimicking his tone.

"This is certainly serendipitous," he said, after a slight pause during which he was doubtless formulating his next lie. "I'm glad to see you. I was hoping for company again at dinner. I've decided I might as well attend the auction. Dr. Xie will be there. He's going after that poet's folio, as I think you know. He said he was treating to champagne afterward in celebration if he was the successful bidder, or a wake of some kind if he wasn't. It sounded good to me, either way."

"I thought you were heading back to Toronto, Burton," I said, in a perhaps somewhat snappish tone.

"I was, but I seem to have developed an aversion to the idea of going home empty-handed. I thought I'd see if there was something else I could purchase. The auction goes ahead tomorrow night as planned, minus one box, so I thought there might be something else. Courtney Cottingham pretty well gives me carte blanche as far as purchases are concerned."

"And you thought Liulichang Street was the right place for museum-quality antiquities, did you?" I asked, voice dripping with disbelief.

"Not really," he said. "But the auction does present a possibility or two."

"I decided I'd go to the auction, too. I can't get a flight for a day or two. Dr. Xie invited me for champagne as well, and perhaps young Mr. Knockoff will show up and we can sound the alarm."

"Mr. Knockoff?"

"The fellow who was at Molesworth and Cox in New York, and who I think stole the box here. The fellow you can't remember."

"Hmmm. That would be something of a long shot," Burton said. "I expect the thief knows better than to show up."

"You never know," I said. "How about we get a cup of tea? I'm finding it a bit cold now that the sun is going down."

"Why not?" he said and we picked a little tea shop nearby. Once again, Burton ordered. I suppose it made sense, given he spoke the language, but I have a real aversion to men who order my food for me, particularly when they don't ask me what I want.

"What have you been up to, Burton? Did you get your hand stuck in a car door or something?" I said. He'd taken off his mittens, and now was carefully peeling off one set of surgical gloves, and had another pristine pair waiting. I suppose he couldn't possibly hold a tea cup with the same pair he'd worn in the street.

"What?" he said.

"Your nails look bruised. Both hands, actually. Hard labor, perhaps?"

"They do look a little blue, don't they? But no, I can't recall having them smashed or anything. I'm sure I'd remember it." He quickly put his fingers in the new gloves. I noticed he didn't remove his sunglasses.

I didn't believe him, but there didn't seem to be much point in pressing him on the subject. There was so much about Burton's behavior that was perplexing, to say nothing of just plain annoying. "What are you doing?" I asked as the waiter brought the tea, a pot, and cup for each of us. Burton had fished a plastic bag out of his jacket pocket, and was dipping a tea bag into the single pot.

"I've brought my own tea," he said. "I ordered Chinese green tea for you and hot water for me."

"That tea of yours stinks, I'd have to say." Perhaps it didn't actually stink, but it sure overpowered the delicate scent of my green tea.

"It does smell a little strong, but it's very efficacious," he said. "Fights bacteria, keeps the blood running properly, eliminates blockages in the qi. You would get used to the strong flavor, and it would do you a world of good."

I was tempted to say that when it wasn't eliminating blockages in the qi it could probably be used to clear clogged drains, but I restrained myself. Instead, I returned to a more important subject, first tucking into one of the scrumptious custard tarts he'd also ordered, although he wasn't eating them himself. I might have to concede that it had not been such a bad idea for him to order on my behalf if this is what I got. "What are you planning to do tomorrow?" I said. "Just the auction?"

"Probably. I'll take it easy during the day, maybe visit the hotel's fitness room. You can't use a trip as an excuse not to keep in shape, you know. Then I'll go to the auction and see you there."

He didn't do that either. At this point, I was starting to take these lies of his personally, and was therefore ready for them. I'd given him ample opportunity over tea to confess what he was doing. He'd chosen not to do so. That fast led me to the conclusion that he was not just an eccentric genius of overweening ambition, but essentially a slug.

The next morning, I watched as he scanned the lobby quickly when he got off the elevator, probably looking for me. I was strategically placed behind a potted palm, and had been just about to give up and move on when he appeared. Once he got going, though, he moved fast, out the door and into a cab in a matter of seconds. I took the next one in line and followed him, which takes some doing in Beijing traffic, but the driver managed it once he understood what I wanted, thanks to the hotel doorman who didn't bat an eyelid when I asked for his translation services. Burton headed north and west from our hotel, skirting the north end of the Forbidden City, but after that we began to wend our way from street to street and I got hopelessly lost. My only consolation was that I had a card from our hotel with its name in Chinese, so at least I could get back. Finally, the cab ahead stopped and Burton got out. After giving him a minute's head start, I did the same.

We were on a lively street, lined with gnarled old trees and many shops. It was crowded, which made it difficult to keep him in view, but it also afforded me some protection once again, necessary given he and I were the only non-Chinese on the street. He never looked back, but occasionally looked up to read the signs or numbers on the shops or peered in the windows, as if he were looking for something specific. There were no antique stores around that I could see, which begged the question, Why were we here? I had a sudden crisis of conscience, thinking I might have been wrong about him. Maybe he was visiting some Chinese herbalist for a consultation on the state of his health, or for another supply of vile-smelling tea. I mean, what would I say if he looked behind him and there I was?

Rather abruptly, Burton turned into a little grocery store. I stood across the street and waited for him to come out, but after several minutes, he hadn't. Finally I followed him in. He wasn't there. I'd lost him, although I couldn't figure out how I'd managed to do so. I wished I could ask someone, but of course I couldn't.

Annoyed, I turned to go, and almost tripped over a tiny old woman who was sitting by the door. She had a lovely face, deeply wrinkled but beautiful. She also had teeny little feet. I was appalled, my feminist hackles rising. Technically, foot binding in China had been outlawed in 1911, and I never thought I'd ever see someone with bound feet. Bound feet were often referred to as "golden lilies," and the perfect foot an appalling three or four inches. Despite being outlawed, the practice probably went on in the country long after 1911, and it took the Communist Party, when it took over in 1949, to put an absolute close to this revolting practice. This woman clearly predated that time. I apologized, although I'm sure she couldn't understand a word I said. But I smiled at her, and she smiled back, several teeth missing. Then she gestured toward the back of the shop.

At first I thought she wanted me to buy something, but then I noticed a rough wooden door at the back of the shop. The woman had assumed that a white woman on her own was almost inevitably looking for a white guy, and was pointing me in the right direction. My crisis of conscience was over: if Burton was sneaking out back doors, he was up to something. I planned to see what he did this time. And so, like Alice in Wonderland, I stepped through the door and into another world.

Four

I was fourteen when my life took a different turn. The first distur-
bance to the pleasant enough existence I had—with effort and some
ability I believe—forged for myself, came with a drunken revelation
by Wu Peng, who told me that I had become his adopted son, not be-
cause of a long-standing tradition in my family for imperial service,
but because my father had sold me to Wu in order to pay off some
gambling debts. Wu's "wife" had wanted daughters-in-law to do
her bidding and grandchildren by way of the two sons they'd
adopted, so it was necessary for him to find someone else for imperial
service. My father's affliction had presented just that opportunity. It
was a jolt to my complacency, yes, but it also forced me to call into
question everything I had been told by my father, most especially
what I had chosen to believe about my sister. I began to think she was
dead. Perhaps, I thought, it was Number One Sister who haunted
the well at my home. It was she who plagued Auntie Chang's sleep!

One evening I was privileged to be able to stand in the shadows while the emperor's own musicians, the Pear Garden troupe, performed for the Son of Heaven and his friends. The musicianship was inspired, and evidently met with the emperor's approval. He did not find it necessary, as he often did, to correct them. The women—for the Pear Garden Orchestra consisted only of beautiful women—performed a piece of music that the Son of Heaven himself had written for them. It was exquisite, of course. I confess that I was beginning to think of myself as something of a connoisseur of the arts, and enthralled as I was, I drew closer perhaps than I should have, coming out of the shadows. The Son of Heaven did not seem to mind. At the conclusion of the performance, the emperor presented a silk pouch to each of the women of the orchestra in turn. Wu Peng, who had joined me, told me that all the women would receive a coin. One of them would receive a jade disk that indicated they were to share the Son of Heaven's bed that night.

It was shortly after that performance that I received a summons to the apartment of a woman known as Lingfei. I assumed this was a name she had been given in the palace and not the one she was given at birth. Ling is the sound of tinkling jade, so I expected she might be a musician, although I could not recall having made her acquaintance. Her reputation had, however, preceded her. It was to Lingfei that other women turned for help with certain medical problems, blemishes, for example, that they felt would detract from their beauty and turn the Son of Heaven's favor from them, or conditions of a womanly nature. There were medical experts of all kinds in the palace, of course, but the emperor's women seemed most comfortable discussing their problems with Lingfei. I wondered what she would want with me.

I was shown into a hall, quite austerely decorated, considering it was part of the palace, and waited. I had a sense that I was being watched, that there was someone in the shadows. I could not see anyone, but there was the faint whiff of cloves that I associated with the cosmetics favored in the harem, and of sweet basil and patchouli. After several minutes of waiting, however, I decided that this was a trick of some kind, and turned to go.

"I have not dismissed you," a voice said. I turned toward the voice to see a woman in simple dress, yet luxurious of fabric just the same, of the Western style, which is to say it lacked the long, hanging sleeves that many in the palace preferred. The only adornment to her tunic was a belt from which pieces of jade dangled, appropriate enough given her name. Her face was tinted white, her forehead, as was the fashion, yellow; her lips and cheeks were rouged, and her eyebrows were plucked, then redrawn and tinted blue-green to resemble moth wings. Her hair was piled high on her head, held in place by an elaborate hairpin from which, once again, pieces of jade hung, tinkling as she moved.

"I have an errand for you," the woman known as Lingfei said. "I understand you can read and write. I would ask you to write down this list," she said, gesturing to brushes and ink. When I had complied, she continued. "You will go to the lane of the apothecary, and thence to the stall whose name I will give you. Ask the proprietor to give you the powders that are listed and bring them back as soon as you can. There is more than enough money in the pouch for the purchase. You may keep for yourself what is left. There is plenty there for you to indulge your passion for dumplings and fried pastries," she said. "There will be another coin for you if you return quickly." With that she tossed the pouch, which resembled the ones distributed the previous evening by the emperor, toward me and disappeared into the shadows.

This was perplexing, to be sure. This woman knew far more about me than I did of her. It was true I liked the dumplings from a certain stall in the market, not far from the apothecary lane. It had been pointed out to me more than once that I was no longer the skinny child I was when I had first arrived at the Imperial Palace. How would a royal concubine like Lingfei, whose acquaintance I had just made, know that?

It was the first of many surprises during the time I knew Lingfei. It was also the first of many errands. I was regularly sent to the markets to fetch what she needed, most often to the apothecary lane. I often had to wait for some time, while she attended to some young woman or another, but it was a pleasant enough place to wait. It was many months before I summoned the courage to ask her if she would tell me about these potions, but to no avail: she declined, saying that time would tell whether or not I could be someone with whom she shared this information.

It took me a moment or two to get my bearings. I was in a narrow lane lined with high walls. The buildings were gray brick with gray roof tiles, so the place had a monochromatic aspect, punctuated here and there by a brighter sign and on one side by a lone red Chinese lantern that seemed to glow in this setting. It was quiet, the bustle of the street I had just left only a muffled sound behind me. Two men were sitting on the street playing chess, two birdcages hanging near them, the birds chirping away. Another man was repairing a bicycle nearby.

For a moment I just stood enjoying myself, drinking in this place so different from the new Beijing of traffic and towers. This is what Beijing used to be, a city of tiny streets like this one, called a hutong or lane. I was in a hutong neighborhood. This was the Beijing I'd loved twenty years ago, the one of little neighborhoods, and I was happy to have rediscovered it. The residents themselves run these neighborhoods, electing their own leaders, and setting the rules for everyone. Many things are shared, I was reminded, as a teenage boy came out of a doorway in his pajamas and a well-worn terry bathrobe, walked briskly along the street, and then into what was clearly marked, with the international man and woman symbols, as a public toilet. That made me smile for some reason. There were wires for electricity, and aerials for television, but there were also communal bathrooms.

It was all quite lovely, in an understated way. The rather stately gray walls of the lane were punctuated by doors, some ramshackle, others much more elaborate. In the latter case, the entrances were painted, often red, and they had lovely old door knockers. Sometimes I could look through to the courtyards beyond; in still others, my view of the interior was blocked by a decorated wall or screen, attractive in its own way.

I was enchanted. It was all coming back to me: the houses are called *siheyuan*, a typical northern Chinese style of home. The Forbidden City uses this same design writ large. The houses are a series of single-story buildings built around courtyards, sort of like a family compound. You go through a door, a gate really, called a "good luck gate," and then you're in the first courtyard. You can tell how important the person was who originally lived in the siheyuan by the number of crossbeams at the entranceway. You can see the rounded ends of the beams, some of them painted and decorated, protruding out of the gate over the door. No beam or one beam signifies a very ordinary family. Five beams and you're in the presence of a pretty important person. Nobody got seven beams because seven is an unlucky number in China, and nine was a number reserved for the emperor.

It was captivating to be sure, but unfortunately there was no sign of Burton. I'd given him too much of a head start when I'd waited for him to come out of that shop. I decided I should just savor the experience and look around, and with any luck he'd turn up. If he didn't, then I'd had an enjoyable time, and I'd just go back to the hotel. Knowing I was in a hutong neighborhood technically meant I couldn't get lost, as the houses in hutongs are aligned as the Forbidden City is, in fact as all of Beijing is, or at least used to be, on a north-south axis. The main avenues tend to also run in that direction, the hutongs run east-west by and large, linking them. If I kept going, I'd hit a main thoroughfare, and transportation back to the hotel.

Still, after a few minutes, I was feeling a bit anxious. Yes, technically hutongs ran east-west, but there were side lanes that didn't, and I didn't have a clue where I'd started. It was now a bit overcast, and a light snow was beginning to fall, making all the streets look even more the same. After several minutes, I still hadn't come upon a main thoroughfare as I had thought I would.

I began to think that not only had I lost Burton, I was pretty much lost myself. Still, luck was with me on both counts. My first break was a very loud drumming sound that began quite suddenly not that far away. It had to be the Drum Tower, which marked the north end of the old city of

Beijing, and I knew where that was. Realizing that the drumming would not continue for long, I started off at a fast pace in the direction of the sound. As I rounded a corner, I realized all was not lost on the Burton score either. I backed up a few paces in the direction I'd come, and then carefully peered around the corner again.

Burton was standing in front of one of the more elaborate siheyuan, talking to someone in the doorway. This home had a rather large, richly ornamented good luck gate flanked by imposing stone sculptures, guardians of the gate. The wall of the compound stretched along the hutong for many yards, and I could see a rather impressive roofline inside the wall. If I were a betting person, I'd say whoever lived there had his own bathroom. After all, there were five beams on that gate. And to all appearances, the lucky person in question was the man in black.

This was all very perplexing, to say nothing of irritating. As personally rewarding as touring the hutong neighborhood might have been for me, following Burton everywhere was not my idea of a good time, and his constant obfuscation as to his plans was definitely getting up my nose. Still, I too had a plan, one that involved finding my way back to the hotel and then ambushing him. With the Drum Tower, a fabulous structure that was used to sound the time both morning and evening for the inhabitants of ancient Beijing in the Yuan, Ming, and Qing dynasties, located, and a taxi hailed to take me to the hotel, I put my plan into action. I rather hoped the army officer hadn't recognized me. I seemed to be the only Caucasian woman in the neighborhood, and therefore more obvious than usual. I'd worn a hat and scarf against the cold and snow, and I hadn't noticed any glimmer of recognition on his face in the second or two before I'd hightailed it out of there. Indeed, he and Burton had been very deep in conversation. I was reasonably sure that Burton, with his back to me, had no inkling of my presence.

I ordered myself a coffee in the lobby and waited for Burton to return. I gave him about five minutes to get to his room and get his coat off before I pounced. I knew which room was his. He'd bought the drinks when we'd met in the bar, and I'd noted it when he signed for them. He answered my knock with a can of disinfectant spray in his hand. I held my breath for a few seconds in case he decided I had to be hosed down before I would be permitted to enter. He didn't look happy to see me, but at least he didn't blast me with the disinfectant, and after a long pause, he stepped aside and gestured for me to come in.

"I have a proposal for you, Burton," I said.

"Could it not wait until this evening? I'm going to see you at the auction. I was hoping to have a bit of a rest. I'm not feeling completely well." Actually, he didn't look well, now that he mentioned it. He kept his head down as he spoke, and still had his sunglasses on. This did not stop me.

"Your qi is no longer harmonious, is that it, Burton? I'm sorry to hear that. Here is what you are up to. You aren't looking for a substitute for the T'ang box. I think you're looking for the box itself. Mira Tetford, whom you met the other day, has had all the newspapers checked, and there is no word of the theft from the auction house yet. You think if you put the word out, the thief, who may think he's relatively safe given the lack of publicity, will come to you. You are following every lead. Am I right?" Actually, although I had decided not to mention it, the lead he'd been following that morning had been mine: the idea that the man in black had deliberately blocked the view of the custodian at the auction house so that the thief would have a head start. The man in black might even have given the doorman the wrong impression as to which young man to tackle.

He shuffled uncomfortably in his chair. "I suppose I might be doing that," he said. "There's a chance, you know."

"I think it's a really long shot, and probably a waste of time. But I want that box, too, as much as you do, if not more. What I am suggesting is that we look for the box together. It will save time. If one of us finds it, the deal is that it goes back to the auction house. We both get to compete for it again, and we'll let the legal process take its course. May the best person win, as you would say. You might as well agree. Purchasing it is one thing, but you would have trouble getting it out of the country if it has been reported stolen."

"I could probably get it out."

"They definitely don't want stolen antiquities taken out of the country. If you got caught, they'd assume you were the one who stole it. Even if you legally purchased it at the auction, China probably doesn't want you to take it out."

"That's ridiculous. I mean, yes, the Chinese government is asking the U.S. to ban imports of Chinese antiques and antiquities over ninety-five years old. Hypocritical if you ask me."

"What's hypocritical about wanting to protect your heritage for your own citizens?"

"Protect your heritage? Surely you know that during the

Cultural Revolution people were encouraged to destroy much of the country's heritage—antiques, temples, tombs, you name it. It was state-sponsored hooliganism, if you ask me. Almost everything of value from an historical perspective was a target."

"That was then, this is now. Now they want to protect it."

"They have a funny way of doing it. You wait until tonight at the auction. You'll see. There'll be dozens of Chinese collectors paying large sums for the merchandise. The biggest market for Chinese antiquities is the Chinese themselves."

"So?"

"So these bidders will by and large be private citizens, the new wealthy class, young and aggressive. These objects are not going to museums where they can be shared with the proletariat, I can assure you. They are going to people like Xie Jinghe, who, elegant gentleman though he may be, will be the only viewer, unless of course he lets some of his equally wealthy friends have a peek at his treasures every now and again. So why shouldn't we, as North Americans, either individual collectors or dealers or museum curators, have the same access?"

"What about—?"

"Please don't give me the argument about buyers and collectors encouraging looting. The Chinese government urges its citizens to get out there and collect Chinese art and antiquities. If anything is encouraging looting, that is it."

"Okay," I said. "Let me put my feelings on this subject another way. If I found out you were trying to smuggle something out of the country, I would report you in a flash. Despite what you say, I believe the penalties here have become quite harsh for exporting something of real cultural significance, which this arguably is, particularly when it's been stolen. The death penalty, isn't it?"

He paled. He should have, too, because people have in fact been executed for smuggling fossils out of China. "How do I know you won't find it and not tell me?" he said, after he managed to compose himself.

"You don't. I'm just giving you my word that I will play fair here. Personally, I think I'm the one taking the greater risk."

He thought about it all for a minute. "Okay," he said. "Deal. Let's shake on it."

We shook, my bare hands to his surgical gloves. "Do you want some tea?" he said, gesturing toward a rather complicated bit of tea paraphernalia and a box of some kind of tea that I didn't recognize. "I've brewed a pot. This one helps remove blockages of the qi."

Once again, it smelled like drain cleaner. I declined. "What is that thing?" I asked, pointing at a small cylindrically shaped machine of some kind that was humming away rather noisily.

"It's an air filter," he said.

"You travel with an air filter?" I asked incredulously.

"I do," he said. "Dual voltage, of course, with a set of international plugs so I can use it anywhere. The same goes for my tea kettle. You can't count on a hotel to have them in the rooms, and anyway, who knows who's used them and what they put in them."

"You travel with an air filter," I repeated.

"What's your point?" he asked in a peevish tone.

"No point, I guess."

"It's flu season. Everyone is coming back from Asia with these horrible bronchial conditions."

"I see. I'll try not to do that. To get back to the real point of this conversation: where are we going next?" I asked.

"Panjiayuan Market," he said. "Do you know it? It's south and east of here. It's big, so we'll go tomorrow morning and spend a good part of the day if we have to."

"Let's go together," I said, determined not to let him out of my sight. "I'll meet you in the lobby whenever you say."

"Good. We'll share a cab. No, wait. I have an appointment for a therapeutic massage first thing. Spot of tummy trouble I want to get under control. It's on the way. I think the market opens early, but why don't we meet there at nine thirty. Does that work for you?"

"Sure," I said. "I'll meet you there. We can divide it up and get it done in half the time. I'll bring my copy of the photograph, and I'll get myself lots of cards from the hotel, and just put my name on them."

"Get the taxi driver to take you to the antique section, not the curio part of the market. I'll meet you there. We'll stick close together. If you have language difficulties, I won't be far away." I wanted to say that I was perfectly aware that the reason he wanted me close was not to help me with his Chinese, but to keep an eye on me at all times. That suited me just fine. I wanted to keep tabs on him, too. I also wanted to ask him what he was doing talking to the man in black, but that would have meant letting him know I'd been following him. I thought it best not to do that, given that at the moment I appeared to have the upper hand, ethically speaking, no matter how undeserving I might be. He hadn't mentioned that he knew I was following him, which either meant he hadn't seen me, or that he was being as cagey on that subject as I was.

We didn't talk about our arrangement again that day. In fact, we were not to talk about it ever again. I did see him at the auction, however. There was a good crowd, which included Mira Tetford, who said working on this project with me had gotten her interested in Chinese art, something she was sure was going to cost her money. I told her there was no turning back.

The bidding was fierce. I had to admit, painful though it might be, that Burton was right about one thing: most of the bidders were Chinese, young, ostentatiously dressed, and doubtless buying for themselves, not a museum. Dr. Xie was the oldest bidder in the room. He was also the high bidder for the folio, paying an astounding three million dollars U.S. That went a long way to explaining why the mystery seller had decided to move the box to Beijing from New York. He or she would definitely be doing better here than in New York. I did think about bidding on some lovely porcelain, but Burton, who saw that I was about to put in a bid, stopped me. "Not worth it," he said. Again, he was probably right. Mira, however, did bid, and managed to acquire a very lovely nineteenth-century painting with advice from both Dr. Xie and Burton. She was thrilled.

Dr. Xie was determined to celebrate his acquisition, and celebrate it we did. It was not quite the quiet glass or two of fine champagne that I'd been expecting. Rather it was a sumptuous party at his penthouse apartment. Once again, the view over the Forbidden City and the lights of central Beijing was spectacular. The apartment was gorgeous, all gold and blue, with silk carpets everywhere, and very beautiful hand-carved furniture. The art was breathtaking. I could have spent days there examining every piece. There was a cabinet of Shang bronzes, beautiful porcelain, lacquerware, and jade objects that were just exquisite, and some gold and silver objects as well. He had an entire glass cabinet filled with T'ang dynasty funerary objects, terra-cotta figures of horses and camels and riders, servants, and soldiers, glazed in yellow and green. I almost forgot to drink my champagne.

Dr. Xie was particularly fond of his collection of scrolls and folios. A nicely masculine den with dark furniture had almost every square inch of wall covered with beautiful scrolls. He joined me in that room. "You have an extraordinary collection, Dr. Xie," I said. "I heard about the collection you donated in Canada, but I haven't had a chance to see it yet. If it is half as beautiful as this, then the museum is indeed fortunate to have it."

He acknowledged the compliment modestly. "I've been very successful both here and in Canada, and happy to have found a way to share that. I admit I've become somewhat addicted to collecting. Eventually I will give all of this to a museum, but I want to enjoy it myself for now. Shall I show you where I'm going to put the folio I just purchased?"

I followed him to a sort of antechamber off the den. In it was a glass case, humidity and light controlled. "This is where it will go, my little sanctuary," he said. "Now I must join my other guests. Dinner will be served shortly."

I was admiring the T'ang funerary figures in the living

room one more time when it occurred to me that as lovely as they were, not one piece in the cabinet, and possibly the entire apartment, could really hold a candle to a set of nesting silver caskets, not because the figures in front of me weren't absolutely top-notch, because they were, but because there was something very special about the boxes. Every now and then, there are pieces of art that somehow capture our imagination, because they encapsulate an age, perhaps, or because there is a story attached to them that continues to have resonance for us, or because they carry some symbolism that is profound. Art like this can move us deeply. Yes, the funerary figures in front of me were particularly lovely, and undoubtedly authentic. Yes, the workmanship was superb. Yes, both the funerary figures and the boxes dated to the same era and chances were both had come from a T'ang tomb. Somehow, though, the silver boxes with the rather poignant, indeed hopeful, formula for the elixir of immortality stood head and shoulders above the rest. Burton was right. It was just that kind of antiquity that a museum like the Cottingham would want to have as the anchor piece for its Asian galleries. Any museum would.

I hadn't heard Burton come up behind me until he spoke. "Fabulous stuff," he said. I nodded. "But not as fabulous as that silver coffret."

"No, it isn't."

"We have to find it, Lara. It doesn't matter which museum gets it, mine or the one your client plans to donate it to. But we have to find it."

"Yes, we do, Burton. We really do."

"And we will. Time to eat," he said.

There were several people there I knew, and several I didn't. Mira and Ruby were there, as were Burton and David. Mira pulled me aside and pointed out some of the people, including a gentleman on the far side of the room. "Big man in the government," she whispered. "Very influential. Son of a close friend of Mao Zedong. Harvard educated."

"I thought you didn't get to leave China to go to Harvard," I said. "When I was here twenty years ago anyway, which I suppose would be about the time the man you're pointing to went to Harvard, you had to get special permission to leave the country, didn't you?"

"Anything was possible if you were the son of a friend of Mao's," she said. "Does the term red prince or red princess mean anything to you?"

"No it doesn't."

"It's the offspring of someone who was closely associated with Mao. I'd say several of the people in this room would qualify. Friends of Mao got special privileges, a better place to live, they were allowed to accumulate wealth where other people couldn't, and yes, their children could go to Harvard."

"Now that the country is opening up a little, maybe the concept doesn't have as much relevance."

"They're still around. Ruby would like to leave the country to study. Do you think she'll get a passport instantly? No, she won't. I'll do my best to get it for her, because she's talented and should be doing more than simply assisting me. I would miss her. She found the office for me, and she deals with the bureaucracy that I don't understand. But if she wants to go abroad, I'm going to try to get her there. I brought her tonight because I want her to meet the influential Dr. Xie. I'm here to chat up the government big guys."

"I guess if Dr. Xie put this party together, he was pretty sure he was going to be the successful bidder on the folio. He did say he would hold a wake if he didn't, but this looks pretty much like a victory party to me. If the people here are as important as you say, you wouldn't just call them up from the auction house and tell them to come on over."

"No, and you wouldn't have food like this just sitting in your refrigerator, either," she said, as a waiter passed some really delectable shrimp hors d'ouevres. "When you can outbid anybody in the room, and you are absolutely determined to get something, then, yes, you can plan your victory party in advance. Dr. Xie is that wealthy and that determined."

"And the Chinese government doesn't care if he owns all this art? I mean there are objects here that have got to be five thousand years old! That cabinet of Shang bronzes would make any museum proud."

"As long as he keeps it in the country, and as long as he has such influential friends, I don't think it's a problem. Really, the government just wants the stuff kept in China, and Dr. Xie is doing that." That pretty much confirmed what Burton had said earlier in the day.

I found myself sitting between Mira and David, which was nice, because several people were speaking Chinese. Mira whispered to me that she was going to have to chat up the man on her right, the red prince she'd pointed out to me. That left me to talk to David, who was on Burton's right. That was fine with me. David turned out to be an interesting man.

"So how do you know Burton?" I asked. "He said you were assisting him while he was here."

"Nice of him to say that. I met him a year ago at an auction. We chatted and spent some time together. He got in touch when he was coming here to purchase the T'ang silver box, and I'm really just tagging along. To be perfectly honest, I wanted to meet Dr. Xie, seeing as he is an extremely important man and therefore a great contact for me. Burton was good enough to suggest he'd introduce us. I was quite unexpectedly about to meet him at Cherished Treasures House, but when the silver box got lifted, there wasn't a chance to talk about much else. Burton then brought me along tonight. It is a blatant attempt on my part to get ahead in life."

I laughed. "Do you collect art?"

"I'd like to. I think I need to learn more about it, to say nothing of make more money, before I get into it."

"Very wise. Most people just leap right in, and learn through their mistakes. So what do you do for a living, then?"

"I'm a lawyer by training. I went to law school in California. I work as a consultant to businesses in, I suppose, the same way Mira does, except that she is retained by the foreign firms, and I represent the Chinese firms."

"Does law school in California mean you are one of those red princes that Mira has told me about?"

David laughed. "I suppose so. Second generation, however. Did you enjoy the auction?" I thought perhaps it had been rude of me to ask the red prince question, which was why he was sidestepping the whole issue, but we had an enjoyable

chat nonetheless. Despite what he said about his relative ig-
norance about art, he was very knowledgeable about Dr. Xie's
collection, certainly more so than I, and I'd had a good teacher
in Dory Matthews. We exchanged cards at the end of the evening, and David told me if I came back to Beijing, he'd be
happy to show me around. I thought he was adorable.

We left Dr. Xie about one in the morning. I headed back
to the hotel with Burton, who'd worn sunglasses the whole
evening, citing a migraine. "Don't forget," he said, as we
parted for the night. "Panjiayuan Market, nine-thirty in the
morning. Be there or be square." As if I needed reminding!

The trouble was, morning didn't come as soon as it was supposed to. We were up very late, and I'd had a fair amount of
champagne. I admit it. That morning, of all mornings, I
overslept. I had tried to set the hotel telephone alarm, and
had obviously botched it, because it was 9:45 when I awoke.
Having spent much of the night wandering around the room,
I had managed to fall asleep shortly before I was supposed to
get up. Jet lag and champagne will do this to you. I leapt
out of bed, and was bolting through the lobby at about five
minutes after ten. As it turned out, my timing was perfect.
Burton was getting into a cab. Thinking he was late too, I
headed for the door, but stopped as the doorman loaded
Burton's luggage into the trunk.

The slug had lied again! I stood motionless, absolutely
fuming, as the taxi pulled away. When I had recovered a
measure of composure, I went to the front desk. "My colleague from Toronto, Mr. Burton Haldimand, hasn't checked

out yet, has he?" I said in what I hoped was a panicky voice. I'm not entirely sure I was faking it.

The very pleasant woman at the desk typed away at the computer in front of her. "Yes," she said. "I'm afraid so. Just a few minutes ago. Is there a problem?"

"He's forgotten his papers," I said. "He's going to a meeting in . . . in . . . I can't pronounce it, sorry."

"Xi'an," she said. Xi'an is very easy to pronounce, or at least to approximate the Chinese pronunciation, which is to say more or less *see ahn,* and most tourists in Beijing would know how to say it, given its fame for the terra-cotta warriors, but I didn't care how dumb I looked. I'd got what I wanted. "He is coming back, though," she said. "He asked us to keep any phone messages he received while he's away. I would be pleased to take a message from you as well. Here, I'll get you a pen and paper."

"This can't wait until he gets back. I have to get him these papers." I pulled a packet out of my shoulder bag. It actually contained my travel documents, but what did she know? "He needs them for his meeting in Xi'an. Did he tell you what hotel he's staying in? I'll phone him. Perhaps I could fax some of the material. You could help me do that, couldn't you? I'd be very grateful."

Bless her. She told me what I wanted to know. She offered to fax the documents if I brought them back later in the afternoon when Burton would have arrived in Xi'an. I didn't, because later that afternoon I was on an Air China flight to Xi'an, heading for what was once the capital of the T'ang dynasty, and therefore quite possibly the home of Lingfei, original owner of the silver box. I was also heading for a big dustup with a slug. To say that I was annoyed with Burton would not come close to capturing my feelings, after all that garbage about how we had to find the box no matter which of us got it, how we had to work together. I was really ticked.

Five

I remember the exact moment when I decided that there was a distinct possibility that Lingfei was my long lost sister. After Wu Peng's revelation, I spent as little time as possible visiting my family. The necessary obligations met, I sought no further opportunities to see them. My feelings about my family did not extend to Auntie Chang, who had been a most devoted and beloved servant, and a very distant cousin of my mother's. A chance encounter with Auntie Chang as she was leaving a Buddhist temple after prayers provided the impetus. (My family is Buddhist, my mother devoutly so. Indeed my great-grandfather purchased an ordination certificate from a particularly grasping member of the imperial family of his day, one Princess Anle, for thirty thousand coppers in order to be exempt from taxes, as all priests are. He did not live in a monastery however, nor was he celibate, as his numerous offspring would attest. The current Son of Heaven revoked his exemption and put us back on the tax rolls, which upset my family, but rather impressed me now that I was old enough to understand it.)

Auntie Chang did enjoy a tipple or two, her favorite being Courtier's Clear Ale of Toad Tumulus. It was an inferior brew, I knew from my sojourn at the palace, but Auntie Chang liked it, and I took her to a pub for a goblet or two. She drank. I ate dumplings. When she was feeling happy, I took the opportunity to ask about my sister.

"All I know," Auntie Chang said, "is that your father was very angry with her when she stayed out all night. He guessed, and I knew, that there was a young man involved. Your sister had fallen in love with a member of the Gold Bird Guard, one posted to the station at one of the eastern gates. That is why she had no worries about staying out on the streets after the ward had closed. Your father had other plans for her. She was an accomplished musician, and he wished to enhance his status through her, persuading someone in the Imperial Palace to accept her. If the emperor liked her, then your family would rise in status. They might be invited to the palace, become a confidant of the most senior mandarins."

"Is that what happened then? She is somewhere in the palace?"

"I do not know," she replied. "I know only that she left with your father. He came back. She did not. That is what also happened to you. Unlike you, I have neither seen nor heard of her since. Your mother never mentions her at all, never utters her name. Nor will she permit others in the household to do so."

It had never occurred to me until that moment that I should be searching for my sister where I myself labored, in the harem of the Son of Heaven. From there it was, I suppose, a fairly easy leap to suspicions about Lingfei. On every occasion that I saw her, I looked carefully at her features, searching for something that would tell me *whether or not she was indeed Number One Sister. There were two difficulties. One was that she always wore makeup in my presence. The other was that I had not seen my sister in almost ten years. Indeed, I had been only five years of age when she left us. Her face was not clear to me, except perhaps in my dreams. I listened most carefully to Lingfei's voice, but that told me nothing. Hers was the voice of a mature woman, not the young girl's voice I recalled.*

I had more and more opportunity to study her, however. After several months of doing errands for her, she asked me if I would write something for her. I thought it would be a letter to her family, perhaps, which would resolve my dilemma, but it was not. Instead I began writing what I soon realized was a very detailed formula for making artificial pearls. I gave no indication that I understood it, although I did try to memorize it, pearls being a rather valued commodity in the harem.

I was disappointed by her request, however. My sister had learned how to write just as I and my brothers had, so this seemed to indicate quite conclusively that Lingfei was not the woman I sought. I was desolate, until she told me that I had saved her many hours of writing, and allowed her to consult the notes resulting from her experiments. That could only mean that she could read, and I went forward with renewed hope. She asked me to come back two days hence.

From that day on, I spent at least one day a week with Lingfei, writing for her. I would sit cross-legged on one of her wooden couches with my writing table before me while she paced the room, stopping occasionally to consult her notes. Most of the formulas I wrote were for medicines, I decided, for the treatment of various ailments resulting from an excess of either yin or yang, caused by wind, cold, heat, damp, dry, and fire. She told me when I questioned her that she had been a Taoist nun before she caught the Emperor's eye, and had studied with a master. These formulas that I was writing for her were based on her notes of that time, and the work she had done with the master, and also her observations from the treatment of the women in the harem. It was the first of several confidences that she shared with me.

Different city. Same routine. At least it was a really interesting place. Xi'an and its environs are considered by many to be the cradle of Chinese civilization, and justifiably so. With a history that stretches back at least four thousand years, and its status as capital of several Chinese dynasties, including that of the first emperor, Qin Shi Huangdi, it is a wonderful repository of art and culture. Best known worldwide as the home of the magnificent terra-cotta army of Qin Shi Huangdi, it is a city that seems to me to have managed the transition to the new economic reality better than Beijing, having preserved the old with the new to a much greater extent, as compared to the wholesale leveling of much of old Beijing. It is a walled city, although the urban area has expanded way beyond the walls.

Burton had chosen a hotel within the beautiful old city walls, a little east of the Bell Tower, which would have been the center of the ancient city, positioned where the main north-south and east-west axes meet. He headed out of his hotel around 9 AM when this part of town was just waking up. Once out the front door he stopped briefly to add a surgical mask to his attire, which already included a hat pulled down over his ears, a long scarf that was wound around his neck a couple of times, azure of course, and heavy jacket and gloves. It was cold, that's for sure, and for once the surgical mask did not look entirely out of place. Xi'an's air is unfortunately highly polluted, and even some Chinese wore masks.

Health thus attended to, Burton sidestepped the taxi driver who wanted to take him wherever he wanted to go, and headed west on foot along the rather prosaically named Dong Dajie or East Street, past the restaurants selling steamed dumplings and buns from their front windows, past the many clothing shops, most still boarded up for the night, past the banks with their charming English signage—like "Evening Treasure" for their night depository chutes—and then past the man washing the sidewalk in front of the establishment with the inspired English moniker of Sunny Half Past Eight Friend Changing Club. The street was not crowded at all, and as always I was worried Burton would see me. And as always, he never looked back.

When he came to the Bell Tower, he paused only briefly to look at the impressive and beautifully colored structure before taking an escalator down to the subterranean passages that linked the major streets of the city's central square. During the time that Xi'an, then known as Chang'an, was the capital of the T'ang dynasty, it may well have been the most populous city in the world. These main thoroughfares would have been extraordinarily wide, particularly the main north-south street, wide enough, indeed, for the emperor to leave his Imperial Palace to the city's north, and make his way south to go about imperial business. City residents would have had to cross huge drainage ditches that lined these impressive avenues. Then they used bridges built over the ditches; now we pedestrians are sent underground to avoid the traffic, and from the underground passage can choose to surface north, south, east, or west of the Bell Tower.

Burton chose to continue moving west, surfacing right near the Drum Tower on the west side of the intersection. He kept to the same street, now called Xi Dajie, or West Street. Suddenly, though, he paused for a few seconds, causing me to find cover behind a staircase leading to a shopping plaza. Then Burton turned north.

I continued to follow him into a quite extraordinary market area. There were tea shops and grocery stores, dumpling stalls, and vendors of piles of sweets of some kind. As we went deeper into the market, the lanes became narrower. Gradually the signs that were in Chinese were replaced, or at least supplemented by signs in Arabic, and the women covered their heads. The smells were now that of mutton. We had entered the Muslim Quarter of Xi'an. Burton stopped to purchase a ticket, and entered a mosque. After a few minutes, I did the same.

Xi'an's mosque, purportedly the largest in China, a fact I did not doubt, was a soothing, quiet place, with lovely arches that integrated Arabic and Chinese design, pleasant wooden buildings and gates, old gnarled trees, stone stela and fountains. It seemed to me to be a place best suited to quiet contemplation, too quiet, of course, if you happened to be following someone. I had to be very careful not to be seen.

It was also a perfect place for a clandestine meeting. Just in front of the prayer hall, Burton stopped and waited. I held back and watched. For a few minutes he did nothing other than stamp his feet against the cold and pull his scarf tighter around his neck. At one point he removed his surgical mask, there being no germ-ridden person in sight, and his breath could be seen against the cold air. About five minutes after we got there, a man of indeterminate age, not young but not old either, strode right past me and went up to Burton. I ducked into one of the side halls and waited. In a moment or two, I could hear their voices coming toward my position and strained to hear. They stopped right outside the hall in which I was cowering. To my profound irritation, they were speaking Chinese. I had no clue what they were talking about, only that they both sounded angry, as if they were negotiating something and it was not going well. I did manage to catch a glimpse of the face of Burton's acquaintance, enough that I thought I would recognize him if I saw him again. A moment or two later, they moved on, leaving me wondering whether to wait or go. When I screwed up the courage to look out, neither man was to be seen. Burton had managed to slip away again.

I did go looking for him. One of the covered souks in the Muslim Quarter had a high preponderance of shops selling what were purported to be antiques, and that was as likely a place as any to pick up Burton's trail, if he was following his now normal routine of asking about the silver box and handing out his business card with an accompanying request for them to get in touch if they had it to sell or knew someone who did. When that proved fruitless, I had another idea: the antique market just outside the Baxian Gong. Presumably Burton would be hitting every antique market or stall in town.

The Baxian Gong is a Taoist temple located not far outside

the eastern city gates of Xi'an and dedicated to the Eight Immortals. Across a narrow road from the temple is an antique market that is held every Sunday and Wednesday, and Sunday it was. To get to it, you go out the eastern gate at the end of Dong Dajie, then turn left and walk along the outside of the city walls where a narrow urban park has been created between the walls and the moat. On this cold and bright Sunday, a group of older men sat together and listened to their birds singing away in cages that they had hung from branches of the trees along the path. A group of men and women were practicing tai chi. Farther along there was a group of musicians playing traditional instruments and singing. They appeared to be rehearsing, and it was inspiring. I would have liked to just watch and listen, but I was a woman on a mission.

At the northern-most east gate, I crossed the busy roadway that runs parallel to the walls and headed into a much quieter and older district. Guidebooks tend to refer to the area outside the eastern gates and around the temple as shabby, but I didn't see it that way. What I view as shabby are the rows of hugely unattractive high-rise apartment buildings that tower over the city walls. But slip past them, and you will find real people doing real things, shopping for food, having their bicycles repaired, visiting the cobbler, consulting the doctor.

I had some difficulty finding the Baxian Gong, despite having a map. I took several wrong turns, and nearly got flattened by a man on a scooter, but every corner revealed something new. There were piles of brightly colored plastic washtubs piled up in front of one shop, mountains of oranges and green onions at another. There were pyramids of eggs of the most beautiful soft-blue hue, each one in its own tiny straw nest. The butcher had his meat hanging from hooks outside his shop. Dumplings steamed away in bamboo baskets. All along the street there were fires in old metal drums over which people cooked noodles or steamed vegetables as their customers chatted as they waited.

The market at the Baxian Gong is not large, and definitely not fancy. In a courtyard across from the temple, vendors have laid cloths and bamboo mats on the ground and simply spread out their wares. It was a far cry from the antique markets I usually frequent, but I liked it just fine. The amazing thing was that, unlike Beijing, there really were antiques here. There was old jade and porcelain, some bronzes, beautiful drawings and scrolls; in short, many very attractive objects. There were very few foreigners here, maybe one or two other than me, and vendors kept shouting "Lookie, Mother" at me over and over as I stepped past their displays. One woman in Mao jacket-and-pants with a faint scar across her left cheek was particularly persistent, actually grasping my sleeve tightly at one point. In truth, she had some very interesting merchandise, and I was tempted to buy, but there was also a sign warning purchasers that we required an export stamp if we wished to take any purchase out of the country. What I didn't see was either a T'ang box or Burton Haldimand. I seemed to have lost him completely.

Still, I kept looking, not because I thought I was going to see Burton, but because I was enjoying myself. To either side of the informal stalls were antique shops, and I visited every one of these. I tried asking about a silver box, but no one could understand me, even when I took out the photograph of George's box and waved it in front of them. Only in Beijing could I manage such a task in English. I was envious of Burton for his facility with the language.

Burton wasn't in the temple itself, either. He would have liked it, too, especially a hall devoted to Sun Simiao, a master pharmacist of the T'ang dynasty, and one of the earliest practitioners of Chinese medicine, now worshipped as a Buddhalike god. Sun Simiao was the first to write on the subject of medical ethics, and wrote several texts on medicine with many, perhaps thousands, of formulations for just about whatever might ail you. Apparently he was a sickly child, and managed to cure himself along with everybody else. The walls of the hall were covered in a colorful mural that depicted scenes from the sage's life. All in all, he seemed to me to be Burton's kind of guy.

Beyond his more conventional medical talents, though, Sun Simiao was an alchemist who secluded himself on Zhong Nan Mountain to perform practices that would allow him to become immortal. He also believed in exorcism. He wrote a text on these subjects called, more or less, "Essential Instructions from the Books on the Elixirs of the Great Purity," which was probably based on texts called *Taiqing Jing* or "Book of Great Purity," one of the first books anywhere on alchemy, now lost to us. These formulations quite possibly included elixirs that contained mercury and arsenic, which the master pharmacist was said to have administered to himself. Apparently it worked. Legend has it that his corpse had not begun to decompose some months after he died.

This alchemy business I found interesting, given the T'ang

box. I'd thought the formula for the elixir of immortality contained in the box was unusual at best, laughable at worst. But
clearly no one in T'ang times would have agreed with me. Its
loss was more than just the theft of a valuable object, as I had
begun to realize that night at Dr. Xie's celebration. It clearly
was an artifact of some great importance, and I felt sad not
just for Dory, not just for China, but really for all of us who
value the past. I also realized that I had known only two people who were true experts on T'ang China and would not
think it odd if I asked them about alchemy. One was Dory
Matthews, and it was too late to ask her. The other was Burton Haldimand. To ask him would take much swallowing of
pride on my part. I wasn't sure I was up for it.

Burton was not answering his phone when I got back to
the hotel. This annoyed me even more, if that was possible.
I chose to deal with this aggravation by going out for the
rest of the day, visiting the truly awe-inspiring terra-cotta
warriors of China's first emperor, Qin Shi Huangdi who
reigned from 221 to 210 BCE. The terra-cotta warriors are
a World Heritage site, deservedly so. They are as spectacular
as you might imagine them to be, row upon row of hundreds of men, all life-size and no face the same: generals,
archers, light infantry, heavy armored soldiers, cavalry complete with horses, and in a special place, two wonderful
chariots for the emperor. The actual mausoleum of the emperor, the place where presumably his body was laid to rest,
has never been opened. All we can see is a pyramid-shaped
structure near Mount Li. The historian Sima Qian reported,
however, that a whole world had been created for the First

Son of Heaven, with representations of the Yellow and Yangtze Rivers dug and filled with mercury, flowing somehow mechanically, the heavens above him complete with representations of the constellations. Automatic crossbows were set to kill any tomb robbers. It would be a difficult place to break into. Whether as a tomb robber or an archaeologist, the hazards would be many. Even at the time it was a decidedly unhealthy place to be. Qin Shi Huangdi's successor had the first emperor's childless concubines buried with him, and all who worked on the enormous tomb were sealed in it to die. Protecting him through all eternity were the terra-cotta warriors we see today.

Qin Shi Huangdi believed in immortality, and may have taken far too much of the elixir that was supposed to guarantee it. He was reported to have sent several expeditions in search of an island where the Immortals dwelt. The Immortals lived, if that's the right verb, in special places befitting their status, secret islands or underground cities or, for Taoists especially, on mountaintops. None of these expeditions of Qin Shi Huangdi's came back. One has to wonder why. Perhaps they couldn't resist the temptation of escaping the emperor, who was undoubtedly not the most benevolent of rulers.

All in all, Qin Shi Huangdi didn't have much luck in the immortality department if the stories of his death many miles from home are anything to go by. Rather than making the leap and leaving his clothes behind, his corpse was put into his carriage and began the journey back to the palace. Those in charge did not want anyone to know he had died, so they packed the carriage with rotting fish to cover the smell of rotting emperor. It was an ignominious end, I suppose, for the man who had united China.

Still the warriors are a remarkable sight, and I felt immeasurably better when I got back to the hotel. This pleasant feeling lasted for about ten minutes. Burton still wasn't answering his phone. After fuming for a while, both about Burton and the sheer uselessness of this trip to Xi'an from a silver-box point of view, I decided that once again the only approach was to go directly to Burton's room. I'd managed to inveigle the room number from the hotel operator, again with the colleague-from-Toronto story. By the time I'd left to see the warriors, I'd asked her to put me through to him so often that I'm sure she was glad to just give me the number so I'd go away.

The door was open when I got there, a housekeeping cart right outside. The maid was scrubbing the bathroom. I took a quick peek inside. The room was empty. There was no suitcase, no portable air filter buzzing away, no tea apparatus, no clothes, no toiletries in the bathroom. The slug had slipped away from me again!

I stomped back to my room. First I called Air China and tried to get on a flight back to Beijing the next day. That didn't work, but I could get out the following day. Then I called the hotel in Beijing to tell them when I was coming back. The woman at the desk asked me to hold for a moment, and then came back on the line to tell me there was a message flagged to my room. She had it still, given that they didn't want to put it in the room until I returned. It was in a sealed envelope. I asked her to open the envelope and fax it to me at my present location. She agreed to do that right away.

While I waited for the contents of the mysterious sealed envelope to be put into my hands, I went to the hotel bar. The lobby was a hive of activity. The staff was putting up Christmas decorations, garlands were being strung from every pillar and post, an enormous fake tree already fully decorated was being set into place, and Christmas carols, sung by Chinese children, were being piped through the whole place. This did not improve my mood. The bar didn't either. It was the off-season, December now, and the bar, despite the frenzy of Christmas cheer elsewhere in the hotel, was far from a happening place. In fact, it was empty. I ordered a glass of the house red, something nonspecific from a company called Dragon Seal. If I thought wine would help, it didn't, but there was nothing that was going to make me happy that evening, that much was certain.

As I sat there in solitary splendor, the staff whispering to each other over in a corner, occasionally casting glances my way, I gave myself a stern talking to. First off, I told myself to calm down. Why exactly was I in Xi'an? What exactly had I hoped to accomplish? Why was I letting Burton Haldimand get to me? Yes, he was scum—lying, deceitful scum, that is—obsessed with getting that silver box ahead of anyone else, including me. Why, though, was I falling into the trap of becoming just as obsessed as he was? Rob tells me that occasionally I am like a little dog with a bone. That's his polite way of telling me that at times I can be stubborn, willful, and occasionally even obsessed beyond all reason with something. It seemed to me that where Burton Haldimand

and the silver box were concerned, this was one of those times. I told myself to take a few deep breaths and let it go.

I was making some, albeit minimal, progress, telling myself how much fun I would have in Taiwan with Rob and Jennifer, when I was joined by two other visitors. That I should know them, in fact know anyone in Xi'an other than Burton, came as a surprise.

"Lara!" Dr. Xie exclaimed when he saw me. "What a pleasant surprise! You know Mira Tetford, of course. May we join you?"

"Hello, Dr. Xie, Mira," I said. "Please do. It is an unexpected pleasure for me, too."

"I left a message for you at your hotel in Beijing this morning before I flew down. They said you were still registered. Did you get it?" Mira asked. "And what brings you to Xi'an?"

"The terra-cotta warriors, of course," I said, without missing a beat. "I decided I couldn't leave China without seeing them. They are as fabulous as everyone says they are." I'd seen them on my previous visit many years earlier, but why bother to mention that small detail?

"They are one of the wonders of the world," Dr. Xie agreed.

"And how about you two? What brings you to Xi'an?" I asked.

"I have a manufacturing facility here," Dr. Xie said. "I come here frequently. I have an apartment in town, in fact. And Mira is helping me with an acquisition of a company in this area. We meet with the company representatives tomorrow, and have been working on our strategy all day. I have promised Mira that I will take her to one of our famed dumpling buffets. I insist that you join us. My car and driver are right outside to take us when we're ready."

I did join them. It's difficult to imagine a buffet where your meal consists of a choice of twentysomething different Chinese dumplings, but in fact, it was delicious. I tried not to think about either Burton or the silver box, but there was a floor show with song and dance from the T'ang dynasty, which as interesting as it was, I'd just as soon have skipped under the circumstances.

It was on the way back that something interesting happened. My seatbelt had slipped down between the top and bottom of the seat. When I managed to pull it up, something unpleasant-feeling came up with it. I held it up to find a surgical glove.

"Has Burton Haldimand been in this car by any chance?" I asked, wiggling it.

"It would be difficult to think it would be anyone else," Dr. Xie said, smiling at the glove. "I had my driver take Burton sightseeing this afternoon. He wanted to see the imperial tombs west of the city and tours do not regularly go there this time of year. Not," he added, "that Burton seems a tour kind of person."

"I thought I was going to meet him here," I said, stretching the truth just a tad. "But he doesn't seem to be in the hotel any longer."

Dr. Xie spoke to his driver, whose English name was Jackie, chosen for his hero Jackie Chan apparently. "Jackie says that he dropped Burton at the train station at the end of their tour."

"The train station? I guess he's not going back to Beijing."

"That would not be the ideal way to get there, no." Dr. Xie spoke to the driver again. The man shrugged at first, and Dr. Xie looked about to tell me Jackie had no idea, when the man spoke again.

"The driver thought Burton a little odd," Dr. Xie said.

"I can't imagine why," I muttered.

"Burton told him that the trip to the tombs had been most educational, and that now he was going to see the Jade Women, something about meeting someone where the Jade Women live. No accounting for tastes, but Burton's a grown man, and he can do whatever he wants. I'd be happy to have Jackie take you to see the imperial tombs tomorrow. They are worth seeing, and I'm sure you would enjoy them as much as Burton did."

"Thank you, but I can't accept your kind offer. You will need the car." Actually, the new me wasn't going to look at anything that would get the silver box back on my personal agenda, nor did I think that anything that Burton might like would appeal to me in the slightest.

"Nonsense. I insist. Here is my telephone number in Xi'an, and my mobile as well. I'll have Jackie take Mira and me to our meeting in the morning, and he will show you around the rest of the day."

"Thank you," I said. It seemed churlish to refuse such a gracious offer.

The desk clerk at the hotel called out to me when I came through the doors, having said good night to Mira and Dr. Xie. "Your fax from Beijing is here," he said. I'd completely forgotten about it.

I opened it in the room. Based on my chance meeting with Dr. Xie and Mira, I had already concluded it was from Mira, telling me she was traveling to Xi'an for a day or two. Instead it was a message from Burton.

Lara, I hope you weren't waiting for me too long at Panjiayuan Market. My apologies! No doubt you were standing in the cold, cursing my name. I have good news, however. I have received some information about the whereabouts of the silver box. It was too late to call you because you would already have left for the market, hence this note. I am flying out to Xi'an today if I can get to the airport in time for the flight, and will call you from there. Burton.

He'd got the cursing part about right, but the rest of it left me dazed. In fact, I read it three times to make sure I'd understood it correctly. Having concluded that there was only one possible interpretation, I reached two obvious conclusions. The first was that Burton had not intended to lie to me about Panjiayuan Market, and the second was that in this instance the slug was not Burton, but a certain antique dealer.

I called the Beijing hotel again and asked to be put through to my voice mail. Burton had said he would call me. Had he done that as well?

Yes, he had, as had Mira, just as she said. As expected, her call was merely to say she was out of town for a couple of days, but if I needed anything to feel free to call Ruby. There were three messages from Burton. In the first, he said he hoped I'd forgiven him for the Panjiayuan business, and that he would call again. The second indicated that he was making progress, and thought he knew who had the silver box. The third was considerably more unsettling. As soon as I heard it, I headed for the business center and looked up the Jade Women. Apparently they were Immortals who protected alchemical texts, and probably the alchemists, too, and who dispensed cups of the sacred elixir of immortality to those of us below deemed worthy. They awaited the arrival of adepts on the top of the Western Mountain, one of the five sacred mountains that held up the sky. They also came down to Earth from time to time. Apparently they were recognizable because of a tiny grain of yellow jade above their noses.

So where was this sacred Western Mountain? It is now called Hua Shan or Flower Mountain, and it is about seventy-five miles east of Xi'an. I called Dr. Xie. Thirty minutes or so later, Dr. Xie and I were hurtling through the darkness toward Hua Shan in his Mercedes.

The train from Xi'an had come and gone. It was dark, though, so I was almost certain Burton would not yet have headed up the mountain. In the village of Hua Shan, there were a few not-so-choice hotels. That had to be where he was staying.

You wouldn't think hotels would reveal whether they had a guest by the name of Burton Haldimand, but Dr. Xie is a persuasive, indeed imposing, man. It was at the third cheap hotel near one of the entrances to the route up the mountain that we found Burton. There were no phones in the room. Dr. Xie spoke sharply to the man at the desk. "I've told him it is a patient of mine who has called for assistance. As soon as another staff member comes to accompany us, we will go up."

Burton did not answer to our knock. The hotel employee was persuaded with cash to open the door. We found ourselves in a tiny room with only a cracked sink and two small cots. To find someone like Burton in a tiny room with toilets down the hall, a room that would never come even close to passing his standards of hygiene, was somehow really disturbing in and of itself. But that was by far the least of it. Burton was dead, curled up in the fetal position on a tiny cot. If he met someone, there was no indication of it. If he saw the Jade Women as he passed to the great beyond, we would never know. Most terrifying of all, his face was a horrible dark blue-gray color.

Six

In addition to serving Lingfei, I was going about acquiring considerable wealth. So disturbed had I been by Wu Peng's revelation of what I saw to be my father's perfidy in selling me to pay his gambling debts, I had overlooked for a time the other piece of information the man had offered me. He told me that his position in the royal household, which I might well take over on his death if I showed true merit, presented many opportunities for profit, that the access eunuchs had to the emperor was a highly valued commodity that I might exploit with care. I decided that I would not wait until Wu Peng died to take advantage.

There was a very good reason why eunuchs inclined to do so could enrich themselves, and that was that all was not well in the Imperial Palace. The Son of Heaven was revered as a wise and just ruler. Early in his reign, he stabilized the food supply throughout the Empire, thus bringing terrible famines under control. A benevolent leader of his people, he distributed government lands to the common people, and ended taxation for the poorest amongst us. He was strict in his insistence upon law and order, making the Empire safe for his subjects, yet merciful in the administration of justice, approving executions only for the most heinous of crimes, and finally abolishing the death penalty. He was a patron of the arts, but also a man of enormous personal accomplishment, a gifted musician, an artful poet and calligrapher, an outstanding sportsman. He was a ruler of cosmopolitan tastes, having introduced the music, the costumes, and some of the customs of the peoples of the Silk Route to Chang'an.

But the Son of Heaven was spending very little time on the business of his empire. He was, you see, enamored of his Number One Consort, a young woman of the Yang family, one Yang Yuhuan, now known as Yang Guifei. Number One Consort brought her family to the palace, most notably her sister and her cousin Yang Guozhong, who rose through the ranks of power with incredible speed. More and more, affairs of state were left to people like Yang Guozhong, and First Minister Li Lin-Fu, a most unpleasant man according to my confreres, as the Son of Heaven spent most of his time with Yang Guifei, indulging her every whim and his. While the Son of Heaven and his Yang Guifei wiled away the hours at the imperial hot springs outside the city, other men were quietly flexing power. And it was into this void that those of us within the palace who wished to do so moved.

There was another man of much interest to Chang'an. That was the Sogdian, an accomplished soldier from the north, one An Lushan. Despite his bravery and tactical prowess in dealing with troublesome incursions on the northern boundaries, he was out of his element in Chang'an. He was uncouth, enormous in size, voracious *of appetites of all sorts, and yet he was a favorite of the Son of Heaven. Perhaps the emperor enjoyed teasing this barbarian; I cannot tell. But the barbarian was named prince, was given a huge estate in Chang'an, and generally enjoyed access to the emperor that was the envy of many a minister and senior mandarin. An Lushan also seemed to enjoy the favor of the Yang family, except perhaps Yang Guozhong. That might well be because both An Lushan and Yang Guozhong were ambitious to a fault. It was perhaps inevitable they would clash, but who would have guessed the outcome of that political battle? I most certainly did not. A storm was gathering, but most of us were unaware of it.*

"Argyria, almost certainly," Dr. Xie said the following morning after he'd managed to extricate us from the police in both Hua Shan and Xi'an. "Completely preventable."

"What's argyria?" I said. "I've never heard of such a thing."

"It's a condition resulting from excessive intake of silver," Dr. Xie replied.

"You mean Burton once worked in a silver mine or something?"

"Minute silver particles in suspension in distilled water," Dr. Xie said.

"He drank it?" I said. "Are you kidding?"

"I regret to say I am not," Dr. Xie replied. "He ingested it in some form."

"You said preventable. He drank silver on purpose?" I said, aghast.

"There are those who believe it to be an extremely effective antibacterial, antibiotic agent," Dr. Xie said. "Silver was used for centuries in the treatment of disease."

"But an antibiotic that kills you, obviously," I said.

"Not in my experience, no. Under certain circumstances, it does color the skin, as you now know, especially the nails and sometimes the eyes."

"Is there a cure for this argyria?"

"The color of the skin, you mean? Again, not in my experience. I would have to consult the literature, and I believe there are those who claim it is reversible, but I have not seen any indication it can be done."

"But it did kill Burton?" I insisted.

"We'll have to wait for the autopsy," Dr. Xie said. "It could have, but I repeat I do not know of any cases where ingesting it has killed someone."

"Where do you get silver you drink?"

"You can buy it on the Internet, or you can make your own. All you need is distilled water, silver, and a battery, really."

The things you learn! "Maybe it was a combination of things," I said. "He was always dosing himself up with something or other: special teas, pills, tonics. Maybe they interacted in a fatal way. He was very big on traditional Chinese medicine, the Medical Classic of the Yellow Emperor, disharmonious or blocked qi, that kind of thing. He seemed to know a lot about it."

"Burton talked a good line about traditional Chinese medicine, but clearly he did not understand it," Dr. Xie said, with an impatient gesture. "It is possible that he took something in a lethal combination, or merely took a lethal dose. You recall I told you that poisons are used in treatment of illness all the time, but in minute and controlled quantities. Perhaps he just took too much of something. It is also possible that he had an underlying condition, and that condition got out of hand. You see the body would regard silver as an invasive agent."

"No kidding," I said.

"I'm simplifying here, you understand, but the body would attempt to rid itself of this foreign substance, and in doing so, neglect, as it were, the other condition, which might then run rampant, get the upper hand. That might kill someone."

"An underlying condition like what?" I said.

"HIV/AIDS? I shouldn't speculate, nor should you. We will wait for the autopsy results. There is no question in my mind, however, that the blue-gray color of his face and chest is argyria."

"Potable silver," I mused. "Do you remember that recipe for the elixir of immortality in the T'ang box? It had potable gold in it. I thought . . . I guess I don't know what I thought. That it was just silly, maybe?"

"I believe it did mention potable gold," he agreed. "That might have meant the mysterious yellow, though, the *hsuan huang*, which was the material from which the elixir was made, the starting point. Many alchemists tried to make potable gold from other substances. Some claimed to have been successful. Silver could also be used. You are not saying, are you, that our colleague Burton was trying to join the Immortals?"

"No, but he did want to stay young and healthy," I said. "Maybe that's the modern equivalent of wanting to become immortal."

"Philosophically speaking, I suppose it is. At the heart of alchemy is the process of transmutation. In Europe, it was the transmutation of base metal into gold by means of the *prima materia*, the starting point for the process. Others saw it as a spiritual transmutation of some sort. The idea of an old body transmuting into a young body would not seem out of place in the study of Chinese alchemy. There are recipes for substances that if taken for a short period make you weigh less, look younger. Take enough of it and you float away, literally. You became an Immortal. Yes, in ancient times, there were people fixated on the idea of becoming immortal, of either preserving their existing body beyond death, or actually living forever in some state or another, but how different is that, I ask you, from botox injections and plastic surgery, liposuction, and everything else we do to try to hold back time?"

"Not very," I said.

In truth, if Burton had to go, I was relieved it was something like this. I hoped he hadn't suffered, but when I got his last phone message, I had feared something much more violent. Because the message from Burton, left, according to the time recorded by the voice-mail system, at 9 PM on the day I'd found him, and delivered in a panicky tone that I can attest was contagious, went as follows: "Lara! Get out of China right away! Please believe me, it is very dangerous for you here, for both of us. Do not look for the silver box. You must leave immediately. I'll be back in Xi'an tomorrow. I can't get a direct flight to Hong Kong, so I'm flying to Beijing, and transferring to the international terminal. I'll sleep there if I have to. I'll get on the first flight anywhere that I can. I'll call from the airport in Beijing to explain if you're there, but please don't wait for me. Get out of the country as fast as you can. I'll tell you everything when we get home." There was a pause, during which I heard the sound of a door slamming nearby. Just before he hung up, he said in a shaky voice, "This is not a trick, Lara. Please do what I say."

"Does this argyria make a person delusional or anything?" I asked.

"Not that I know of," Dr. Xie replied. "Why do you ask?"

"Burton left a message for me in which he sounded frightened by something. I just wondered if he was out of it."

"What did he say?"

"He just said it was dangerous here, that he was going to fly back to Beijing as soon as he could, and then proceed directly to the international terminal to wait for any flight out. He said I should do the same. He told me to stop looking for the silver box."

"Who knows what was going on in his body and his head?"

"But didn't you tell me that the desk clerk mentioned to the police that Burton had had an earlier visitor? Jackie said Burton was planning to meet someone. Could it have been someone who threatened him? Perhaps even killed him? Who could he possibly know in Hua Shan?"

"I wouldn't believe a word that clerk said," Dr. Xie replied. "Let's wait for the results of the autopsy, all right? We shouldn't leap to any conclusions."

"Of course. You're right. It was exceptionally good of you to come with me, Dr. Xie. I don't know what I would have done if you hadn't been with me. I shouldn't have called you that late I know, but I didn't know where else to turn. I have imposed on you. I'd still be in the police station if you hadn't been there. You are obviously much admired and indeed revered here."

"Nonsense," he said, waving that off as if I'd said something preposterous, but it had seemed clear to me that everyone was practically bowing and scraping in his presence, even kowtowing, a form of obeisance that had been outlawed by the Communist Party and rightly so. "Why wouldn't I help you? We're both Canadian residents, after all, and you are a guest in the country of my birth. I gave you both my home and mobile numbers so that you could call me at any time. As you know perfectly well, I was here. It was no inconvenience whatsoever. As it turned out, regrettable though it might be, you were quite right to worry about Burton. I wish we had managed to get there in time to save him, but I suspect that perhaps at that stage, even if he were still alive, there would have been little that could have been done.

"I'm glad I could help," he added. "Not just because you are a friend of Dory's and George's, but also because I have enjoyed your company here. I should tell you that I have given the authorities my word that you will not leave China. You will have your passport shortly and can travel in the country, but should not attempt to leave just yet. We will work on that part of it, Mira and I."

"Don't worry. I won't make a run for it. I wouldn't dream of it, given that you have been so kind."

"That is why I have no hesitation speaking on your behalf. Now I think you should get some rest, don't you?"

"I'm afraid to go to sleep. I know I'll dream about Burton. He looked terrible, Dr. Xie."

"Yes, he did. It was an unpleasant sight even for someone trained to deal with it. I think that if we find that Burton died trying to stay young and healthy, that will be a very tragic end, indeed."

"Oh, it's worse than tragic. It's criminal. I laughed at him, at the way he carried his air purifier every place he went, at how he wiped down the chopsticks even though the restaurants had perfectly clean ones, at the way he disinfected every hotel room, his desk at the office. His staff made fun of the way he wouldn't use the facilities at work, and went home for lunch every day. But he must have had a compulsive or obsessive disorder of some kind, a pathological fear of germs. He needed help, and I laughed."

"It would be difficult for most of us not to laugh. We would see Burton as eccentric, not ill."

"It wasn't just his health he was obsessed with. He was obsessed with the T'ang box. He came to Xi'an to try to find the box, you know. I'm certain he also went to Hua Shan for the same reason."

"Did he?"

"I'm sure he did, even though I thought it was a ridiculous idea. He was looking for the box all over Beijing. He had this idea that if he showed antique dealers the photograph and then left his business card everywhere, someone would contact him, and he'd be able to purchase it. He was convinced he could get it out of the country, stolen or not. He hinted that he knew how to do that."

"It can be done, I regret to say," Dr. Xie said. "And why did you come to Xi'an, if this idea of Burton's was so ridiculous?"

THE CHINESE ALCHEMIST

"The short answer would be that I lost my temper. I don't mean that I was yelling at him or anything, but he kept lying to me, over and over, and it got to me. I thought we'd established some sort of rapport over dinner one evening. He told me he'd booked a flight home the morning after we went to Cherished Treasures House to watch the videotape. But he hadn't."

"You know, I believe he had," Dr. Xie said. "I could not help but overhear him speaking on his mobile phone. His Mandarin was execrable, but he did ask for a reservation the next day, and certainly sounded as if he had one."

"You're saying he didn't so much lie as change his mind?"

"Quite possibly. That is certainly the way it sounded to me."

"I guess I was wrong. I wonder what made him do that? That wasn't the only time, though. He told me he was just going to rest, visit the fitness room in the hotel before going to the auction, and instead he went to a hutong neighborhood and paid a visit to the man in black, the fellow in the army who didn't feel the need to help the police with their enquiries. That still bugs me, by the way. If anyone could pull rank and get out of it, that would be you, Dr. Xie. You didn't choose to do so."

Dr. Xie ignored that last remark of mine. Suddenly he leaned forward and clasped both of my hands in his, a surprising gesture for a distinguished Chinese gentleman who would not tend to use physical contact to make a point. "Do not go there, Lara," he said. "Please!"

"Burton did."

"Burton is dead. Believe me, there is army and there is

army. There is the real Chinese army, well-trained professionals, and there are those who set themselves up as rulers of their little fiefdoms, a town, for example, or a sector of Beijing. They are not real army, you understand. They may well be in the army, but that is not what gives them their power. What gives them their power is fear. They brook no opposition. Those who do oppose them often come to a bad end. I regret to say that the system here almost encourages such behavior on the part of those they abuse. It is drilled into us from a very early age. A man respects his father. The father respects the mayor. The mayor respects the governor, and so on, all the way up to the emperor, or for that matter, Mao Zedong, or whoever else is in charge at any given point in time. That is why things like the Cultural Revolution happen. This is a system where obedience to those in charge, whether they are there legitimately or not, is so deeply ingrained as to be almost impossible to change. It is for this reason I do not believe democracy can be achieved here, at least not in my lifetime."

"I suppose a woman just respects everybody, is that right? What do you mean people come to a bad end? You make these people sound like the Mafia, or something."

"Not a bad analogy, Lara. I do not know this man. I do not wish to do so. At my age I am just happy that, with the economic changes in the country, I have been able to benefit rather considerably. I can afford to live the good life. I don't look for more than that. I hope that the system will change, but I am not optimistic. I live my life and that's it."

"Somebody knows who that man is. I'm sure Burton

didn't know him at first. There wasn't the slightest hint of recognition when the man first came into the auction house, for either Burton or that man. So somebody told Burton who he is, and maybe he's the one who gave Burton the idea of coming to Xi'an."

"Lara! You are not listening to me. Leave this alone. The T'ang box is but one historical treasure in a country that has several millennia's worth of treasures. Either the police will recover it, or they will not. If they recover it and it goes back on the market, then you get another chance. If it doesn't, you don't. I agree with you that it was a particularly beautiful object, but only one of many beautiful objects to be found here."

I sighed. "You're right, Dr. Xie. I am a foreigner, someone who does not understand what is happening around me. I got into a competitive situation with regard to the T'ang box, and neither Burton nor I looked good competing for it. It's just that I had a client who wanted it, and I guess I wanted to prove something. I will drop this. I'd really like to go to Taiwan to see my stepdaughter and my partner. May I impose on you once again to continue to urge them to let me leave soon?"

"Of course," he said. We sat quietly for a minute or two, and then he said, "Is it possible your client was Dory Matthews?"

"I'm not supposed to say," I replied.

"I will take that as a yes. That is indeed very interesting. She is dead, remember that. I realize that a request from the deceased is a difficult one to give up, but there is no reason to pursue this. Dory would have no way of knowing the box would be stolen. Surely that absolves you of further responsibility. It does explain something, though."

"Which is?"

"George Matthews called me in Beijing and asked me to keep an eye on you. That posed no difficulty, you understand. I was going to the auction anyway."

"That's nice of him, I suppose, but why would he do that?"

"I think that is a very good question. I thought at first you must be someone very young and perhaps a very inexperienced traveler, or had never visited China, but you are none of these things. Forgive me! You are young, of course, but hardly inexperienced. You seem to be able to manage all by yourself quite well."

"You were right the first time, Dr. Xie. I am not that young anymore, but yes, I travel all over the world, usually by myself. I did express some reservations when I met with him in Eva Reti's office about not speaking any Chinese, and not being entirely sure how the auction system worked here, but arrangements had already been made for Mira to help me with that."

"Perhaps he was just being neighborly."

"I'm sure that's right, and I am grateful to him, because as it turns out, I rather desperately needed your help. It's funny you should mention this, though. I was dreading phoning George to tell him that Dory's silver box had been stolen. I felt I should be the one to do that, and not leave it to Mira and her partner in Toronto. The call went much better than I thought it would. If anything he sounded a bit relieved."

"I got the distinct impression that he thought this was—how to put this politely?—that it was not the best idea she ever had," Dr. Xie said. "But he felt he had to respect her wishes under these sad circumstances."

"That's exactly what my partner Rob says."

"Whatever the reason, it doesn't matter now," Dr. Xie said. "You need to go back to the hotel and get some rest. Doctor's orders! Promise me you will forget all about this wretched silver box, that you will no longer pursue it."

"I am no longer pursuing this," I said. "I have had enough."

But life is rarely that simple. I did stop pursuing the T'ang silver box, for a while anyway, but though I did not yet know this, by now the evil presence that swirled around the silver box was in fact pursuing me.

I tried to sleep. I really did. My legs just ached from tension, though, and when I drifted off for a moment, they twitched. More serious, I also saw Burton's blue-gray face hovering in the corners of the room as I sank into sleep. After an hour or so of this, I decided the only thing I could do was try to walk the tension off.

As always seemed to happen whenever I left the hotel, a man rushed up to ask me if I needed a taxi. As usual, I told him no. He was a good-natured fellow who always seemed to be there. I suppose business wasn't that good. He told me his name was Peter. I told him mine was Lara. I took his card and promised if I ever needed a cab, to the airport or anywhere else, he'd be the first person I'd call. He beamed. That hurdle overcome, I then had to bypass the woman who swept the street in front of the hotel. The streets of Xi'an were very clean, actually, surprisingly so, perhaps because of this small army of women who sweep away all day and into the evening.

I rambled for awhile, looking into the shops, and just watching the people. I climbed the stairs to the balcony of the Bell Tower, which afforded me a view of the traffic and not much else. I tried to imagine what Xi'an would have looked like in the days of Illustrious August. The current city walls are Ming dynasty, not T'ang, although the Ming walls follow some of the ramparts of the older city, and the Bell Tower is not in quite the same spot. In T'ang times, the city would have been larger, hugely populous, and it would have been a city of walled neighborhoods or wards. To the north would be the Imperial Palace and just south of it the Imperial City where the mandarins and others worked. The wealthy by and large lived in palatial estates on the east side of the city. There would have been markets, east and west, pubs, temples, shops of all kinds, just like now, except there'd be no neon. At the moment I was standing there, the sun was low in the sky. Soon the city would be awash in neon. At sunset in T'ang times, the palace drums would have sounded to announce the palace was closing. Then the drums of the Drum Tower would beat, and when they had finished, it was required that the gates of the wards be locked.

It was a beautiful sight, but I was very much laboring under the weight of Burton's death, and felt that it required some kind of appropriate recognition. I could not think what that might be, but I knew I wasn't going to rest until

I'd done it. It was then I had the idea that I should go to the Baxian Gong, the Taoist temple, to light some incense for him in the hall of Sun Simiao, the physician and alchemist. If ever there was someone who would look after Burton in the afterlife, it was Sun Simiao. He might even have understood, as I could not, why Burton drank silver.

I took the same route I'd taken the previous time I'd gone there, through the eastern gate at the end of Dong Dajie, and thence along the narrow park that ran along the city walls. It was dusk now with the remains of one of those brilliant orange skies that seem to exist only in winter. The tai chi practitioners, the practicing musicians, the men with their birds were all gone. There were only a few young couples wandering along in a languid way, holding hands.

Waiting to cross at the light where a smaller road led into the area around the Baxian Gong, I caught sight of a familiar form, at least I thought I did. I decided it was Mr. Knockoff, this time with a bicycle with a wicker carrier basket that contained something wrapped in brown paper. To my mind that package was exactly the right size. I tried edging my way through the throng of cyclists and pedestrians, but he saw me before I could get to him. In what looked to be a suicidal gesture, he'd pedaled straight into traffic, jumping the median in the busy street running parallel to the eastern city wall, and heading into the old area behind the apartment towers.

I hailed a pedicab at the corner, and tried to tell him to follow the man on the bicycle. He had no clue what I was saying. Consequently I told him I wanted to go to the Baxian

Gong, which he did understand, given that was roughly in the direction that Mr. Knockoff was going. I hoped I would see him on the way.

I didn't, but when I got to the temple, there was a bicycle that I was almost certain was his parked in the entrance courtyard. The wicker basket was now empty. Either the package was deemed sufficiently valuable that it couldn't be left at the entrance to a temple, which seemed to say a lot about its contents, or the man was doing something with it in the temple. I paid the driver and followed, but by the time I'd purchased my ticket, there was no sign of the young man.

I was reasonably sure there was only one way in and out, but then when I thought about it, I remembered—at least I thought I did—a back gate. The question was, would he leave his bicycle? When there was no sign of him for several minutes, I entered, crossing a lovely arched stone bridge in the first courtyard, before systematically checking every hall that was open and crossing the next courtyard to another hall. The place was absolutely silent. I seemed to be the only person who did not belong there. There were the faithful few lighting incense sticks and kneeling in prayer, and from time to time a priest in black hat and tunic, short black pants, and white socks hove into view before disappearing again. There was no sign of my prey.

It was in the hall devoted to Sun Simiao, the physician and alchemist, that I found him. He was kneeling, hands clasped around burning incense sticks, bowing and murmuring as he rocked back and forth, and I still couldn't see his face well enough to positively identify him. The package was at his side. On the inside of the wooden railing that separated the worshippers from the worshipped, a priest was sitting on a low chair, chopsticks in hand, slurping a bowl of noodles. I suppose that, given we were in a Taoist temple in Xi'an, it was all perfectly normal, but I found it disconcerting, the idea of interrupting a man at prayer. I hung back, uncertain what to do, just long enough for him to see me. He leapt up, dropping his incense sticks as he picked up the package and, roughly pushing past me, made for the entrance and his bicycle. I followed as quickly as I could.

The bicycle wasn't there. Before I could even begin to fathom what that meant, the young man gave a cry and bolted into the street. I went after him, just trying to keep him in sight as he moved deeper and deeper into the old neighborhood that I had thought appealing before, and now found menacing. It kept getting darker and darker, twilight coming upon us very quickly. I couldn't both follow him and keep track of where I was, so the longer this went on, the more lost I became. I couldn't read any signs, and everything was starting to look the same. I, however, was standing out in this crowd more and more. By this time, a lot of people were staring me. They would not forget me.

Just then the man turned into what looked to be an alley. Gasping for breath, I followed. At the entrance to the alley, I stopped, taking a second or two to get accustomed to the light, or rather the lack thereof, and to come to grips with what was playing out before me. I thought at first it was a dead end, that there was nowhere else for the pursued man to go, that perhaps I might somehow convince him to talk to me. At the far end of this laneway stood the man, whose face I still couldn't see in the dim light, his back to the wall and package firmly held against his chest with both arms. He kept looking first in my direction and then at something else around the corner to his right, his head swiveling first one way, then the other. He looked as if he was trying to choose between the lesser of two evils and didn't know which way to go. Suddenly, decision apparently made, he turned my way, and starting running straight for me.

It was all over in seconds. First I heard the roar of a motorcycle engine, and then saw two riders take the corner from what had been the man's right. The first rider had his right arm straight out at shoulder height, and slowed slightly as he passed the young man with the package, now pressed against the wall to the right of the rider. There was a brief scream, a screeching of brakes, and the young man fell. The package flew out of his arms. The second rider came straight at me. Able to move at last, I ducked into the first doorway I came to, and the bike and rider swept by.

I heard the motorcycles turn for another run at me. This time they were going to stop, and I knew what they would do. The young man lay face down, almost certainly dead. Judging by the splash of blood against the wall and the widening pool under him, his throat had been slit. I staggered back from the sight, leaning hard against the door where I was standing. I almost fell through it into a little courtyard when it opened behind me. There were no lights in the buildings on the three sides of the courtyard, and no sign anyone was there. I pushed the door closed and locked it as the motorcycles swept by.

I was holding my breath when I heard the motorcycles stop, and then the crunch of footsteps coming right to the door behind which I stood. Someone tried the door. A few seconds later, something or someone slammed against the door with some force; the door bulged slightly but the lock held. I didn't think it would hold for very long. As I looked about for somewhere else to hide, I heard a man shout, then many voices coming into the alley. Whoever was out there trying to break down the door stopped, as someone started to scream. In an instant I heard the motorcycles race off in the direction from which they had first come.

I waited for a few seconds, opened the door, and took a quick look outside, ready to hide again if need be. A crowd had gathered in the alley, all staring at a huge spray of blood splattered against one brick wall, a pool of blood on the ground, and the young man, facedown. There was no sign of the package he'd tried to protect.

I just stood there, tears burning my eyes, my legs absolutely leaden. I simply did not know what to do. Then someone with a very firm grip grasped my arm and started pulling me out of the alley. "Lookie, mother, lookie, mother," a voice said. It was the woman from the Sunday antique market, the one with the scar on her face. She drew me rather forcefully out of the alley, and thence straight into a pedicab. She said something to the driver and he was off like a shot. I tried to get out, but he wouldn't stop long enough to let me. A few minutes later, he dropped me at the door of my hotel, and pedaled away before I could pay him. The idea that he and the woman should know where my hotel was without my telling them absolutely terrified me.

Seven

The first indication that Wu Peng had been right about my ability to make considerable sums of money came when Number One Brother asked for a meeting with me. Thinking he planned to berate me for not sending money to our father, I was reluctant, but it was diffi-cult to refuse. He made no mention of other members of our family; he merely discussed an issue in the ward in which my family lived that would benefit from palace attention, and gave me a petition. I said I would see what could be done. When I had in fact, despite my reservations, spoken to one of the eunuchs who would know more about this matter, it was suggested to me that a gift would do much to ease the required petition through the system. Number One Brother obliged.

I was on good terms with many of the more influential and pow-erful eunuchs in the palace and after that episode with Number One Brother found that my advice was sought on many matters. Gifts came my way in a satisfying manner. Many petitions passed through my hands and it was very simple for me to expedite one and delay another. One in particular, though, caused me much consternation.

It was from Lingfei. In it she asked leave to marry a man that she loved. She did so, she said, because she recognized that she no longer enjoyed the favor of the Son of Heaven, now that Yang Yuhuan was Most Favored Consort. She said she begged his indulgence in permitting her to spend her remaining days with this man, a member of the Gold Bird Guard. As astonished as I was that she would have the temerity to ask to leave the emperor's service—it spoke of a rash and unsettled spirit, it seemed to me, however evident her pain—still I felt a shiver of excitement. Had Auntie Chang not told me that Number One Sister had stayed out all night with a member of the Gold Bird Guard? Surely if I needed proof of our relationship this was it.

To be sure, her request was not without precedent, something she would have known. There were imperial concubines who had been given their freedom to marry. Certainly Yang Guifei was dealing with other former favorites with dispatch. The Plum Concubine had already been exiled to the second capital in Luoyang, one that the Son of Heaven had not visited in years. Yang Guifei was extraordinarily beautiful, and she was also intelligent and ambitious. The Son of Heaven spent more and more of his time with her. I was not entirely sure why. I am perhaps not the best person to comment on this, but my feeling was that Lingfei's slender form was rather more attractive than that of Guifei, who was rather plump. Evidently the Son of Heaven did not share that opinion.

More than just recognizing the reasons behind Lingfei's petition, I also felt a pang of jealousy. I planned, like my adoptive father, to take a wife when I had accumulated sufficient funds, and perhaps to adopt children as well. But I would never know the thrill of love, or its loss, of the sort Lingfei had expressed so passionately in this letter, of that much I was certain. Despite this unpleasant feeling, I moved Lingfei's petition forward expeditiously.

I did several things that evening, which given my state of mind was something of an accomplishment. I asked to change rooms, making up some lame excuse to do so, and then bolted myself in the new one, barring the door with a chair. I wanted to move to another hotel, but without my passport, that was not possible. No visitor got to check into a hotel in China without first producing this document.

Next I called Mira Tetford's office in Beijing, given I didn't know if she was still in Xi'an, and left a message asking her how she was doing getting my passport back to me. I gave her my mobile number, and told her I'd pick up the passport whenever I was allowed to do so. I also left a message that evening at Dr. Xie's office to the same effect.

Then I called Rob in Taiwan. He didn't answer. I wanted to leave a message, but I knew I shouldn't. I would have sounded absolutely hysterical. What would I say? That I had locked myself in my new hotel room in Xi'an because I'd witnessed a terrible murder and that a colleague from Toronto had either managed to poison himself by drinking too much silver, or had been dispatched by some other means, possibly malevolent? The poor man might have a stroke. I figured I'd better calm down first and talk to him directly.

Then desperate for something rational to do, I took a sheet of hotel letterhead, drew a line down the middle so that I had two columns, and put "Don't Know" at the head of one, "Know" on the other. Dr. Xie might say I should stay away from it, and perhaps he was right, but that was easier said than done. People were dying around me, and there were other people out there I didn't know, but who appeared to know me all too well. Somehow I had to understand this.

There were a lot of things I didn't know. I really didn't know how Burton had died, but given the terrible events of the day, I could not assume an accidental death. I was no longer putting any effort into convincing myself that he had somehow inadvertently managed to poison himself with silver. Even though there had been no blood, no obvious trauma, I believed he had been murdered, just as surely as the young man with the package had been murdered. It was a matter of waiting for the autopsy results to confirm that. As much as I tried to tell myself that I was just being hysterical, I could not rid myself of that belief.

I did know that Burton had been in Xi'an and presumably Hua Shan on the trail of the silver box. Logically if Burton were following his normal routine, that is to say visiting every antique dealer he could find, he would have gone to the antique market at the Baxian Gong that day just as I had. But he didn't. He went to the western tombs in Dr. Xie's Mercedes, then straight to the train station and on to Hua Shan to meet someone. In the morning he had met with the man in the mosque. As far as I could tell, Burton hadn't gone there to pray. He had gone there because it was a quiet place at that time of day, where he could meet someone he didn't want to be seen chatting with in the hotel lobby, which while perhaps not nearly so evocative, was considerably warmer and more comfortable. Who was the man in the mosque, and what if anything did he have to do with the silver box? Given Burton's obsession with the box, it didn't seem to me he'd be having discussions like that about anything else, except perhaps how to get the box out of the country illegally. But if the times logged in to my Beijing hotel room voice mail were accurate, Burton didn't have the box then, if he ever did. Was the man in the mosque the person who convinced Burton to go to Hua Shan?

It had not escaped my notice that Burton had been much better at tracking the silver box than I had. All I had done was follow him. What did that mean? Certainly his facility in Chinese had made a huge difference. But who had talked to him? I had seen him speaking to two individuals I couldn't identify, the man in black and the man in the mosque. Was it possible that the former had sent him to Xi'an, and the latter to Hua Shan? It seemed to me that if I could backtrack on his trail, I'd possibly learn what he had. Whether or not this was a good idea was open to question.

I didn't have a clue who the hapless young man in the alley was. Of his demise I was certain. He was not going to spend the night in a hospital and then be sent home. His throat had been slit. His heart would have stopped in seconds. Could it have been a random robbery that ended in murder? I didn't think so. He had looked to me as if he knew very well who was around the corner in that alley, and he'd chosen to come to me. This was quite possible because, of the two, I was clearly the lesser evil, and he probably thought he'd be able to push me out of the way easily enough, which

I suppose he could have. He just never got the chance. The other horrible thought was that if I hadn't been there, standing in one entrance to that alley, he might have gotten away from the motorcycles by retracing his steps and blending into the crowds of a main street. I had stood in his way, slowing him down long enough to doom him.

I had not seen enough of him in the Baxian Gong to clearly identify him with real assurance as the man in New York who had looked to be interested in bidding, nor as the person who had stolen the box in Beijing, just as I didn't know if the package he held contained the silver box. I did not let this lack of clarity stop me from leaping to conclusions. He was Mr. Knockoff, and the fact that he'd wanted the box, maybe enough to steal it, pointed once again to this entire situation being about the silver box. If that was true, then two people had died for it.

Another big question mark was the identity of the man in black, the smirking army officer. Who was he, and what if anything did he have to do with this? How had Burton known him? Burton apparently knew him well enough to know where he lived. He'd gone to a house in the Beijing hutong neighborhood and, lo and behold, there the man in black was. Did Burton have an appointment? Did he go to confront the fellow about the box? Had the man in black told him something that had sent Burton on a hasty and fatal trip to Xi'an?

I was more and more convinced, again with no real facts to back me up, that the man in black had been blocking the view of the box in the auction house. If I was right, then he too was tied to the silver box. Dr. Xie had told me not to try to find out who the man in black was, but surely I didn't have much choice now. Someone had told Burton who the man was, and presumably it had been someone in the room when the box was snatched or, I suppose, when the video-tape was shown, which would add three police officers. The police seemed unlikely, so that left Dr. Xie, Mira, Ruby, David, or the hapless employee of Cherished Treasures House, who had looked guilty all right, but surely for dere-liction of duty and not theft. He had been devastated at los-ing his job. Dr. Xie had said he didn't know who the man in black was. Maybe he didn't, maybe he did. Maybe he was simply trying to protect me when he said he didn't know.

After almost an hour of pondering all this, one ear cocked toward the hall outside my room, my heart leaping into my throat every time a door opened or closed, I had a "Don't Know" list that covered the entire column and then some. The "Know" side of the ledger was distressingly short, only one entry in fact: a number of people associated with this silver box were dead.

Along with that came the unwelcome conclusion that I too was now inescapably linked to the silver box. It was not a pleasant thought. Here I was in a country where I didn't speak the language, didn't understand anything that was going on around me, and therefore didn't stand a chance of getting out of the place in one piece unless I thought of something fast. Where to start? Given the hour and the fact that I was afraid to leave my hotel room, it had to be some-thing I had with me. That was the file on the silver box that I had put together an eternity before. I had made a copy of the photograph of the box in the Molesworth & Cox catalog, and had several photographs that Dory had given me of the silver box George had purchased some time previously. I had also kept the translation of the box up for auction that Justin at Molesworth & Cox had given me at the preview in New York, and I had gone to both New York and Beijing with a translation of the box already in Dory's possession.

I had not paid any real attention to the file, because I hadn't needed to. Dory was certain the box on offer at Molesworth & Cox was authentic, and once I'd taken a good look at it myself and chuckled at the recipe for the elixir of immortality, I'd shoved the pages into the file. Now I needed to revisit the file.

I got out a small magnifying device I always carry with me in case I need to examine some antique or another closely, and looked carefully at the photographs of the two boxes. George Matthews's box was lovely. On the sides and the top were a group of women musicians in a gazebo. They were all beautifully dressed, and their instruments were quite discernable—a lute, a flute, chimes of some sort, and so on. The workmanship was very fine. The smaller box showed a woman in a garden talking to another woman while a line of women waited. Once again, they were all well dressed.

It was very clear these went together. The rounded tops of the boxes were the same, both in shape but also in what was depicted on them, unlike the sides of the boxes, on which the scenes were different. I had at first seen only the bird on the lids, a crane, but when I looked more closely, I realized there was another scene, or perhaps more accurately, three of them, one on top of the other. At the bottom was a woman who looked to be laid out in a tomb of some sort, or perhaps she was sleeping. In the middle there was a woman seated in a pavilion while other women stood in line in front of her, and at the top, yet another woman floated above the rest of them, hovering over a mountain. The woman in each scene wore an identical robe, and could quite possibly be the same person. Woven into the design were flowers, possibly chrysanthemums, but more likely roses or peonies. What was also very interesting to me was that fact that it was quite possible these boxes had been done by different artists, even if they depicted the same thing, or at least something similar. There were variations in the strokes, tiny deviations really, but discernible nonetheless. I'd want to see the originals again and examine them closely, but I thought I was right. I wondered why there would be two artists working on these boxes if they were meant to fit together.

I decided that these three vignettes were of the same woman, in life in the middle, dead at the bottom, and floating above us all, as an Immortal at the top. Justin at Molesworth & Cox had said the box belonged to someone named Lingfei, a person of some importance in the court of Illustrious August. Could I safely assume that the woman on the box was Lingfei? I hadn't given much thought as to the gender of Lingfei before this moment. I'm not really familiar with Chinese names, so that hadn't been a clue, but there wasn't a single man depicted on either box that I could see. It wasn't absolutely conclusive, but from now on, Lingfei, at least in my mind, was a woman.

Next, I read the translation carefully. There the recipe for the elixir of immortality and instructions for its preparation as I already knew. A more thorough reading of the translation of the text convinced me that someone had cared very much for Lingfei and was perhaps drawing some consolation from the thought that she wasn't really dead. This conclusion seemed to rest on the fact that her body had not been found, which is to say that she was one of the lucky ones who had made the leap to immortality. I wasn't prepared to accept these immortal leaps, so what, I wondered, had happened to her body? Had it been stolen along with treasures that had been buried with her? Or had her body not really been buried where the author of the text thought it had? The text did, however, make it pretty clear there was a tomb somewhere with, if not Lingfei's body in it, then something else.

I then looked at the measurements of the two boxes. The one at Molesworth & Cox and again at Cherished Treasures House in Beijing would fit into the box that George owned, as Dory had predicted that it would. However, because of the tight fit, only the smaller box could have contained something. Burton had called the box a coffret à bijoux, or jewelry box, but I didn't think that was right, or if it was, then there was some very special piece of jewelry in the smallest box. It wasn't big enough to contain a great deal of anything.

Dory had said there was a bigger box that she remembered. She had not hesitated at all on the subject. Now, I think relative size is a difficult thing to remember over many years, particularly given how close in size the two I'd seen were, so despite what she said, the missing third box could have been either larger or smaller than the ones I had seen. I wondered how long there had been between the auction at which George Matthews had bought the silver box he had, and the second one coming up in New York. Dory had implied that George had had his box in his collection for many years. Could I safely assume that was true? I wasn't sure the answer to that was relevant in any way, but I had so little information that it seemed to me I just had to go on a data search and see what came up. I could simply phone up George and ask him, I supposed. I wasn't sure yet whether or not I wanted to do that.

Dory had also said there would probably have been an external wooden box, although it was long gone. How did she know that? Was there something about these nesting boxes that required such a thing? Were there other nesting sets like this I might learn from? I wasn't going to find that out in my hotel room.

I wished I could hold Dory's box again, or the one that was stolen, to study more carefully the tableaux carved on the outsides. Having concluded that one of the women depicted there—women I'd once just glanced at, being more interested in the workmanship than the content—had been Lingfei, I suddenly wanted to find the missing box even more than I had before. Somehow this had gotten very personal, not just because of Dory, but because of the mysterious Lingfei herself. I suppose, like Burton, I was hooked.

As I contemplated all this, the telephone rang, a sound that jangled right through me, and caused me to jump up in dismay. I stared at the ringing phone, willing it to tell me who was calling, and finally picked it up. I said nothing, however.

"Lara? Are you there?" Dr. Xie said.

"Yes, Dr. Xie," I replied.

"I woke you up, didn't I?" he said. "That's why you're having difficulty speaking to me. I am truly sorry."

"No, I'm awake," I said. "I can't sleep."

"I was afraid of that. I am in the lobby. May I come up, or would you like to come down?"

"I'll come down," I said. There were two reasons for that decision: I wasn't going to be in my room alone with anybody, even the lovely Dr. Xie, and I suddenly realized I was really, really hungry. I thought maybe food would settle me down a little.

I met Dr. Xie in the bar. He had a scotch, I had a hamburger and a glass of wine. I'm a firm believer in eating what the locals do, and have been known to make fun of tourists who insist upon eating their own food no matter where they go, but right now what I needed was a hamburger and fries—lots and lots of fries. Having said that, when the food came, I couldn't eat it.

"Have you slept at all?" Dr. Xie asked in a disapproving tone.

"Not really, no."

"Then I have a plan, one I hope you will agree to. First of all, let me tell you that Mira thinks she will have your passport by tomorrow evening, or the following morning at the latest. They are holding it only until the preliminary autopsy results are known, and we believe that should be late tomorrow. Of course, it will show death by some sort of misadventure, and you will be able to go. But I can see you are in some distress. First, you must get some sleep. I have brought you," he said, pulling a small plastic bag out of his pocket, "some of Xie Homeopathic's finest. You have a kettle and a mug in your room, no?" I nodded.

"Good. There are five or six teabags here. One teabag per cup, please, and one cup should do it. It will help you sleep. It smells a little strong when the boiling water first hits it, but let it steep for three minutes. It is all natural, no narcotics. You will find it tastes quite pleasant, and it will help you sleep. As for tomorrow, while we wait, I don't want you sitting around thinking about Burton. I repeat my earlier offer. Jackie will pick you up tomorrow morning at, say, nine-thirty after the traffic settles down a little, and take you west of the city to see Famen Si, a quite extraordinary Buddhist temple, and some of the T'ang and Ming tombs."

Tombs, I thought. *There might be some merit in this excursion.* Burton had found this trip educational. Perhaps I would as well. I'd be safe with Jackie. He'd already shown himself to be a good man in a crisis. "Thank you," I said. "I appreciate the tea, and the offer of your car and driver. I accept both."

"Good," he said. "Now eat. I may not approve of your choice from the menu, but you need to eat something." I did the best I could.

Later, door barred, I took out a teabag and did as I was directed. Dr. Xie was right. I drifted off to sleep fairly quickly and slept much of the night. It was a disturbed sleep to be sure. Inevitably, I kept dreaming about Burton. He was dead in my dream, dark blue of face, but he was still wearing gloves and making himself cups of tea.

Jackie was waiting for me at nine-thirty the next morning. He handed me a copy of *China Daily*, the English-language newspaper. One of my questions was answered right on the front page where, in addition to a story about a peasant demonstration not far from Xi'an where poor farmers were protesting corruption in government, and a mining disaster that had killed hundreds of workers, it was reported that a man had been murdered in Xi'an. This man, who had been identified as Song Liang, was an employee of the Cultural Relics Bureau. It was not known whether Song was in Xi'an on official business or vacation. Some vacation! The police believed he had been murdered by two men on motorcycles. The police had a good description of the perpetrators, and the investigation into this brutal crime continued and was expected to be brought to a speedy conclusion.

I was glad the article didn't mention they were looking for a female foreigner. At least the people who had talked to the police about the crime knew who the culprits were. If Song Liang really was an employee of the Cultural Relics Bureau, then his presence in New York could be explained. He was attempting to purchase the silver box for the people of China. Governments indeed do such things. It certainly did not explain why he'd steal it, unless he'd been given a limit on how much he could spend and despaired of being able to purchase it at the price it might fetch, and just grabbed it on impulse, thinking he was doing his country a favor. Then what would he do? Take it to his employer and beg forgiveness? I didn't know enough about how this all worked to say. If he had the silver box with him in Xi'an, then he had certainly not 'fessed up in an expeditious fashion. The other possibility was that he was basically corrupt, had been in New York just to see who purchased it, and then planned to rob the purchaser. If you think that sort of thing never happens, you kid yourself. He'd certainly been unhappy when the object was withdrawn from sale, as unhappy as Burton and I had been.

This put me in something of a dilemma. There was no photograph of Song Liang in *China Daily*. If there had been, I could tell Mira or Ruby to call the police and tell them that the person I thought had stolen the box might be the employee of the Cultural Relics Bureau who had been killed in Xi'an. But there was no photograph, so if I said that, they might quite rightly wonder how I knew of it, and I would have to say I was there, something I was extremely reluctant to do, not the least because I thought being linked in some way with two suspicious deaths was going to keep me in China for the rest of my life.

Our route took us past the statues that mark either the beginning or the end, depending on your geographic and political point of view, of the fabled Silk Route, through the burgeoning modern city that spreads outside Xi'an's old city walls, thence past miles of farmland to the place where the emperors and their families centered in that area went to spend eternity.

The tombs were interesting to be sure. We visited T'ang Princess Yongtai's tomb, a young woman who may have been executed by a rather nasty piece of work named Empress Wu Zetian, or may, as her tombstone related, have died in childbirth. Perhaps Empress Wu had the tombstone carved with her version of events. Princess Yongtai was the granddaughter of the Emperor Gaozong. She was also the granddaughter of Empress Wu, the woman who may have ordered her killed.

These were dangerous times to be a princess, it seems. Was Lingfei a princess? That might explain why her body had disappeared, stolen by an unpleasant rival.

To reach the sarcophagus, you descend a long ramp sloping quite steeply downward, past a few badly faded frescoes depicting the princess's maids in lovely gowns and elaborate hairstyles, little niches filled with terra-cotta figures of servants and so on, infinitely smaller than the life-size warriors the first emperor, Qin Shi Huangdi had formed for himself, and past a shaft that had been cut by tomb robbers at some point in the distant past. The air was unpleasantly damp, almost fetid, at the bottom where the sarcophagus stood, and there was nothing much to see other than a large stone sarcophagus, but at least I knew what a T'ang tomb looked like.

I also learned that several hundred objects had been found in the princess's tomb, including lots of gold and silver. Could I safely assume the silver boxes had at some point been in Lingfei's tomb, even if her body had disappeared? Yet another question for the "Don't Know" side of the equation.

Quite unexpectedly the most interesting part of the visit was that to Famen Si, a Buddhist temple an hour or so west of Xi'an. During the T'ang dynasty, emperors went to Famen Si to worship, and the temple's most famous relic, a finger bone purported to be that of the Buddha himself, was also carried in a great procession to Chang'an, now Xi'an, from time to time. It seems that an Indian prince, determined to earn celestial points in his lifetime, had dispersed a number of such relics, and Chang'an had one. The relic was essentially forgotten, but when the stupa at Famen Si collapsed in 1981, an underground chamber was found, and in it, the relic.

What was interesting to me, and had perhaps been for Burton as well, was an exquisite little museum on the site in which I found a series of silver boxes with hinged and rounded lids that were supposed to contain said finger bone. All of these boxes looked to contain a finger bone when they were opened, but only one of them had the real thing. These boxes were not unlike Dory's missing box, and I found myself wondering once again whether the smallest of Lingfei's boxes had held anything. There certainly hadn't been anything in it when it went up for auction, but that didn't mean much. Whatever it was could have disintegrated over the intervening centuries, or it could have been something more permanent, a particularly costly jewel perhaps, that someone had decided to separate from the box at some point. Was it the contents, and not the box itself that were so important to someone? It did lead me to believe, given the finger bone of the Buddha, that silver casket boxes held important objects.

Once again I was filled with regret that the silver box was gone. I wanted to know who Lingfei had been, partly because it might be relevant to what was happening now, but also because I was interested in her, assuming I was correct in considering her a woman. If she was a princess, I stood a chance of finding her; if not, it would be much more difficult. History records the famous, the victorious, the wealthy, and by and large, the men. If Lingfei was none of these things, her voice might remain silent forever, except, of course for the words and the pictures on the boxes. That made them all the more important.

When I was safely back at the hotel, my first order of business was to call Ruby in Beijing. I asked her if she knew who the man in black at the auction house that day was. She said she didn't. I said that somebody had to, somebody other than the police.

"I wonder if David knows him?" she mused.

"Can you ask him?" I said, as casually as possible. I didn't want to ask him myself.

"Sure," she said. "I'll call you back."

She did call back, but only to say that David was in Shanghai for a couple of days. She didn't know him well enough to have his mobile, so she'd call him in a day or two. I had his mobile number. He'd given me his card at the party at Dr. Xie's after the auction. I still didn't want to phone him myself, but I didn't seem to have any choice. I called, but got his voice mail. I didn't leave a message.

Next, I went to the business center and searched for Lingfei on the Internet. As always zillions of entries came up, but nothing that helped me. There was a Chinese appliance manufacturer with Lingfei in its name, that's about all. Then I tried famous Chinese women of history. Once again there was no Lingfei, but there was a Meifei and a Yang Guifei. The latter two were concubines of Illustrious August, Yang Guifei a woman he neglected affairs of state to spend time with, and who was known as Number One Consort. All three names had "fei" as a suffix. I knew two were concubines. Was "fei" a job description as opposed to a name? Was Lingfei a concubine, too? You wouldn't think an appliance company would have "concubine" in its name, but that, I thought, might be due to the lack of subtlety in translating Chinese

into English. This Meifei, for example, was called Plum Concubine, but "mei" also meant rose, so maybe there were two
meanings for something we would write as "fei," but which
would actually be two different Chinese characters with different corresponding meanings.

I had a flashback to New York, to Burton's exit from the
auction house preview. Had he not said something like
"Farewell, my concubine"? Had he been talking to Lingfei
and the box rather than to me? It would have been a relief at
the time to know that, but even now it was useful. Lingfei
was an imperial concubine!

If she was, I was soon to learn as I searched further, she
was in serious danger of being lost in a crowd. According to
what I read, Illustrious August had a harem of approximately
forty thousand women. Apparently there was something
called the Flank Court where the wives of men who had displeased the emperor were sent. New emperors tended to free
the women held by the previous emperor, but since Illustrious August had reigned for more than four decades, from
712 to 756, there were a lot of women in his harem by the
time he passed on. They were there on sufferance as it were,
both acquired and discarded at his whim. Being of a feminist bent, the whole idea of a harem made me distinctly nauseous, but I read on.

Other than his propensity to keep forty thousand women
around for his personal pleasure, Illustrious August looked
to have been a good emperor. He had several names; all emperors did. He was born Li Longji. The T'ang dynasty was
founded by the Li family, and he was a Li. His dynastic title
was T'ang Mingdi, also known as Minghuang. We know him

best as Emperor Xuanzong. Emperors got special names after their deaths that encapsulated their reigns. If someone was a bad emperor, he got a bad name. Xuanzong is remembered as Illustrious August, or Profound Ancestor, which spoke well of him. Contrary to my earlier impression, perhaps he hadn't named himself. From my perspective, he seemed to have had the most glorious reign of all in terms of culture. He loved music, and he even wrote some himself. There is a song he is supposed to have written when he was on a journey to the moon or something like that.

It was interesting to speculate what it would take to become an imperial concubine. People fanned out across the kingdom to find lovely young girls—virgins were esteemed as always—for their emperor. Fathers would want their daughters to be chosen. But being chosen or perhaps offered to the emperor just got you into the pool, as it were, sort of like the secretarial pools of old. Then you had to claw your way up through a ranking system in hopes that you would be an imperial favorite, get your own luxury apartment in the palace and an annual stipend that was generous enough to keep you in cosmetics and finery, and maybe even acquire the opportunity to bestow favors, like homes and titles, on your family. For the few who managed this, others, perhaps the majority, probably never got to even see the emperor. So there had to be something exceptional about this Lingfei. Perhaps she was a singer or dancer, or she wrote exquisite poetry. That would appeal to Xuanzong. Above all, she must have been extraordinarily beautiful.

After about an hour of searching, I gave up. I'd have to have another go later. But I did look up argyria. Yes, it existed; yes, it was exactly as Dr. Xie had described it; and yes, you could make colloidal silver yourself with some distilled water and a battery to run a charge through it and the silver somehow. I didn't spend a lot of time on this. It didn't seem to be a useful life skill from my perspective.

I made another attempt at eating and was marginally more successful than the day before. There was a message on my hotel phone from Rob saying his mobile wasn't working very well, so he might be hard to reach, but given I'd been delayed for a few more days—that was an understatement—he and Jennifer were taking a short cruise. He said he didn't know whether his phone would work there either, but he would try to get in touch. Jennifer came on the line at the end to say how much she wanted to see me, and that I was to hurry up and get there. It was all I could do not to sob uncontrollably. Then, after watching Chinese television, hoping to see a photograph of Song Liang pop up on the screen even if I couldn't understand a word, I decided to try once again to get some sleep.

I boiled the water for my bedtime cup of Dr. Xie's tea. It did smell a little strong, as he had said it would, but I had not found it that difficult to drink the previous night, and it certainly worked. As I took a teabag out of the plastic baggie in which Dr. Xie had given it to me, I had a sudden flash of memory: Burton taking a similar plastic baggie out of his pocket that day we'd had tea on Liulichang Street when I'd caught him checking out the antique stores. He'd brought his own tea bags.

I got out my magnifier and had a really good look at the teabag. It was of the sort that has a string attached to it to help you dunk it in the water, with a little tag at the end where you hold it that usually gives the manufacturer's name and the type of tea. This one was blank. The teabag itself was not of the type that is sealed all around. Rather, the staple attaching the string to the bag also sealed the bag. I painstakingly removed the staple, being careful not to tear the paper in any way. Were there two separate staple marks? There were not. Was it possible that the teabag had been stapled twice? I looked at the holes very carefully through the magnifier. I thought it possible that the teabag had been stapled twice.

I decided then and there that Burton had been poisoned, not through his own actions, his pathetic although understandable desire for good health. No, there was something in that awful tea he drank, something that shouldn't be there, something he would not detect because of the extremely strong and bitter flavor and aroma of the tea. The burning question was, had Xie Jinghe given it to him?

I didn't drink the tea.

Eight

Lingfei's petition to have leave to marry the man of her choice was denied. There was to be no further appeal. The reason given was that the emperor's Pear Garden Orchestra would be diminished by the loss of her voice and her consummate artistry on the lute. I thought back to that evening when I had watched the orchestra perform, and in my mind tried to place Lingfei there. Perhaps she had seen me that evening, creeping out of the shadows the better to see and hear. Perhaps that was why she had chosen me.

The next time I went to visit Lingfei, I took sweetmeats and flowers, peonies in remembrance of my sister. I had decided before I went that I would make no reference to her petition. When I arrived there, however, I was in for a terrible shock.

She was standing, hair disheveled, several locks of it scattered about the floor, a pair of scissors on the writing table nearby. She *held a cleaver in her hand. "Wu Yuan," she said. "You will cut one finger off each of my hands."*

I was aghast. "I will not, madam!"

"I demand it!" she said. "You are my servant."

"You will not be able to play the lute," I said, rather naively.

"That is exactly the point," she said.

Light dawned. "And will you also ask me to pour acid down your throat so you will be unable to sing, madam?" I said, no longer caring if she might guess that I knew of her petition. "Or cut off your feet so you will be unable to dance?" I was very angry now, almost as angry as she. "I will not do that, either."

She raised the cleaver, as if to cut off her own finger. But then she dropped it, and burst into tears, collapsing onto a couch. I did not know what to say. I did not know what to do. I simply sat beside her and held her hand for a very long time. When I left her, I reached down and picked up a lock of her hair from the floor and took it with me.

I got my passport back the next morning. Mira and Dr. Xie had obviously been persuasive, because they were still sorting through the toxicology reports on Burton. According to Mira, his blood was a toxic soup. She said he could be the poster boy for a campaign on the risks of self-medication. His suitcase had contained a very large plastic bag full of all sorts of stuff, from vitamins and minerals of every description, to the silver goo, to teas and infusions for almost every ailment you could think of, and some you've never heard of. Over and above the nasty substances in his blood like mercury and lead that all of us who live in developed nations can acquire just by living, there was the silver, of course; arsenic, perhaps acquired along with the lead through some environmental pollutants; and a host of other things. It sounded as if he'd been taking the elixir of immortality for far too long.

However, the cause of death was very probably hepatitis C. Burton had been suffering from this terrible condition, acquired who-knew-how and when. Perhaps that explained why he was so obsessed with his health. Sadly, many of the substances he took to make himself healthier just made him worse. As Dr. Xie explained to me, and as he'd hinted when we'd discussed the subject earlier, Burton's body had identified these substances, such as the silver, as invaders and had in some sense turned their attention to them, neglecting the hepatitis C, which had gained the upper hand.

It was very sad, but I also felt like a fool. I had suspected Dr. Xie of poisoning Burton. He had been nothing but generous with his time with me, and that's how I'd rewarded him. I had thought my life was in danger because Burton had been murdered. Instead, Burton had very foolishly managed to kill himself. I was very glad I hadn't left an hysterical message for Rob. He would be too polite to say anything, of course, but he would have been puzzled by my reaction, I was sure.

As for Song Liang, the victim in the alley, did I know for certain that he was the same man who had been at the auction in New York, or had stolen the silver box in Beijing? I was beginning to think maybe I didn't. I had to admit that I'd been more interested in his suit than his face, and for sure he wasn't wearing fake Hugo Boss or Armani in that alley in Xi'an. He was better dressed than most of the people in that neighborhood, but that could be because he was from Beijing. I'd found that most of the people I saw in Beijing were well dressed, particularly the people in the part of town I spent time in, around the hotel and the auction house. The only information about him that was a link to Chinese art was his position at the Beijing Cultural Relics Bureau, and given that he died in Xi'an, just how relevant could that be?

I had to go to the police station to retrieve my passport. I had also received a call from a brother of Burton's I'd never heard him mention, who asked me if I would have a look at the contents of Burton's suitcase, and make a decision as to whether or not anything there was worth sending home. This brother had tracked me down through the Cottingham, Burton having apparently told his employers that I too was after the box for a client, and then to the Beijing hotel where I'd now left a forwarding number, and thence to Xi'an. I took the suitcase back to my hotel and after sitting around staring at it for about an hour willing myself to open it, got around to the unpleasant task.

It was an instructive little exercise, and very, very sad. Where the rest of us put clothes, Burton had a box of surgical gloves, his portable air purifier, disinfectant spray, a large economy-size bottle of hand sanitizer, and another box, this one of surgical masks. There were also two boxes of tissues. Hotels do provide tissues, but I guess Burton wasn't about to risk the ones in the dispenser in a hotel bathroom. The police had told me they had kept the pills and other potions, a very large plastic bagful. Presumably they had kept the tea apparatus and the teabags, too, because there was no sign of them in the bag.

I figure I'm a good packer, and I travel light, but believe me Burton would have had to do laundry every night. If anything he had fewer changes of underwear than I did in my carry-on bag, which was all I'd brought to Xi'an. He also had five azure scarves, considering them more important than clean underwear, I guess. It was cold, yes, but somehow I'd managed to get along with only one scarf. If it hadn't all been so awful, it would have been funny. I sent an e-mail to the brother saying there was nothing worth keeping, and I'd see to it that Burton's clothes, what there were of them, went to a worthy cause. I told him I'd try to find out if Burton had checked any luggage at the hotel in Beijing when he'd flown to Xi'an. The surgical gloves, masks, air purifier, disinfectant spray, and the like I tossed in the waste basket.

Life went back to normal almost immediately. My capacity for self-delusion is as bad as the next person's, and it must have been in high gear that day. All it took was a tentative finding of accidental death in Burton's case, and I was prepared to believe all was well and that I should just get on with my life. I would forget the search for the silver box, I would do something appropriate to mourn poor Burton, and I would go to Taiwan as soon as they'd let me.

First order of the day was to deal with the demons. It was Wednesday, another antique market day at the Baxian Gong. I decided to go. I walked slowly through the park outside the city walls, and into the neighborhood beyond the ugly high-rises, telling myself over and over that I could do this.

I wasn't sure I could bring myself to revisit the alley, but that wasn't a problem because I was pretty sure I would never be able to find it. However, the person I did want to see was the antique dealer with the scar on her face. It was pretty clear that she wished me no ill. Indeed, she was my guardian angel. She'd dragged me out of that alley and got me to my hotel when my legs had turned to lead. I'd have been standing there for a long time if she hadn't, maybe long enough that the police would have wanted to spend more time with me than they already had. Still, I really wanted to know how she knew where I was staying. There was always a possibility that she didn't, that she'd just sent me to one of the closest tourist hotels to get me out of there. At the very least, I owed her a thank you.

Looking back on these thought processes of mine now, from a safe distance, I am amazed at how proficient I was becoming at rationalizing just about everything. I felt almost euphoric, as if this huge weight had been lifted from my shoulders with the news that Burton's death was an accident. My life had never been in danger at all.

In any event, the woman with the scar on her face wasn't there. I looked everywhere, including the shops that lined the little plaza. And then, given that I was having no luck with the task I'd set myself, I started doing what I said maybe an hour earlier that I absolutely would not. I began to look for the silver box again. I mean, I was there anyway, wasn't I? Somewhere in the back of my mind, I must have been planning this, because I had put the copy I'd made of the photograph in the Molesworth & Cox catalog in my bag before I went out. It was ridiculously rash, of course, but having been told Burton had essentially killed himself by accident, the threat had receded from my mind. I got out the photograph and started negotiating the narrow aisles between the stalls, by which I mean sheets on the ground on which the items were displayed, asking each of the dealers in turn if they had seen such a thing. Some of them understood the question, others did not. All shook their heads.

In the middle aisle I came upon a dealer who had some very interesting objects on display, including a lovely jade disk that I thought, despite a crack, would make a truly unique piece of jewelry with minimal effort. I picked it up and then looked into the face of the dealer who had it on offer, planning to try to purchase it, and also to show off my photograph of the silver box.

The man was dressed in a rather scruffy-looking padded jacket against the cold, worn boots, and pants. He had a cap pulled down low, and his face was a little smudged with dirt. It was, however, Liu David, lawyer and business consultant from Beijing, the same man who couldn't call me back because he was in Shanghai, or if not David, then his identical twin. I opened my mouth to say something, and he gave me just the very slightest of shakes of his head. I closed my mouth, set down the jade disk, and moved on.

This was perplexing indeed. I supposed there were several possible explanations for Liu David's presence there, but there was only one I liked. Regardless, I'd obviously seen something I wasn't supposed to, and the best course of action was to get out of there. Trying not to look too hasty, I made my way along the aisle stopping occasionally to look at something, on to the street, and then, at as stately a pace as I could muster when my inclination was to run, back to the city walls. I liked the idea of big, high city walls between me and the antique market at the Baxian Gong.

I didn't get far, however. I was about a block or two away from the antique market when a man, one I recognized from the market, and to whom I had shown the photograph of the silver box, approached me. His English was such that we could make ourselves understood, if not exactly converse about the problems besetting the planet. He suggested he had some objects I would be interested in seeing. I asked him about the silver box.

"Yes," he said. "T'ang. You come with me. I take you to box."

"Why didn't you tell me this when I asked?" I said, just a tad suspiciously.

"Too many ears," he said. "Also police always watching us. They are corrupt," he added. "They want money not to arrest me."

I didn't know whether that was true or not, although it was depressing to think it might be. Part of me assumed this was a variation on what I refer to as the tax-collector pitch, which goes something like this: dealer notices you admiring something, whispers in your ear that he will give you a very special price because the tax collector is over there, whereupon he gestures somewhere indeterminate, and he has to pay him or her off or he will be in trouble, and he is a man with a family, etc., etc. I've heard this one all over the world.

I wasn't sure how far I was going with this man, my newly discovered confidence in my safety not stretching so far as to enter a blind alley with him, but I did follow along. He kept to well-crowded streets, which helped, and as he chatted away to me, I began to feel more confident.

He stopped at a tiny house on a very small street, opened the door and gestured to me to go in. I didn't think that was a good idea, but I looked in, and saw a woman playing with a very young child. She, too, gestured me in. An older woman, the grandmother, I expect, immediately went to a pot over a fire and started to make tea. It seemed pretty harmless. In fact, it was playing out the way it so often did when I was on a buying trip, with the approach in the street, the ritual cup of tea at the home of the dealer, and then the unveiling of the merchandise, for a special price, of course, just for me.

The Chinese version of this time-honored and nearly universal ritual included excellent little pancakes with green onions in them that the grandmother made, something I thought added to the occasion considerably and might happily be picked up by salesmen elsewhere. The rather stilted conversation from the dealer, the only family member who spoke English, was sadly familiar, however. After the social niceties had been observed, I was led out a back door into a little courtyard, and then to a padlocked door in the building to one side of the courtyard. There was no way I was going any further with this man, and I said so.

He grabbed my arm. "Please," he said. "T'ang."

I peered into the room, being careful to stand just in the doorway so I could run if I had to. There was T'ang all right, several pieces, in fact, including *sancai*, or three-colored glazed earthenware pottery, in this case four ceramic figures of musicians, all women, each about eight inches tall. The earthenware is called sancai but in fact it often employs more than three colors, as was the case here. The colors, red, green, blue, yellow, and a soft purple were faded, as were the facial expressions, but if anything this enhanced their beauty. They were undoubtedly authentic. There was a dusting of dirt on them, which is a pretty easy way to give the impression, to the uninitiated at least, that the objects were old. In this case, however, I was pretty sure they really were. They were almost as certainly looted merchandise. "T'ang," the dealer repeated, as he whipped out a calculator. It was his favorite word. He keyed in a few numbers and showed the result to me.

Despite my conviction these were stolen artifacts, something of which it would be almost impossible to convince oneself otherwise in such a setting, I wanted them. I admit it. In fact, I would have given my firstborn for them. I could have bargained him down to something I was prepared to pay—of that I was sure, given his starting position—just a few hundred dollars for the lot. They were exquisite. The women were slim and graceful, the faces charmingly expressive, the little instruments perfect in almost every detail. Figures like this, I had learned from Dory, came in the slim variety and the well-rounded. Dory had told me the latter came into vogue because one emperor rather fancied a little excess flesh on his concubines. These women, though, followed the more traditional svelte lines.

Who would know I had these? I found myself asking. There are lots of T'ang tomb figures to be had on the open market in North America. Once out of China, they would look perfectly legitimate. Furthermore, if Burton had been right, I would have little trouble getting these out of the country. I was reasonably sure that any moment now my newfound friend would offer an export stamp as part of the deal. Reluctantly, I told myself to get a grip. What was I thinking? In the first place, I really enjoy not being in jail, most especially a jail in a foreign country. Furthermore, one can only imagine what my Rob would think if he found out. Not only that, but I rather fancied myself as an ethical antique dealer. Clearly my commitment to ethical behavior is not as robust as I like to think it is.

"Where did you get these?" I asked.

"Tomb," the man said. "What you pay?" I told him I wasn't going to buy them, as beautiful as they were. It was not easy to do so, and predictably he took this as my opening gambit rather than a firm decision on my part. "How much?" he demanded again. "T'ang. Very beautiful."

"No," I said, taking the photograph out of my bag. "Silver box."

"T'ang," he said again. He picked up one of the musicians. "T'ang. Stamp for export, yes. I will give you."

"T'ang, yes, but not a silver box. I want this silver box." I wondered what an export stamp would cost me in addition to the price of the musicians.

He continued to wave the musician under my nose. "Special price for you," he said over and over. "You tell me what you pay." In retaliation, I kept waving the photo of the silver box under his nose. There was a lot of arm-waving going on.

It was a fruitless gesture, however, on both sides. As lovely as these pieces were, it was pretty clear I'd been brought to this house under false pretenses. He didn't have the box.

He'd have brought it out by now if he had. It was time to go. The man looked disgusted as I walked back through the courtyard and through his house, pausing only to say thank you to the two women and to smile at the child. I handed the wife a few coins, which I hoped she wouldn't give to her husband.

It was only as I left the house that I realized that I was very near the spot where Song Liang had died, at the other end of the L-shaped alley in fact. When I turned right, I could see that the alley was blocked off with tape at the end. I took a quick look and, sure enough, it was almost certainly the same place where I'd witnessed the murder. There was a dark stain on the ground where he'd fallen. I'd just come at it from the same direction as the motorcycles, rather than the way I'd entered it before, which was probably just as well, because I would never have followed the man into the alley from that direction. Had that happened, I would not have learned what I had from the visit, which is to say that T'ang tombs were being looted somewhere nearby.

This proximity did lead to some interesting questions, however. Assuming Song Liang was indeed Mr. Knockoff and furthermore had stolen the box, and if he had had it in his possession the day he died, as I had surmised he might, was he bringing it to the man I had just met to sell for him? Did the man have the silver box even if he hadn't shown it to me? Or had the men on the motorcycles stolen it from Song before he could get there? Did the dealer I'd just visited have an inkling of any of this, or was Song just trying to unload the box as fast as he could? There were many questions I would have liked to ask the dealer, but I didn't think there was any way he'd answer them, and furthermore I wasn't sure it was in my best interests, given that I wanted to get out of this country in one piece, to pursue it with him.

When I got back to my hotel room, I dug Liu David's card out and called his cell again. I'd been reluctant to call him directly, but there was nothing for it. Not entirely unexpectedly, he didn't answer, but his message was in both Chinese and English. "Nice to see you today," I said after the beep in as neutral a tone as I could manage. "I would like you to call me back, please. Here is my mobile number. It works intermittently here, but if at first you don't succeed, keep trying, and please feel free to leave a message. I will pick up my messages regularly. I think you owe me one. There are perhaps other things we could discuss at the same time—for example, the murder I witnessed in the alley close to where you were today. I believe Song Liang was the man who tried to buy the silver box in New York, and stole it in our presence in Beijing. Now you owe me again. Here is how you can repay me. I would like to know the name of the army officer who was present when the silver box was stolen. I am tired of people telling me I don't want or need to know. I look forward to your call." I left my mobile number, not telling him where I was staying in case I'd completely misjudged the situation, and hung up. He probably knew where I was staying anyway. Everybody else seemed to know.

I figured that should do it. If it didn't, I'd tell him where he could find a stash of looted T'ang tomb figures. Then, still protected by the bubble I'd created that insulated me from the realities of this world, like murders for example, I headed out one more time. I moved west along Dong Dajie and soon found myself once again underground at the main square, at which point I headed up the stairs toward the Drum Tower, intending to visit the market behind it again.

I was close to the Drum Tower when I was approached by a beggar on crutches. There are unfortunately a lot of beggars in China. The burgeoning economy has created an enormous gap between rich and poor, between city- and country-dwellers, that is quite evident for anyone to see. This man, however, was particularly aggressive, frightening really, and not the kind of person I would stop to help under any circumstances. He kept pace with me, even though I tried to wave him away. I was walking faster and faster trying to get away from him, but I couldn't do it. I reversed my direction heading back to the steps that led down to the underground passage at the Bell Tower, thinking the stairs would certainly stop a man on crutches. They didn't. He kept right beside me, matching me step by step, his entreaties getting louder and louder. Call me crazy, but I didn't think he needed the crutches. I was getting really anxious, and didn't know how I would get rid of him. Then I saw the door to a rather fancy department store on the tunnel level and ducked through it. I knew the two doormen were not going to let the man, dirty and disheveled as he was, into this fancy establishment.

I felt safe for a few minutes, surrounded by familiar cosmetic counters and bright lights, and decided I had overreacted. It was a zealous and possibly desperate beggar, that's all, one who used crutches as a ploy for sympathy and therefore cash. I was annoyed at myself for being frightened by someone who clearly needed some money, but in truth there

LYN HAMILTON

had been something about him. When I was certain the
man was gone, I went out another door, and continued my
way west and then north into the market area behind the
Drum Tower.

I'd been so intent on following Burton when I'd last been
in this area that I hadn't really savored it at all. It was a vi-
brant and exciting place. People thronged the streets, their
children running and jumping along with them, the merchants outside the shops trying to lure customers in. Soon I
was back in the Muslim Quarter. I'd learned enough about
the Chang'an of T'ang times to know that it had been a very
cosmopolitan city, a magnet for traders from far and wide.
The people of the Muslim Quarter were said to be descended
from Arab soldiers who'd arrived in the eighth century,
right about when Illustrious August was emperor.

I had left the puppets I'd purchased for Jennifer in Beijing, but thought I should get something for Rob—
although I had no idea what—if I was going to arrive in
Taiwan bearing gifts for his daughter. I found some lovely
inkwells, and had a beautiful jade stamp carved with his ini-
tials in Chinese while I waited. I doubted he'd be stamping
his correspondence with it, but it's the thought that counts,
and it would look nice somewhere in his place. If we ever got
around to moving in together, it would be something I'd
permit him to keep, too, unlike, say, his red-and-green plaid
recliner with the duct tape on the left arm, no matter how
hard he tried to persuade me the nasty thing was an antique.

I made my way to the lane that featured antiques, and
started going from shop to shop, trying to make myself understood. Everybody shook their heads no. Most of what they

called antique wouldn't have qualified as such in my shop, so I held little hope for success, particularly when one dealer who spoke a little English told me someone else had been looking for the same box. I assumed that person was Burton.

I kept an eye out for the man in the mosque, not really hopeful of success. Still, I looked, and I asked, and eventually a woman directed me to a shop down one of the little lanes. My heart soared, my pace quickened. I was getting closer, I just knew it. Burton had just had an easier time of it because he spoke the language. I, however, had persistence on my side.

It was a particularly large stall, one that you actually entered as opposed to stood in front of, and to my surprise, I found some real antiques once again. There was no one there, however, to assist me. That seemed a little strange to me, as an antique dealer. I wouldn't have left my stall unattended. That would be way too much temptation for locals and tourists alike.

I called out, but there was no answer. I then noticed there was a teapot, and I could smell the tea, so perhaps the proprietor had made a quick dash to the communal toilet down the street. I waited a few more minutes, standing in the doorway. It was then I saw the beggar with the crutches again, the man who'd aggressively followed me down the stairs. I recognized him despite the fact that he'd apparently made a miraculous recovery, no longer requiring the crutches.

He was standing a few yards from the shop I was in. I couldn't tell whether he'd seen me or not, but I knew I didn't want to risk another confrontation with him. I ducked back inside and moved as far into one corner as I could so that if he happened to look in, he wouldn't see me. There was a pile of carpets on offer, and I decided if I moved behind it and stayed down low, he would pass right by.

It was in the corner near the carpets that I made a horrible discovery: a hand, and a hand only. I reeled back, then ran out of the shop, getting several yards along the lane before my rational self regained a measure of control. I stopped a man on the street, and with hand gestures and sounds that were possibly tinged with hysteria, I convinced him to follow me.

Police were called. They found the rest of the body behind a curtain. Despite the body's bloodless aspect, I recognized him as the man in the mosque. In addition to having both of his hands severed, his throat had been cut.

Soon I was back at the police station. "Violent events appear to follow you, madam," said the interviewing officer, the same one, in fact, I'd spoken to before. His name I believe was Fang, Officer Fang.

"Burton Haldimand killed himself by accident," I said. "You are the ones who decided that. This was a terrible crime. I'm calling Dr. Xie."

At the sound of that name, the man blanched. Apparently Dr. Xie did not even have to be there for his power and influence to be felt. I was very happy to have him on my team.

"That will not be necessary," Fang said. "What were you doing in the shop?"

"Shopping, of course. What else? I was looking for souvenirs, and also some things to sell in my own antique shop in Toronto." I wished I hadn't said that. It would have been better to let him think I knew nothing about antiques. On the other hand, maybe he knew all about me anyway, and it was just as well I'd been forthcoming on that subject. "I called out, but there was no answer. I didn't think he'd leave the shop unattended for long, so I waited for him. I was looking at the carpets when I saw the, you know, the hand. Who was he?"

Fang grimaced. "Just a shopkeeper."

I wanted to chastise him for saying just, being just a shopkeeper myself, but I resisted the temptation. I also declined to ask him if this is what regularly happened to shopkeepers in his town. It didn't seem politic, and I just wanted to get out of there.

"You don't know this man?" he went on.

"No. How could I?"

"I'm asking the questions," he said rather tartly, but then perhaps he recalled my relationship with Dr. Xie. "I apologize for this inconvenience. Please be assured that this does not happen here often. We expect to arrest the killer or killers very soon."

"I don't know what you mean by not happening often. Didn't I read in *China Daily* that someone else was murdered here a couple of days ago?"

Fang gave me a look that would have frozen the Yellow River solid. "That crime, too, is unusual, and it also will be resolved shortly." I hoped he was right.

There was some good news. Fang did not take my passport this time, and he had a policeman drive me back to my hotel. The bad news was that Liu David had not returned my call. There was, however, another voice mail awaiting my return. It was a message from a man who sounded as if he had a sock in his mouth and an accent I now recognized as Chinese saying he'd like to book an appointment to measure me for the suit I needed for the funeral. I had no doubts that it was my funeral he had in mind.

Nine

Neither of us said anything about that unnatural incident ever again, nor did I mention it to anyone else, tempting though the prospect of sharing such juicy gossip might be. The next time I saw Lingfei, she looked as she always had. She had covered her mutilated locks with an elaborate wig so no one would be the wiser. Our time together went on as before, she dictating formulas to me, I, in my best hand, recording them. I could not fail to notice, though, that after the failure of her petition, the ingredients for which she sent me were not always the medicinal herbs she'd been working with before, but rather others, more costly, like cinnabar and powdered oyster shells, mica, and pearls. I also recorded detailed processes for formulating something, I knew not what. From time to time our work together was interrupted when the emperor moved his court to the hot springs east of Chang'an where he was spending

more and more of his time. While I quite enjoyed the time spent there, Lingfei was impatient to return to her work.

Finally I could contain my curiosity no longer. "What is this you are working on?" I asked in some exasperation, having had to redo, with only the most minor of changes, a formula that I had already written three or four times for her.

She looked at me for some time without speaking. I was afraid I had offended her, and was about to apologize profusely, when she signaled me to be quiet. "Can I trust you, Wu Yuan?" she asked very quietly.

"Why wouldn't you?" I asked rather rudely. "I have been coming here for more than a year now without fail. I believe my work has been satisfactory, has it not?"

"Indeed it has," she replied. "But it is not the quality of your work or your punctuality that I am concerned about. It is your ability to hold a confidence. I know only too well the gossip that goes on in the imperial harem, amongst the women, but also amongst the eunuchs, too. I understand firsthand the deceit, the bickering, the plotting and subterfuge that grip the harem. I defy you to tell me that is not so."

"I cannot," I said. "I can only promise you that I will not betray your confidence." I realized even as I said it, that it was true. Not only that, but I realized in an instant that I loved Lingfei in some way I did not understand. "I . . . I . . . would do anything for you."

That was patently untrue, of course, as I had quite definitely demonstrated when she'd asked me to cut her fingers off. Still, it was unfair of her to ask, as she would have to have known, given the absence of harem gossip, that I had told no one of either her petition or her reaction to its rejection. It is possible these thoughts showed in my face. "Not quite anything," she said, but at least there was a hint of a smile there. "Come with me."

She took me to a pavilion across the garden from her palace apartment. The garden was treeless, of course, so as not to provide a means to scale the wall and make good her escape to the arms of the man in the Gold Bird Guard. Her living quarters were a prison, beautiful to be sure, but a prison nonetheless, I now began to realize. Until that moment, I believe I had misjudged the grip of the golden threads that bound all of us to the palace and to the Son of Heaven.

The pavilion was hot, as a fire burned, over which a cauldron rested. The smell offended my delicate nostrils. There were three tables lined with vessels of all shapes and sizes, and tools as well. "This is my life's work," she said to me.

"But what is it that you are doing here?" I asked. The unpleasant thought that I was in the presence of a witch crossed my mind. I brushed it aside. This was the lovely Lingfei, quite possibly—no, almost certainly—my sister.

"I seek the elixir of immortality," she said. "I believe I am very close to perfecting it. I have solved the puzzle of the mysterious yellow, the foundation of the elixir, and am now proceeding to formulate the elixir itself. I have tried the ingredients I know to be necessary in different combinations, and I believe the secret is within my grasp."

Everything became clear to me, the endless hours writing and rewriting formulations with only the most minute changes, the reworking of the same ingredients over and over, the necessity for the precious ingredients. Still, I was astonished, and felt compelled to remind her that the emperor was inclined to Confucian thought, and might find some of the Taoist arts not to his liking. She pointed out that the Son of Heaven knew the words of Buddha and the Tao as well as that of Confucius, and that while he might favor one, he was not averse to the others.

"Whether you have realized this or not, you have become my apprentice. It is you who have worked and reworked the formulations according to my experiments."

"But how do you know how to do this?" I asked.

"Do you recall I told you of a Taoist convent to which I was sent when I first left my home? It was there that I was trained to be a concubine, but where I was also apprenticed to an adept at the adjoining monastery. Like you, I did not at first realize that I was being initiated into the mysteries of the elixir. However, I was wrenched from the convent too soon. I knew the ingredients for the elixir, but not in what combination. It is only from an adept that one can learn details like that. The exact formulations are never written down, but passed along orally only to those deemed worthy. I tried to contact the adept with whom I studied, but learned that he joined the Immortals soon after I left him. It was a most encouraging event. He was speaking to his new apprentice when suddenly he disappeared. Only his robes remained. It was cause for much celebration, and he is now venerated. Do not forget your promise to me," she said. "And I will share the secret of the elixir with you."

It was terrifying, of course, to think that Golden Lotus, the gang that was causing so much trouble at home, was nearby. When I managed to get my fear under control, however, I realized that the people I was up against had made their first mistake.

Rob once told me that the British secret service had an expression to describe the Russian gangsters on British soil, and that was that they, the gangsters, still had snow on their boots, which is to say that they were not local talent per se, but had very strong ties back to their homeland. I don't know what the Chinese equivalent of snow on boots is, but that one phone call told me that Golden Lotus, too, had ties back to Mainland China. And if I needed more evidence that a gang was operating here, I had only to look at the deaths of Song Liang and the man in the mosque, both of them with slit throats, one of them with severed hands. If ever there was the mark of a gang, surely that was it.

At home, Golden Lotus was, as Rob had told me, engaged in fraud and extortion and was attempting to move into the territory of other gangs, most specifically those who controlled drug trafficking, thus initiating gang wars in which innocent people were being hurt and occasionally killed. Were they calling me in Xi'an because I lived next door to a Canadian police officer, one who spent more time than was absolutely necessary to be neighborly with the woman who lived next door? Had they tracked me all the way to Xi'an to continue to threaten me? I didn't think so. They were calling because of what I was doing in Xi'an.

It was time to call for backup. I left a long and detailed voice mail for Rob. This time I didn't care if I worried him. He should be worried. I told him Golden Lotus was here and was again telephoning threats to me. I told him exactly where I was, and what I had been doing, and that I would notify him of every move I made. Then I set out to figure this all out.

Up until that unpleasant telephone call, I'd judged the facts of the case, and my relative safety for that matter, on what was happening in China exclusively. I was in danger because Burton had been murdered. I was safe because he had killed himself. I should be frightened because I knew the man in the alley, or I was invulnerable because he was not the person I thought he was, and so on.

This call said I was quite possibly looking in the wrong place. What happened if I factored Toronto into the equation? When I had first received the threatening phone calls at my home, I had not yet spoken to Dory about the silver box. Did that mean these events were not related to the silver box? The deaths of two men—one the possible thief of the box and the other a contact of Burton's who was possibly even more determined than I to possess this same box—both killed in a way favored by mobs said they were. The box and Golden Lotus had to be related in some way I did not yet understand. I just had to find out as much as I could about all of them. I decided I could not assume anything, that I had to look very carefully at everything, and not just carefully, but with a jaundiced eye. What part of this whole exercise, right from the first threatening phone call and the moment Dory had invited me to her house for lunch that fateful day, had to be included in my research?

In effect, I had two starting points: the threatening phone calls to my home and Dory's request to get her the silver box in New York. I would look for intersections of those two streams.

I started with the silver box. Dory and I had had many conversations about China, and I had professed my mixed feelings about the country. She had been born there, and there was no ambivalence whatsoever in her view, or if there was, she never let me see it. I had been in China in the

1980s, right out of school, and I loved it. People were wonderful. They didn't live well by our standards, but they all believed in the dream, Mao's dream. I didn't share their dream, but I admired them for having one. I have that tendency, to admire and possibly envy people who are so clear about what they believe in, when I tend to be a little wishy-washy on the subject of just about anything philosophical. To me China seemed less complicated and more real than the life I was used to.

When I told Dory these things, she had countered by saying that when the Chinese espoused Mao's particular brand of communism they had merely replaced one set of despotic rulers, by which she meant two thousand years of imperial rule followed by several decades of the tyranny of Koumintang warlords, for another equally despotic leader.

When I said the country seemed to be moving toward democracy, however slowly, she said that China would never be free, that the one republic that had been created, in the early part of the twentieth century, had fallen into complete decay and despotism within a short time. She believed, as Dr. Xie also professed, that Chinese people somehow could never accept a democracy.

I told her that China, for whatever faults that she might see in it, was the most enduring civilization in the world. She said that was because it resisted change, refused to listen to fresh ideas.

I said that I loved everything I had seen, the Great Wall, the Forbidden City, the Ming Tombs, the hutong neighborhoods, and that I thought Chinese art was surely some of the most aesthetically pleasing there was anywhere in the world. Surely, I had said to her, having devoted her career to Asian antiquities, she could not possibly disagree with that.

She replied that might be true, but that rather than cherishing what they had, the Chinese people, specifically the Red Guard, had set out to destroy all that was most beautiful in the country, that during the Cultural Revolution anyone considered to be an intellectual was hunted down, humiliated, and often killed. Anyone who could read was considered an intellectual. "They burned books, Lara!" she would exclaim. "Books! And they turned beautiful paintings, homes, temples into firewood."

"But for all its faults, the Communist Party lowered the infant mortality rate and raised the level of education in the country," I countered.

"At first, yes, but then there was the Cultural Revolution. Schools were closed, weren't they? What do you think that did for the level of education?"

"But you weren't in China during the Cultural Revolution," I would sometimes meekly protest.

"I wasn't there, but I know," was her standard reply.

It was not that I didn't know what she was talking about. It was just that I didn't share her pessimism for the future. I am not naive. I enjoyed that first stay in China, but was not unaware that there was another China, one that gradually infiltrated my consciousness. This was the China of communist indoctrination. Government guides, who proved extraordinarily difficult to avoid, insisted that I go to so-called model factories, which had frankly appalled me with their poor working conditions. One in particular, a silk embroidery factory where young women worked long hours in poor light and unpleasantly cool temperatures, bothered me more than most. I was later told they could only work a very few years before their eyesight was destroyed. I'd bought an embroidered panel depicting cranes on a gold silk background in the shop there before I'd seen the factory floor itself. The workmanship was exquisite. I didn't know whether I was right to support them to the extent that they would continue to be paid their wages if people like me bought the products, or if I was encouraging exploitation of the women. I have the embroidery still, framed, too, and I still don't know how I feel about it.

I went out into the country, and was shown a bridge that had been built by the common people without the help of engineers. At least that's what the government guides insisted. The trouble was, I knew enough about the terrible period called the Cultural Revolution, where essentially the country had turned on itself in the most brutal way, to know that anyone considered bourgeois—and that included doctors, teachers, and, yes, engineers—was criticized and sent to the country to be reeducated through hard labor. Individually, they had suffered terribly, of course, unaccustomed to the harshness of their new environment, and in many cases separated from their families forever. The country had suffered even more, the school system essentially shut down for ten years, as Dorothy had maintained, people told what to think. This bridge had been built by engineers, all right, just engineers who now picked cabbage.

But those visits to the village and the factory were nothing compared to how I felt when I went to Tibet. I had a rough time getting there, because while the authorities said

I could go, they made it difficult to do so. But I got there, and as spectacular as Tibet is, I was appalled by what I saw. China talks about its "religiously correct" policy toward minorities. They can say all they want. At least as far as Tibet was concerned, it's garbage. The Tibetans were persecuted relentlessly. Monks were considered dissidents and thrown in jail for twenty years for nothing. After that, I had a couple of run-ins with party cadres, petty officials who thought their position entitled them to treat everyone else like dirt. Still, I know you can't equate the people with their government, so I left China, feeling on balance that I liked the place, and that eventually things would get better.

Not long after I had returned home, however, there had been that odious moment in recent Chinese history, the massacre in Tian'anmen Square. I remember watching the television as grainy pictures, a lurid red from the night lenses, were beamed around the world, and wondering if some of the wonderful young people I'd met had been hurt or killed. At that moment, I told myself I would never go back to China. Until Dory Matthews spoke to me from the dead, I never had.

Still, I am an optimistic person. Even before my return to China to try to buy Dory's box, I knew that people clearly lived better lives. The country was modernizing at an unprecedented rate. Where once it had been a crime to be remotely bourgeois, now there was a new government directive: it is glorious to be wealthy. True, there were still the men in black, the army officials who considered themselves above the law, and that continued to make me uncomfortable. Beyond mere wealth, though, the people I'd seen had a degree of freedom they had not had in more than half a century, maybe ever. Dory had heard the same things I had, but it didn't change anything for her. She said that while she loved Chinese history and culture, had made it her life's work, really, she would never go back to Mainland China, that her memories of the place were of a war-ravaged country, with zealots of every stripe so determined to rule that they cared not how many people died in the process.

She had plenty of reasons to feel that way, regardless of whether she was right or wrong. It was difficult for me to argue with her when it came to her own experiences, the ones on which she based her opinions. Yes, I could make a case for the big picture, but what influenced her opinion was what she knew on an intensely personal level. True experience trumps theory every time. Dory had left China with her mother at the age of five. Young as she was, she still had very vivid memories, and they were not good ones. She told me that her father was from Shanghai, and had been a successful businessman. Her mother Vivian, also born in Shanghai to British parents, was well-off too. Shanghai was an enticing city in those days before World War II and the Japanese invasion: Chinese, but with some European influence as well; affluent, but also a little decadent. But the proverbial storm clouds were on the horizon, Japan having occupied Manchuria in 1931, putting the last Qing emperor, Puyi, on a puppet throne.

That must have seemed a distant threat at the time, but it came much, much closer. In July of 1937, the Japanese were at the gates of Beijing, and that city fell to them on July 29, 1937, in an incident known to us now as that of

Marco Polo Bridge. In late 1937, Shanghai also fell to the Japanese and remained under Japanese control until the end of World War II.

On December 13, 1937, Japanese soldiers captured Nanking, then the capital of China, and slaughtered their way through the city for several weeks, an ignominious event called the Rape of Nanking. It is said that during the war with Japan, something between ten and thirty million Chinese were killed, although there are many who believe that number is much, much higher. The Chinese people have come to regard the Japanese occupation of their country, which lasted through World War II, as the Forgotten Holocaust.

Amazingly enough, Vivian and her family managed very well during the Japanese occupation. In Shanghai, whole areas of the cities had in some sense been ceded to the large and powerful nations of Europe, like Britain, France, Italy, and Russia. The Japanese, at this point not willing to rouse the ire of such powerful foes—that would come later—left them alone. Vivian would recall that time as reasonably happy, home with her parents in a beautiful house on a hill complete with servants. The Japanese were not the only problem, however. The Chinese were fighting among themselves. There were two factions, the Red or Communist Army led by Mao Zedong, and the Koumintang, led by Chiang Kai-Shek.

At first Vivian thought the Koumintang would protect people from the Japanese, but in the end the Koumintang was another despotic force. No matter where she went, she found herself surrounded by fighting no matter how cocooned her existence.

It was during this turbulent time that Vivian met the man who would become her husband and Dory's father. He had joined the Communist Army very young, in his early teens, according to Dory. His father had been with Mao in Xi'an when Mao became secretary of the Communist Party, and in 1934 had gone on the Long March with Mao. The Long March was one of the most famous strategic retreats in history, an almost five-thousand-mile march through difficult terrain over the course of just over a year. Only twenty thousand of the ninety thousand soldiers who set out with Mao survived. But it gave the army a chance to regroup, and at the end of World War II, Mao was able to push the Koumintang off the Chinese mainland to Taiwan. Those who had been close to Mao during that difficult time, and Dory's father apparently was one of them, stood to benefit for the rest of their lives.

Dory was born in 1944 in the dying days of World War II. Perhaps Vivian thought that with the defeat of Japan, her life would return to normal. She was wrong. When Shanghai was about to be taken over by the communists, Dory's mother had had enough. She got the last boat out of Shanghai. Dory's father chose not to come with them, something that was a terrible blow to the five-year-old child. Instead he had gone to Beijing to take a senior position with the Communist Party. It must have been difficult for Dory's mother, as well. She might have had British parents, but she'd been born in China and had spent her whole life there. She'd also been married to the same man for a number of years, even if she hadn't seen much of him. Neither Dory nor her mother were ever to see Dory's father again, or even to hear from him. Neither ever went back to China.

Dory's most vivid memory was that of trying to board the ship, a small child surrounded by panicked individuals desperate to get out of the country, and of looking for her father. She'd told me about it more than once, and even after all those years, she'd choked up about it just a little.

And yet, despite all this, Dory wanted to give three silver boxes of inestimable worth back to the country of her birth, one about which she did not have a good word to say. And she wanted to give it to Xi'an, the town where her father formally became a communist. How much sense did that make? I'd felt bothered all along by her request in a kind of fuzzy, unspecific way, sensing that there was something wrong. I still thought so, if for no other reason than it seemed highly unlikely that the box could be first withdrawn from sale and then stolen within a few weeks. I'd tried to tell myself it was a coincidence. Did I really still think it was?

This all said to me that the box had some value way beyond its monetary and historical worth for Dory and possibly for others. But how could that be? As Dr. Xie had pointed out in another context, this was a large country with many millennia of history. There were thousands if not millions of treasures here worth as much, and doubtless a lot more, than one silver box. Yes, it was silver; yes, it was very old; and yes, it was valuable. What else? That it contained instructions for the production of an elixir of immortality? I suppose if you were Ponce de Leon that would be a big selling point. In this day and age, however, it was highly unlikely this fact alone explained anything.

Was it a peace offering of sorts on the part of Dory, an indication she'd come to terms with her past? Maybe, but I hadn't heard anything from her that would indicate this was the case. If anything, her opinion hardened the more we had talked about it.

And if the silver box was so important, was its first owner, the concubine Lingfei, the key to this mystery? I wasn't prepared to accept the leap to immortality that one of the boxes supported. Lingfei was dead. Maybe her body was stolen. Was this relevant? Assuming someone thought she'd made the transition successfully, would she be buried, or if not, then perhaps the clothes she'd left behind? In other words, was this about a tomb? Chances were, absolutely. The dealer who'd led me to his home for tea and a sales pitch had clearly known where a tomb was located, or at least knew someone who did. Had these silver boxes been looted from a tomb? And where might this tomb be? Lingfei hadn't made it into the guidebooks or the Internet, so maybe her tomb hadn't been found—officially, that is. As an imperial concubine in the court of Illustrious August, though, the likelihood of her being buried somewhere near Chang'an, which is to say Xi'an, was pretty high.

What if someone in Xi'an knew where this tomb was? What if several people did? When I'd been in the Muslim Quarter waving the photograph of the silver box around, a shopkeeper had directed me to the stall of the man in the mosque. It was the right place even if I wished I hadn't seen what I had.

I had the feeling I was getting warm here, but I needed a lot more information. I didn't want to leave the hotel to get it, either. Who, I wondered, would help me get what I sought? Anyone who had been in Xi'an at the time of Burton's demise, or that of the man in the alley, or the man from the mosque for that matter, was automatically eliminated as too risky, guilty until proven otherwise. That meant I could not look to Dr. Xie, Mira Tetford, and now Liu David, who wasn't speaking to me in any case. As for Ruby, perhaps that wasn't the best idea either, given that all I had was her mobile number, and she could have been anywhere.

Was it actually going to be possible for me to avoid asking questions of any of these people if I wanted to get to the bottom of this? Probably not, but I was going to try. I really needed to know more about the history of those silver boxes, their provenance. Where had they been since Dory had seen them when she was young? Dory for sure wasn't telling me anything. I didn't want to ask George about it either. So what could I learn without consulting George? That night I called my friend, neighbor, and sometime employee, Alex Stewart. Alex has a deft way of finding out just about anything, and furthermore, he has a good sense of what's relevant and what's not. As a bonus, he seemed very happy to hear from me.

"I have a huge favor to ask," I said. "Is there any way you could go into the shop today?"

"Of course. I was planning to go in any event. Clive could use some help."

"Do you recall where we keep our stash of auction catalogs?"

"Indeed I do. You must have at least ten years' worth there. Pretty soon you'll have to occupy the shop next door to have enough storage space for them."

"And sometimes they come in very handy," I said. "I need you to check the most recent Molesworth and Cox Oriental auction, the one I went to this fall. In it you will find a photograph of a silver box, T'ang dynasty. That is the one I went to New York to try to buy."

"I remember, yes."

"Take a good look at that one, and then if you don't mind, go through the back issues of the catalog and see if you can find an almost identical silver box that is slightly larger." I checked my notes and gave Alex the dimensions of George's box, the one Dory had shown me when I went to visit. "Same shape, same type of decoration, but the smaller one would fit inside the larger. I need to know when that came on the market. It may not be there, but I'm hoping that it will be."

"Easily done," he said. "When will I get back to you? How many hours time difference?"

"Thirteen," I said.

"I'll call you tonight then, tomorrow morning for you."

"Call me in the middle of the night," I said. "I mean it."

"I'll leave right now," he said.

The telephone rang several hours later in the early morning. I wasn't asleep. "I'm sorry to take so long on this, Lara. It ended up being more complicated that I thought, and perhaps you will also be surprised by what I have found. Shall I just begin?"

"Yes, please, and I'm sorry to put you to so much trouble."

"It was very interesting, and I'm glad to help. I had no

trouble, of course, identifying the box you described to me. I then started to look for something similar. I started with the Molesworth and Cox catalogs, just because that is where the box you were attempting to get was to be sold, and I assume people choose auction houses that specialize in the kind of thing they want to sell. That was my theory, anyway. At first I thought that this request of yours was very simple and straightforward. I found a similar box right away, as you suggested I might, in the Molesworth and Cox Oriental auction about eighteen months ago, in the spring. Molesworth appears to hold two Oriental auctions a year. I have the information from that sale, and I'd be happy to give it to you."

"That's great, Alex. I'm glad it didn't take a lot of your time. Except didn't you say this took longer than you thought it would?"

"Exactly. I thought I was home free when I found the listing, complete with photograph, so there was no mistaking the resemblance. But just to be sure, I took the dimensions you gave me, and I compared them to the listing in the catalog. That was when I knew this was not going to be as easy as I thought: the dimensions you gave me are not the same as the one I identified in the catalog; those are about an inch bigger all 'round, in fact."

"Just a minute! There are two boxes in question here, the small one in this fall's auction catalog, and then one whose dimensions I gave you that belonged to George Matthews. I measured it myself."

"That is my point. The measurements are not the same as those that you gave me for the George Matthews box. This box is larger than either the Matthews or the stolen box."

"I thought I was careful. Dory gave me complete access to that box of her husband's to photograph and measure, so I should have gotten it right. I must have screwed up," I said.

"Ah, but you didn't. You usually don't, that much I learned working at McClintoch and Swain. If Clive measures something, measure it again. If Lara measures it, relax. That's what piqued my interest."

"I'm flattered, I guess, but where are you going with this?"

"There is a third box," he said. "Given that the measurements didn't jive, I went on looking for one that did. I found it, too, up for auction about three years ago. These boxes are coming on the market at eighteen month intervals, and there are three of them, not two."

"I see. So if Dory wanted to put the set of three together, she missed one?"

"I have no idea, but there are three boxes. I thought perhaps that meant they are fakes. Having found this anomaly, I started looking for more boxes, just in case. That was when I began to notice something interesting about T'ang dynasty objects. I went back through your entire stash of catalogs, which covers pretty well a decade of the major auctions in New York and Toronto. I can tell you that there has been a sharp increase in T'ang objects offered for sale in the last five years, running perhaps four times the average for the previous five years. Do you see what I mean? Most of the increase is at Molesworth and Cox, incidentally."

"It could be that more people are selling T'ang objects as prices rise, simple as that. They see other items similar to what they have fetching attractive sums, so they put theirs on the market, too. Is there anything you can tell me about the two boxes, other than size and the fact they look right?"

"Both sold at Molesworth and Cox, one in New York, one in Toronto. Both are supposed to have belonged to someone by the name of Lingfei. The seller of the first box to come on the market, the one sold three years ago, was someone by the name of, just a minute, I won't pronounce this well, Dr. Jinghe Xie."

"No kidding," I said.

"You know him?"

"I do. He's here. In China, he's Xie Jinghe, of course, but it's the same man. And the second box?"

"No owner listed. Does this mean something significant?"

"I'm sure it does, but right now I don't have a clue what that might be. What it does do is link Dr. Xie with the silver box, one of them at least. George Matthews obviously bought one of Xie Jinghe's boxes, given the dimensions of the first match the one I saw at his home. It should also mean that Dr. Xie was not the mystery buyer on the telephone in New York, because he'd already sold a box. Why would he want another only slightly smaller than the one he'd had in his possession and chosen to sell? It's also possible that George and Dory just missed the second box up for sale. Dory would just have been leaving the Cottingham, and she didn't purchase in her area of employment on principle, and George might have decided one was enough, not realizing his wife would be more than a little interested in all of them."

"You should know that many of the T'ang objects up for

sale in the past five years are from the collection of this Dr. Xie."

"Not sure what that means either. It was legal to buy and sell Chinese artifacts at that time. He has a tremendous number of them. Maybe he was just unloading a few to make room for more. When we talked about the silver box at the preview in Beijing, he didn't mention that he'd once owned a similar one. I don't know about that. Maybe he simply didn't think it was relevant. Still, you'd think he'd say something. Did he suddenly realize that his box was part of a nesting set, more valuable that way, and maybe he'd try to buy the other one back again? I can't really ask him. What I do need to know, and short of someone getting a court order I never will, is who put the box up for sale in New York and then withdrew it from sale."

"Dr. Xie also?"

"Maybe. Burton Haldimand had Dr. Xie down as a possible buyer, not the seller, but who knows? I can't ask him that, either."

"You are on bad terms with this Dr. Xie?"

"No, but if his name keeps popping up in this connection, I may be. Thank you for this, Alex. As usual you have been wonderful."

"Take care of yourself," he said.

"I plan to do that." I did, too. As I completed the call, I parted the curtains carefully and looked out on to the street, Dong Dajie. It was still early enough that the stores were not open. The street cleaners were out, though, one in particular just sweeping away in front of the hotel. As I watched, she looked up, shielding her eyes slightly. It was the woman with the scar on her face. It occurred to me she'd been there almost every day, except maybe when she was following me to the market. I just hadn't really looked at her. "Whose side are you on?" I said to her through the curtain. I was going to have to be very careful getting out of this hotel.

While I'd been on the telephone with Alex, I'd received some calls. One was from Mira telling me that she was on her way back to Beijing and that she hoped she'd see me before I left. The second was from Dr. Xie saying much the same thing. He added that I should not go out by myself at night, as quite uncharacteristically Xi'an had turned violent. "Tell me something I don't know," I said to the voice mail.

And there was a third call telling me to get out of China or else. At least I think that's what he said. Really, if people want to scare somebody into doing something, they should take the socks out of their mouths and enunciate clearly. Actually I thought getting out of China would normally have been a good idea, but given that I was just going back to the haunt of some of this telephone mumbler's confreres, there didn't seem much point. Beijing, however, sounded like a good idea to me. I called and booked a flight the next day.

Liu David had still not called me back. Maybe he was still kneeling on a bamboo mat in front of the Baxian Gong, afraid to take his fancy cell phone out lest it attract attention. I didn't think so, though. The market would reopen next Sunday. I supposed he just was not in any position to return my call. I was reasonably sure he would, eventually.

I went on with my mulling. Alex had given me some very interesting information. I was certain that Dory had told me that she had seen the three boxes together, but that her stepfather had broken them up and sold them off in the mid 1970s. What had happened to them after that? Dr. Xie had obviously acquired one of them. Dory had also said that there would have been an outer wooden box that disintegrated. That continued to bother me even though I'd seen the silver caskets at Famen Si and learned they too had an outer wooden box. How as a young person would she have known that? Did her stepfather just tell her? And how would he know?

What if all these T'ang objects that were turning up in New York had been stolen from Lingfei's tomb? Was that possible? Was it also possible that this was a business of Golden Lotus, along with their other nefarious activities? Did the fact that many objects had come from Dr. Xie's collection make him a tomb robber as well as a successful businessman and philanthropist? He was certainly besotted with Chinese antiquities. Just how bad was his infatuation? And even if he were a tomb robber, what did this have to do with anything?

Then the telephone rang. I reached for it, but then drew back my hand. Was this to be another of those awful phone calls that would test my nerve? Should I let them know I was in the hotel? Still there were important calls I wanted to receive. I picked it up but didn't say anything.

"Are you all right?" Rob said.

"So far."

"Can you get to Beijing?"

"I think so. I have my passport and I have a flight."

"It will take me several hours to get out of here."

"I know."

"Beijing. Your hotel. I'll be there."

"So will I."

I was out the front door of the hotel very fast the next morning. I'd called Peter, the taxi driver who'd pestered me every time I left the hotel, and had him waiting at the door. The woman with the scar was out there, sweeping away. I hoped she didn't see me because it was pretty clear she was spying on me, whether for ill or good I did not know. She did see me, though, and my bag being loaded into the back. She leaned against her broom and got out a cell phone. Somebody knew I was heading out of town. Still, we sped away the minute my door closed, and the hour plus drive to the airport went without incident. So far, so good.

I found myself in a window seat, with an old Chinese couple beside me. It was immediately apparent they hadn't been on an airplane before. The seatbelt perplexed them utterly. I showed them how to use it. When the flight attendant brought drinks, they couldn't figure out what to do with them. I showed them the tray, and how to operate it. They kept smiling and she, in the middle seat, kept patting my arm, and chatting away. I smiled and nodded. She got out a Thermos and offered me some tea. I declined, having rather gone off tea of late.

I noticed the old man straining to see past me and I offered, via hand motions, to change seats with him. At first he shook his head, but I offered again, and when I'd managed to get both of them out of their seatbelts, in his haste to look out the window he practically sat on my lap. I had to crawl past both of them to get to the aisle seat. The flight attendant had a rather bemused expression on her face, but then came and thanked me. At the window, the old man kept exclaiming and pulling on his wife's arm so she'd lean over and look too. It was a very clear day, and I expect the view was extraordinary. Watching their enthusiasm, I almost forgot my worries for awhile.

The flight was not the end of our adventure together, however. There was still the escalator to be mastered. The woman was about to fall over backward before I realized that they didn't know how to negotiate this newfangled contraption either. I lunged for her, keeping her upright, and then I held on to both of them until they were safely off the escalator. Then there was the marvel of the baggage carousel. I had to help them with their luggage because the old man grabbed one suitcase, a huge plaid number, and was dragged along by it, nearly falling over in the process. Somehow I'd forgotten how complicated these things are.

I was about to take my leave, having managed to get them both, along with their luggage, to the glass gates that separated the passengers from those waiting for them, when I saw something that made me feel ill. It was the man in black, now in uniform, and he was clearly looking for someone. I had a pretty good idea who that someone might be, and even had a notion or two about how he knew I'd be on this flight. I was not yet prepared to meet him.

I slipped in between the old couple, linking arms with them. The man in black, now in green, stepped toward us, but in an instant we were swept up in a crowd, twelve or fourteen people, I think, including babies, the welcoming party for the old couple. At first everyone looked at me with some puzzlement, but the old man was excitedly chattering away, and then the old woman said something, and I was suddenly being much fussed over. I was given a baby to hold while luggage was sorted, and the youngest couple, grand-children of the travelers, parents of the infant in my arms, explained in English that the old couple, who had lived and worked on a farm outside Xi'an all their lives, was coming to live with the family in Beijing. The granddaughter thanked me for helping them, and especially for letting her granddad look out the window. She said, rather unnecessarily, that it was their first flight. I thought it was probably their last, too, and that they'd be talking about it for as long as they lived. She said the family had been worried about how they would manage on the airplane, but couldn't afford to send someone to travel with them. She said they'd hoped that someone nice would look after them, and were grateful I had been there.

All the while, the man formerly in black watched me. Yes, he saw me, and he recognized me, but he didn't make a move. That told me something: he wasn't there in an official capacity, despite the uniform. I found that even more chilling than the alternative. I wasn't sure how I was going to get away, but at least I had cover as far as the curb. I just hoped there was a taxi at the ready.

"Do you have a car arranged?" the young woman asked.

"I'm afraid not," I said.

"Then we must insist upon driving you to your hotel."

Normally I would have politely declined, but this time I decided that I should consider this my reward for good behavior and a timely one at that. Surrounded by my new friends, I sailed right past my pursuer. Mentally I informed him I'd be seeing him soon.

Ten

I kept my promise to Lingfei that I would not reveal the subject of her work. Our life together, however, was soon to come to an end. That is because the gathering storm finally reached Chang'an.

The buffoon, An Lushan, was proving himself a poisonous element in the empire. When Yang Guozhong was made first minister on the death of Li Lin-fu, An Lushan began to fear that he would lose the Son of Heaven's patronage. I could see no reason that he should think that. The Son of Heaven regularly sent An Lushan women from the imperial harem for his pleasure, and still made sure that he was well rewarded financially as well.

Despite or perhaps because of royal favor, An Lushan was sent north to curtail the activities of the barbarians on the northern frontier. It is not possible to know the inner thoughts of someone like An Lushan. Perhaps so far from Chang'an he began to imagine plots against him. For whatever reason, he turned on the emperor whose favor he had so long enjoyed. With a large army, An Lushan began to march, not against the barbarians, but toward Chang'an.

It was possible that the armies of the Son of Heaven might have prevailed were it not for a disastrous decision. Our army was ordered to advance and engage An Lushan. We were defeated absolutely. This left the route to Chang'an undefended, and it became clear that An Lushan would take the capital. The Son of Heaven, who had neglected affairs of state for so long, was forced to flee west. I was one of the eunuchs who went with him. You can imagine the terrible time that was, the chaos, the fear. Before I left I went to Lingfei's home, but she wasn't there. I did not even say good-bye.

At a relay station west of the city, generals killed First Minister Yang and forced the emperor to order the execution of his beloved Yang Guifei. The Son of Heaven had to agree, anguished though he must have been. The Son of Heaven then began a terrible journey to Chengdu, where, in despair, he abdicated in favor of one of his sons.

An Lushan, who had seemed to be in the ascendancy, instead became painfully and desperately ill, and died. Some said it was murder, others merely his just desserts. The rebellion was over. Still, it was a very long time before I returned to Chang'an.

An obsession in the early days of archaeology and anthropology was the hunt for the origins of man and the so-called missing link between Neanderthals and us. Scientists scoured the globe in an effort to find this elusive creature. One of the most exciting finds in this regard occurred right outside Beijing, near a village called Zhoukoudian, where a tooth dating back to something between two hundred and thirty and five hundred thousand years ago was found in 1921. The tooth was followed by thousands of bones. It was different from examples of early man found elsewhere, and some thought it the link they all were seeking, naming it homo erectus Pekinensis, or more popularly, "Peking Man." The story of Peking Man is fraught with intrigue, the skull and bones disappearing as they were being transported for safekeeping as the Japanese invaded. Some said they were ground up as an aphrodisiac, others that they were merely misplaced. Still the story has a spellbinding quality to it, even if they were wrong about it.

It was not lost on me that there was a missing link in all of this for me as well, something that would bring together the two threads, Dory and her silver box and Golden Lotus and indeed everything that had happened over the past several weeks, just one fact that would cause everything to make sense to me, which at that very moment it did not. Yes, I could see where there were intersections between the two, but they could easily be coincidence rather than cause and effect. I did know of one piece of information that I lacked, and that was the name of the man in black, and his relationship, whatever it was, to this whole affair, but whether this was my missing link or not, I had no idea. There was only one way to find out, and that was to ascertain who he was, if only because it was one of the few avenues left for me to pursue. Dr. Xie had said the man in black was army but not army, which is to say he was one of those people who terrified others into doing what he wanted, ruling his fiefdom through fear was the way Dr. Xie had put it. That sounded like Golden Lotus to me. And someone or something had sent Burton to Xi'an.

As scary as the prospect of getting within even a mile of

the man in black was, he had already shown that he was not about to confront me in a public space, so that meant I just had to make sure I was never alone with him. After some thought, I decided that if you can't learn someone's name by any other means, and heaven knows I'd asked everyone I thought might know, then as a last resort, you ask the neighbors. These neighbors would not only yield useful information, but they would also afford me some cover. That at least was my plan.

First, though, I had to find the neighborhood. I knew my chances of locating the little store where Burton had eluded me—eluded me, that is, until the lovely old woman with the bound feet pointed me in the right direction—were not good. I'd been quite lost by the time we got there, concentrating as I was on keeping Burton's taxi in sight rather than keeping track of where I was. I thought, though, that I could find my way in reverse from the Drum Tower.

That is precisely what I did. There was a woman outside the hotel sweeping the driveway. This was beginning to seem not only repetitious but suspicious as well. I found another way out of the hotel, and thence to the Drum Tower and from there into the hutong neighborhood. There were several wrong turns involved, and a lot of backtracking, but in the end I found the doorway with the five posts, the elaborate guardians of the gate, the rather impressive roofline that turned up at the ends, and the long wall that took up most of the lane. This time the man in black was not in the doorway; indeed, he was nowhere to be seen.

I went along the lane to see if I could find someone who might know the name of the lucky residents. My first efforts met with no success, mostly because I couldn't find anyone who spoke English. At last, though, late in the afternoon, I found a little bar with a rather voluble proprietor on the lane that runs along the north side of an artificial lake not far from the Drum Tower. To prime the proverbial pump, I bought an overpriced glass of imported wine, and went on and on about how lovely the neighborhood was. She told me the area was now rather hip, at least I think that's what she said, and while it was good for business, she was afraid the neighborhood might be spoiled. I said there looked to be some really lovely homes in the area. She said most of them were pretty small, and most didn't have toilets.

I mentioned one I'd seen with five posts in the entrance gate, and said whoever lived there must have a truly beautiful home and be very important. She said she expected I was talk-ing about the Zhang residence. I told her I'd seen someone in army uniform at the front gate, and asked if the army was guarding the place. She said no, the army officer lived there. I expressed surprise that someone in the army could afford such a magnificent home. "Zhang Xiaoling," she said. She didn't look as if she liked him. "Zhang Yi important man, much money. Zhang Xiaoling, the son, he spend money. Big car. He is no good."

So there it was, the missing link, one word, Zhang. Dory Matthews, born Zhang Dorothy. Yes, I knew perfectly well that Zhang is one of the most common names in China, maybe even the most common and certainly in the top ten. I didn't care. This was one coincidence too many. Satisfied, I paid the hip price for my wine and headed off to find a taxi at the Drum Tower. It was time to give George Matthews a call. He had a lot of explaining to do on behalf of both himself and his late wife.

I nearly made it. I really did. As I approached the Drum Tower, the drums began to beat loudly and rhythmically. There was a cab in the distance, I had my arm out, and then I felt myself being pulled roughly into the backseat of a car. I tried to call out, but with the din from the drums, I knew no one would hear me. The car pulled away the minute I was in it, the man who had grabbed me pulling the door shut as we careened away. In the driver's seat was Mr. Zhang, Zhang Xiaoling if I had understood my informant properly, formerly known to me as the man in black. His henchman, in the backseat with me, had a gun. He fastened my seatbelt as the car screeched away.

I attempted the requisite protests to no avail. The two men spoke to each other in Chinese and said nothing to me. I tried to keep track of where we were. As far as I could tell, we were heading west. Soon we were in an area that looked a bit suburban, more small town than urban core. There were no signs on the roads that I could read.

A short while later, we were heading into hilly country. I'd seen the hills surrounding Beijing when I'd flown in, but still did not have any sense of where we might be. I looked for clues, but there were no highway numbers, just signs that said, in English, things like "Do not drive tiredly."

Zhang obviously knew where he was. He was driving very fast, and there was no opportunity for me to release the seatbelt and try to get out of the car. Night was falling. I could see the dark outlines of hills, but very few lights now that would indicate a town anywhere near. The road to our left dropped off fairly precipitously, and there were no lights on that side of the road. There were a few cars out, but very few, and those that were soon disappeared behind us as Zhang aggressively passed them all.

It was on a curve that all hell broke loose. Zhang was once again trying to pass another car when a truck appeared on the curve in the oncoming lane. Zhang jerked the wheel hard, just clipping the bumper of the car he was attempting to pass. Our car's right tire hit the shoulder and we spun out of control, first to one side of the road and then the other. We kept hitting rocks and trees near the shoulders, and I could hear and feel pieces of the car being ripped off. I thought we were dead.

The car spun one last time and then started sliding backward toward the drop on the lefthand side of the road, but instead of going over the side, the car slammed against a wall of stone and came to a stop, engine still running. Neither Zhang nor the man who was holding me captive had been wearing seatbelts. Zhang was slumped against the wheel, blood pouring from a head wound that I could not help but hope was fatal, and the man beside me had also hit his head on the roof of the car, I think, and looked to have been knocked unconscious. I couldn't see his gun. Buckled in, I was dazed, but not hurt. It took me a second to pull myself together and move, but then I was out of the seatbelt, and out the door. The headlights of the car, still on, faced down the hill, so I headed uphill into the darkness. The oncoming vehicle and the car that had been clipped by Zhang had disappeared. I wondered why, but didn't have time to think about it.

I tried to be quiet, but it was dark. I kept tripping on brush, and my breathing sounded very loud to me. I kept climbing, though, trying to put as much space between me and those horrible people before they came to their senses. I saw the headlights of another car, which stopped, its beam on the wrecked car. It was a police vehicle, at least it looked that way to me, and for a minute or two, I thought I'd made a terrible mistake moving away from the road. Zhang, who apparently was not badly hurt, got out of the car and spoke through the window to the occupant of the police car. In a minute, the car pulled away. Zhang had obviously pulled strings again. I heard him call out to the man with the gun, who by now had hobbled out of the car as well, and I was reasonably sure, even in the darkness, that he was looking up the hill. He may have been dazed, but he'd seen which way I'd chosen.

I kept climbing, trying not to crash around like a wounded animal, always on the lookout for some place to hide myself. At last I came to what I thought was a ridge, and staying down so that I wouldn't show up against the dark sky, went over the top of it. I fell into a ditch or a small gulch of some kind. Something loomed above me, and I almost screamed. It took me a minute, but I decided what I could see above was the outline of roofs against the dark sky. There was even a very slight glow coming from one of the buildings. It was then I heard a shout from the road below, and the sound of someone coming after me.

I seemed to have found myself in a little town built on the side of a hill. I stumbled up stone steps wondering where I would hide. I tried a door or two that didn't open, and then found one that did. There were no lights inside. I was in a little courtyard with buildings on three sides. There was a large cart of some kind, loaded with something I couldn't make out. I heard someone cough nearby.

In my haste I banged against the edge of the cart, and let out an involuntary gasp. I could hear footsteps outside, whose I didn't know. I tried one of the doors that led onto the courtyard, and it opened. In a second, I was inside. I was in a storage area of some kind, I thought, as I felt around in front of me, one that smelled of cat urine. It certainly wasn't someone's living room. There were sacks piled up and I crouched down behind them, only to feel something furry rub against my legs. I stifled a scream. There was a purr. Apparently I'd found the cat. A few minutes later, I could hear what I thought to be someone knocking loudly on doors. Whoever it was came closer. Then I heard steps in the courtyard, and then the ominous sound of a key turning in the lock of the building in which I'd hidden. I was trapped.

Zhang—I knew his voice well now—was in the courtyard a minute or two later. He called out in a loud and quite authoritarian tone, and a woman answered. There ensued a conversation that I could not understand. I held my breath as someone tried the door, rattling the handle. It was locked, as I very well knew. I thought I was doomed. The woman said something, and a few seconds later I heard footsteps moving away from my hiding place. Soon all was quiet.

I stayed there hardly daring to breathe for what seemed to be hours, absolutely petrified. I was cold, hungry, and scared beyond reason. Who had locked me in? Did they know I was there? Were they holding me prisoner for Zhang, and if so, why hadn't they just told him where I was? Maybe they had, and he was going for reinforcements. Then there were more footsteps outside my hiding place—or my prison, depending on circumstances I didn't understand—and I heard a key inserted into the lock. The door opened. A woman spoke. I didn't have a clue what she said, but I stood up. She couldn't have been speaking to anyone else, and there seemed no point deluding myself with any pretense that I was safely hidden. My legs were aching from the climb and from having crouched down for so long. She took my hand in the dark and led me across the little courtyard and into another small building. This was the house. There was one lantern casting a pale light.

We looked each other over. I expect she saw a very large white woman with fair hair and pale eyes looming over her. I saw a tiny Chinese woman, someone who worked hard, judging from her worn hands. It was a one-room home, with one bed, on which a small child slept. I assume they slept together. She gave me a cup of tea, and even took me in the dark to the communal bathroom—after I said the word "toilet," one she understood—a concrete structure with four holes in the ground cantilevered over a cliff. It was breezy, but what did I care? Then she took me back to the storage room, arranged some sacks as a bed and gave me a blanket. As I more or less collapsed on the makeshift bed, she locked me in again. Again I wondered whether I was a prisoner or a guest. At this point, it didn't matter because I wasn't going anywhere in the dark.

I didn't think there was the slightest chance that I'd sleep, but I did. As the palest of light showed through the cracks in the walls of the house, I heard the key turn again, and the woman offered me a bowl of something. She signaled me to follow her, and I did, to a chair in the courtyard.

The home in which I had found myself was very basic. The cart in the courtyard against which I'd managed to bang my knee was loaded down with drying cobs of corn, dark gold against the green paint of the cart. Bunches of long, thin red peppers dangled from the rafters. A cat, perhaps my companion of the previous evening, was curled up beneath the cart.

The bowl contained congee, a soupy rice dish. To the rice were added some spring onions, and something a bit spicy I didn't recognize. I ate every last bite. I kept saying *xiéxie*, thank you, over and over again. Her child, a shy little boy, kept coming up and staring at me, before giggling and running away.

The woman prattled away to me for a while. I couldn't understand a word. Finally I just said, and I believe there may have been a catch in my voice, "Zhang Xiaoling."

The woman spat on the ground. I said it again, and she spat again. She obviously knew who he was, and she didn't seem to like him.

After breakfast, she offered me a bowl of water to clean up a bit, and picked away at some straw that had attached itself to my jacket. "Lara," I said, pointing to myself. She reciprocated. I think she said Ting, but I couldn't be sure.

I pulled out my wallet, took out all the cash, the equivalent of close to two hundred dollars, and said "Beijing." This elicited a stream of conversation. Ting left the house and came back a few minutes later with another woman, who introduced herself, at least that was what I thought she was doing, as Rong. The two of them talked away, and finally Ting took my watch arm, and pointed to two on my watch. I didn't know what that meant, but I figured she must have thought that this was relevant in some way. It was now only eight.

I spent the next six hours in a state of barely controlled panic. I kept trying my cell phone, but of course it didn't work. I was in the hills, and far from Beijing. I was fed regularly, and pots of tea were always available, but I didn't know what was happening. I also didn't know if Zhang Xiaoling was going to show up again. Every time I heard footsteps crunch against the stones of the lane, I ducked into the storage area.

Two o'clock came and went, and I was getting really frightened. Then, at about two-thirty, I heard a car horn sound several times. Ting gestured to me to follow her, and we carefully made our way down through the village toward the road. She went ahead at every corner, looking carefully about before signaling me to follow. High above the roadway we stopped, and I looked about me. We were in a narrow pass between two dark hills, their slopes brown with winter, in what looked to be a dead end. If so, this could very well be a trap. I tried not to think that way, to concentrate on what I thought had been some real human connection here.

The town clung to the slopes of both hills, with a road at the bottom between the two. The distance between the two hills at this point was just the width of a two-lane road. The town was spectacular. I think it had to be several hundred years old, Ming in style, with lovely rooflines, all gray stone and brick, with only two flashes of color, the red Chinese flag hanging high over the valley, and a red lantern swinging from a porch. Higher up the hill I could see one whitewashed building that looked like a tiny temple of some sort. I could not understand how a village like this got to be here, wherever here was, or how it had stayed like this for so long. The only modern touch was a truck at the bottom of the hill. Far, far below in another direction, on the main road, a white Lexus, at least what was left of it, sat on the shoulder. It was the car, and not the village, that seemed out of place in this setting. There was no one I could see near it. I was surprised how far I'd managed to climb in the dark.

It came to me that the villagers must surely have heard and most likely seen the accident. In a cut in the hills like this, the sound had nowhere to go but up. They may even have seen or at least heard me running away. Ting knew I was in her home. She could have exposed me, but instead she had protected me by locking me in. When Zhang came to her place, he had called her out and tried the door. Finding it locked, he assumed I couldn't have been in it. His tone in speaking to her had been so harsh, and yet she had saved me. She'd waited until she was sure he'd gone, perhaps watching in the darkness from a little open porch I'd seen on the back of her house, a porch that afforded the same view of the road that I now had, and then she had come to make sure I was all right, and to make me tea, and to fashion some sort of bed with a blanket, something that was probably in pretty short supply in this place, to keep me warm. I wanted to cry.

Rong was talking to the driver of the truck, which was loaded down with all kinds of merchandise. There were plastic washbowls, running shoes, towels, sweaters, jackets. It was a kind of moveable general store and several people were gathered 'round it checking out the wares. Others were standing at various places on the slopes of the town. They looked like sentries in a way, and perhaps that's what they were. It seemed possible to me that the whole town knew I was there.

When everyone had made their purchases, Rong gave Ting a signal and we quickly headed the rest of the way down the hill. I felt terribly exposed there, the two hills looming over me like malevolent giants. Zhang or his henchmen could have been up there, and any moment could come swooping down to get me, probably hurting my newfound friends in the process. I thought it was very brave of them to help me. "Zhang Xiaoling," I said again, this time to the driver, and all three of them spat on the ground. The feeling in this town appeared to be pretty much unanimous on the subject of Zhang Xiaoling. I thought perhaps this was part of Zhang's fiefdom, where terrified people were forced to do whatever he asked. These three seemed prepared to defy him, something for which I was exceedingly grateful.

Five minutes later, I was lying on the bed of the truck with sweaters, jackets, pots and pans, and just about everything else piled on top of me. We were underway. It was a really rough ride. I could feel every bone, and at one point the truck stopped, and I heard someone talking to the driver. I held my breath, and soon we were on our way again.

About half an hour later, I think, the truck stopped again, but this time the driver started pulling the merchandise off me, and signaled me to get into the cab of the truck, which smelled very slightly of manure. We sped along for a couple hours that way, he talking to me, me talking back, neither of us understanding a word, but both of us nodding and smiling away.

He dropped me in front of the Forbidden City, at the north end of Tian'anmen Square. I think he would have taken me to the door of my hotel if I could have told him what and where it was. I had given some money to both Ting and Rong, although both had protested. I knew that for these people what was a posh dinner out in my hometown was a fortune for them, and I insisted they keep it. I gave the driver most of what I had left. I had enough for a taxi to the hotel. The woman who swept the sidewalk in front of the hotel was gone. I suppose she didn't expect me to get back. Twenty minutes after the man dropped me off, I was walking through the door to my room.

Rob was there. I could tell he'd been pacing. "Where have you been?" he demanded in the tone he uses when he's worried, but would prefer me to think he's annoyed. "You were supposed to get here first. Was your flight delayed or something?" He looked me up and down with a somewhat perplexed expression—perhaps I wasn't looking as well turned out as usual, what with the dirt and straw all over my clothes—before coming toward me as if to give me a hug or maybe a shake. I gave him a shake of the head of my own. Unless he liked the smell of manure, he'd regret getting any closer to me than he already was.

"Well?" he said.

I didn't know whether to laugh or cry. "No, my flight was right on time."

"Then where have you been?"

"I have no idea. I met some wonderful people, though. It's a long story, but let me summarize it this way: any man who gets between me and the shower is dead meat."

Later, not only clean but safe, I placed a call to George Matthews. Did I care it was rather early in the morning in Toronto? I did not. I reversed the charges, too. When he heard my voice he did not ask why I was calling, nor did he make any attempt at small talk. I didn't think, though, that this was because I'd awakened him. He just waited for me to say something.

"You have not been honest with me," I said, not bothering with small talk myself. "Neither you nor Dorothy have been." For some reason, my tongue and brain would no longer permit me to call her Dory. "Now you will tell me everything I need to know."

"I was afraid it might come to this," George said.

That night I dreamed about Burton and Dorothy. Burton, who was still blue of face and wearing surgical gloves, accused Dorothy of being responsible for his death. Dorothy just kept saying over and over that she was sorry.

Eleven

Lingfei was gone. I searched for her everywhere. In some ways I hoped she had used the opportunity provided by the chaos created by An Lushan to escape the bounds of the imperial harem and join the man she loved. I asked if a message had been left for me. There was none. I confess that hurt me deeply. I wondered if perhaps she was angry because I had not said good-bye to her.

I went to her apartment but someone else lived there now. Her workshop too was gone. I looked in every possible hiding place I could think of, but could find no evidence of Lingfei or of her life's work. It was as if she had never existed.

In many ways, life at the Imperial Palace returned to normal. I found I had more influence than ever before and took full advantage of it. Soon I had a splendid home in the countryside outside Chang'an, a wife of sorts, and two adopted sons, one of whom was to follow me into the Imperial Palace, the other to provide me with grandchildren some time later.

Still, I thought often of Lingfei. Was she my sister? What had happened to her? No one seemed to know, or if they did, they were not revealing that information to me. I looked for her, as I had looked for Number One Sister, in the marketplaces. I looked for her in the brothels of the Gay Quarter.

Life at the palace now was different, of course, with a new Son of Heaven, but in many ways it was the same. There was a ghost though that now haunted the quarters of the harem. It was an angry ghost, someone who had died violently, without the proper rituals to ensure that the cloud soul would be nourished.

One day, several months after I had returned to the palace, a package was delivered to me. Wrapped in a piece of fabric that I recognized as being cut from the plain robe that Lingfei wore when she worked, were a few pages of notes in my hand. It was some of the last work I had done for Lingfei. The eunuch who delivered the package said a stranger had asked him to do so. He did not know who it was. I could only guess what this would mean.

That night, I had a most disturbing dream. In it, Lingfei appeared to me. "Do you not remember me, Di-Di?" she asked. Then she told me her story.

"I was taken as one of the spoils of war by An Lushan himself," she said, tears in her eyes. "He was a loathsome man, not refined like the emperor. He had no real love of music and dance, and he did not really care for me. While I was under his control, he became very ill. Painful boils erupted on his body. He died in agony. One of his men blamed me for his death, accusing me of having poisoned him.

"One night as I slept I was wrenched from my bed and strangled *by this man, who accused me of witchcraft. He buried me under a large tree in the Imperial Park in the garden where the peonies bloom. My cloud soul roams, Di-Di,* she said. *"Help me, please."*

I awoke with a start. She had called me "little brother." I knew then that Lingfei was indeed my sister. I knew what I must do to honor her. The proper rituals must be undertaken to ensure that she could rest.

The gates of the Zhang residence were locked, but I rang the bell as long as it took to get someone to open it. It was Zhang Xiaoling with a bandage on his forehead. He didn't look happy to see me.

"We're here to see Zhang Anthony," I said. He didn't invite us in. I pushed past him, Rob right behind me, Dr. Xie bringing up the rear.

This was quite the spot the Zhang family had. The gardens were lovely and the houses in the two courtyards very elegant from the outside. One didn't need to feel sorry for them at all. They had all the modern conveniences. In fact, in the room to which we were eventually directed, an elderly man was sitting in front of a thirty-one-inch television screen, a basket on his knees.

A maid came with a tray of tea, and some candied jasmine blossoms. We waited for a time, important and wealthy people finding it necessary to put unexpected visitors in their place, I suppose, before a man in his late fifties strode into the room. He was taller than average, although still smaller than his son, and he had a Eurasian attractiveness, a lovely bone structure, and interesting eyes. I didn't think I'd recognize him, but I did. He'd been sitting to the right-hand side of Mira Tetford at the victory dinner at Dr. Xie's Beijing apartment, the man she'd been chatting up for business reasons, as I sat to her left talking to Liu David. I'd been that close and I didn't even know it. I had no idea what I was looking for, of course, not then, and I'd been hampered, as Burton hadn't been, by my total lack of facility in Chinese. I might even have been introduced to him, I couldn't remember. Somehow it seemed to be a very long time ago.

I introduced myself anyway. "Zhang Anthony, my name is Lara McClintoch," I said. "And this is Xie Jinghe, of Xie Homeopathic. I'm sure you've heard of him. With us is my partner, Rob Luczka. I am a friend of your sister Dorothy's, who, I regret to tell you is dead."

Did he speak English? I sincerely hoped so. He'd have spoken English for the first three years of his life, but not, perhaps, after that. But of course his English was impeccable, American-accented. He was a red prince after all, the son of one of Mao's closest advisors, someone who had gone on the Long March. Zhang Anthony had been educated at Harvard.

"I go by Zhang Yi, now," he said. "This is a rather presumptuous opening gambit, Ms. McClintoch. I don't know this Dorothy person. Why should I listen to you?"

"Because your son is trying to kill me."

Zhang Anthony looked sharply at Xiaoling, who couldn't meet his father's eyes. "Well then, why don't you proceed?"

"Thank you. Given that I don't know how much everyone in this room knows of this story, I will summarize. A considerable portion of the information I'm about to impart was told to me by George Norfolk Matthews, Dorothy's husband and now widower, who has confirmed many of the hypotheses I had with regard to this situation."

"I do not know these people," Zhang Anthony repeated.

"Dorothy," the old man said, taking a cricket out of the basket and holding it in his hand. It was difficult for him to do so, as his hands were gnarled with what looked to be arthritis. Still, that one word from his lips seemed a pretty good indication to me that I was in the right place.

"Dorothy and Anthony Zhang were born in Shanghai in the 1940s, Dorothy being three years older than her brother. Children born in those years after the Japanese left were called "peace babies," and that is what both Dorothy and Anthony were. But peace was a relative term then, and an elusive one at that. The Japanese had gone, but there was still civil war between the Koumintang and the Communist Party. While the Communists were seen as saviors in many ways in the late 1940s, not everyone shared that belief. On the eve of the communist takeover in 1949, Dorothy and Anthony's mother Vivian decided she had had enough of war, and perhaps of her husband as well, a man she rarely saw, and someone whom Dorothy believes might have been abusive." When I said this, Anthony looked at his hands. I decided Dorothy's mother had been right about the abuse.

"Vivian decided she was going to take the children and get out while she could. These were difficult times, however. A determined woman, Vivian managed to book passage for herself, her two children, and a nursemaid out of Shanghai on one of the last ships departing for Hong Kong before the takeover. She was not alone in trying to do so. Somehow, in the crowds on the pier, Vivian and Dorothy became separated from the nursemaid who was holding Anthony. Vivian looked everywhere, but she couldn't find her son. She left Shanghai with her daughter only. Vivian came to believe that the maid, who had been extraordinarily fond of young Anthony, had simply kept him as her own, or that the boy's father paid the nursemaid to steal the son."

"Nothing would surprise me about my father," Anthony said drily. "He was, and still is, quite a ruthless man, although as you can see he is constrained by age. Having said that, I'm afraid you have the wrong man." All eyes turned to the old man and his cricket. He looked pretty harmless to me.

"Vivian had very little time to pack, so took what she could. Dorothy, at five years of age, insisted upon taking her very favorite plaything, a small silver box, one of a set of three. She actually wanted to take all three of them, fascinated by the way they fit together, but under the circumstances she was allowed to keep only one small toy. She chose the smallest box. Dorothy could easily recall playing with all three boxes that her father had brought home after one of his lengthy trips away from Shanghai. She didn't know how her father found the tomb, although as an adult she was convinced he must have done so."

"Food," the old man said.

"You just ate," Anthony said impatiently.

I didn't think that was what the old man meant. "I think it might have been found while foraging for food. It was wartime, and soldiers had to fend for themselves. However it was located, it proved to be rather lucrative over the years as the contents were sold off. The tomb I am speaking about was that of an imperial concubine by the name of Lingfei."

"I know nothing about such a tomb."

"Lingfei," the old man said. Anthony grimaced. If this were not so serious a matter, the conversation might have been funny, what with Anthony denying everything, and his old father contradicting him with only one word every time.

"To continue, Dorothy would not leave the little box behind, so into the suitcase it went. Vivian and Dorothy eventually ended up in Canada. While Vivian remarried, and indeed had another son named Martin, she never really recovered from the loss of her little Anthony. She would not speak about him to anyone, and forbade Dorothy to ever mention his name. When Dorothy inadvertently did so as a child, her mother would take to her bed for days, and Dorothy would be wracked with guilt at having made her mother ill. Dorothy learned to say nothing, and soon it was as if the little boy had never existed.

"But Dorothy did not forget her little brother, whom she had adored. It was not until her mother died and China began to open up to the outside world, that Dorothy felt free to start looking for him, which is to say you, Anthony. The trouble was the family name is Zhang, which has to be one of the most common, if not the most common, names in China. She didn't know where to start. Furthermore, she was quite determined not to go to China to do so."

Zhang Anthony had looked a little skeptical up until this point on the subject of his sister, and for that matter everything else I said, but then he nodded. "I remember her," he said slowly. "My sister. I remember my mother, the way she felt and smelled, although I cannot recall her face, but I remember someone else, a girl. What did you say her name was?"

"Dorothy." the elderly man said. His son just looked at him. I didn't know Anthony well enough to read the expression on his face, but I think he was angry.

"Dorothy became a highly regarded specialist in Chinese art and antiquities, curator of the Asian galleries at a small but prestigious Canadian museum," I went on. "One day, in perusing the Molesworth and Cox Oriental auction catalog, she saw one of the silver boxes she had played with as a child. A relatively short time after that, she saw a second silver box that belonged to the set."

"Just a moment," Anthony said rather peremptorily. He then turned to his son and said something in Chinese.

Xiaoling shook his head no. Anthony looked at his son for a moment or two, and then said in a quiet tone that was chilling, "Then where are they?" I suppose he meant the boxes. Xiaoling didn't answer.

"Seeing these boxes on the market told Dorothy many things. One was that almost certainly the boxes had been put on the market by a relative of hers at some point in time. Furthermore, for them to be auctioned in New York at this time could well have meant that they had been smuggled out of the country. Dorothy told me that it was her stepfather who brought the boxes out of China, but it wasn't. While she would not have known at such a young age what she was doing, she herself brought one of them out. Dorothy's brother—her half brother Martin, that is—remembers the little box very well. This was perhaps the first of a series of relatively small lies Dorothy told me

which, while relatively innocuous individually, taken together had unforeseen and terrible consequences." Anthony
looked askance at my choice of words.

"Dorothy's husband actually purchased both of the
boxes on offer at her request. She told me that she did not
collect in her field of employment, but this was another un-
truth. As of eighteen months ago, George and Dorothy
owned all three of the nesting set of boxes. Dorothy said
that when they were all assembled, she was going to donate
them to the Shaanxi History Museum in Xi'an. If she had
really meant to do so, she could have done it eighteen
months ago.

"She didn't, because all of a sudden she had an idea as to
how to track down her brother. One of the boxes on offer
came from the collection of Xie Jinghe. Dorothy and
George contacted Dr. Xie and learned from him that he had
purchased the box several years previously, at least that is
what he told them. They contacted the auction house for information on the second seller, but were refused that information. Something Dr. Xie said to them, however, made
them believe it was he. Dr. Xie also told them that the box
he had sold had been in his possession for many years.
Dorothy, who after all was a museum curator, did a provenance check of her own, and she decided that there was no
evidence that the box had been in Canada in Dr. Xie's collection for any significant amount of time. Her husband,
who by now considered Dr. Xie both colleague and friend,
thought they should take Dr. Xie's word for it, that the results of Dorothy's provenance check must have missed
something. Dorothy disagreed."

"It was in my personal collection for many years," Dr. Xie said rather huffily. "I bought it in Hong Kong before it reverted to Chinese control, perfectly legally, and brought it to Canada with me, also legally."

"That is hardly the point is it, Dr. Xie?" I said. "It was looted merchandise from a very important tomb."

"Carry on, please," Anthony said impatiently. "So far all I have heard are wild and completely unsupported allegations."

"Dorothy," the old man said, putting the cricket back into the basket. I suppose he was a little senile.

"I understand why you would like to think that what I am saying is unsubstantiated, but believe me there are ways of proving all of this, and in addition to George Matthews, there are two lawyers who have heard this story from the lips of Dorothy herself, Eva Reti in Toronto and Mira Tetford in Beijing. To continue, Dorothy decided that she would find her Chinese relatives and put a stop to the smuggling at the same time. I think she had a couple of motives. She had an almost pathological fear, according to George, that someone would find out that she came from a family of criminals and that she would therefore be reviled by her colleagues in her chosen field. One might ask why, given the number of museums lately that have had to acknowledge parts of their collection are stolen goods, but that was the way it was for Dorothy. On the other hand, she really wanted to see her little brother again. She remembers you very well, Anthony. I think she missed you her entire life."

Anthony nodded. He suddenly looked very much older, as if weighed down with regret, maybe, or experiences lost. "I would have liked to have a sister when I was growing up.

I was only allowed one son, of course. That's the way it is here in China, one couple, one child. Is she really dead?"

"Dorothy dead?" the old man said. He certainly seemed to be following this conversation in English all right. "Sons are better."

Well there it was, wasn't it? Vivian could take the daughter, but she would never be allowed to take the son. It had not escaped my notice that almost all the Chinese children put up for international adoptions are girls, which says a lot about Chinese priorities.

"Yes, she's dead," I said, through clenched teeth. "To accomplish her plan, Dorothy took the box she had brought with her from China as a child, and had treasured all these years, and put it up for auction at the same place that the other two boxes were sold, assuming the seller would be checking prices in catalogs and would not only see it, but be curious enough to try to purchase it, or at least to find out who was selling it. You may not have noticed it, Anthony, but others did. In a way, though, this all happened too late for Dorothy, who suffered greatly from arthritis and was therefore not sufficiently mobile to fully put her plan into action." Anthony looked again at this father, particularly his misshapen hands.

"Going to New York to the auction would have been difficult for her, and George, her husband, who was supportive but not actually too keen on this obsession of Dorothy's, refused to go. Therefore, Dorothy conscripted me to go to New York to buy the box. She didn't want to lose it, you see, but she wanted to know who intended to purchase it, whoever came out of the woodwork as it were. I think I should have known that Dorothy was not being entirely honest with me. She told me that the set of nesting boxes would have had a fourth box, the largest, that was wood. A wood box couldn't survive over several centuries, particularly once removed from the tombs. The only way she would know that is if she'd seen the remains of the wooden box before it disintegrated, which means she saw it when it was in the tomb or immediately after. It would have fallen apart when it was moved.

"She asked me who I thought might be bidding on the box. I told her that Burton Haldimand, her successor as curator of the Asian galleries of the Cottingham Museum was trying to purchase it for the museum. I told her there was a young man, too, who seemed interested. That man was Song Liang, an employee of the Cultural Relics Bureau who was sent to purchase it on behalf of China. There was also a telephone bidder, who could have been anyone anywhere, but I am reasonably sure will prove, once courts subpoena the auction house records, to be Dr. Xie here."

"Ms. McClintoch!" Dr. Xie protested, but Anthony motioned him to be silent.

"When Dorothy realized she might lose her precious box, and still be none the wiser, she got cold feet and she herself withdrew her silver box from sale at the last minute. She told me she had to get a drink of water, but she went on another line and faxed the auction house. George told me she had a fax ready to go just in case."

Anthony turned to his son. "You have sold Lingfei's boxes!"

Xiaoling didn't answer.

"Actually he's sold more than that," I said. "He's sold a rather impressive number of other T'ang dynasty artifacts that may or may not have come from the same tomb. In fact, he has a rather effective antiquities smuggling operation going on, feeding a North American market that is panic-stricken that Chinese antiquities will soon not be available for sale in their countries.

"Sadly, Dorothy died shortly after she took the silver box off the market. George had told his wife he would support this project of hers, and somewhat reluctantly continued on with it after she died. He put the box up for sale again, this time in Beijing. Once again he sent me to try to purchase it. And, given that he had some qualms about this whole venture, he asked his friend Xie Jinghe to keep an eye on the box and on me."

All eyes now turned to Dr. Xie, who nodded. "And this is how I am to be repaid?" he said, his voice dripping with acid.

I ignored him. "Dr. Xie was happy to oblige, because, unbeknownst to Dorothy and George, he was part of Xiaoling's antiquities-smuggling scheme. The arrival of a third silver box on the market had certainly attracted his attention, and this was a way to find out what exactly was going on." I heard a sharp intake of breath from the man at my side. "Isn't that right, Dr. Xie?" This time the man did not answer.

"I have no idea why someone as wealthy as Dr. Xie might want to do such a thing, except to ensure his own supply of priceless artifacts, some of which I believe I saw in a decorating magazine a year or so ago. Perhaps, Dr. Xie, you, like others, were worried that the door would really slam shut on Chinese antiquities. I also don't know why Song Liang stole the box in Beijing. I suppose we might give him the benefit of the doubt and assume that he started out with the best of intentions, hoping to purchase the box on behalf of his country. Later the temptation got to be too much for him. He was approached by Xiaoling and he agreed to simply steal it. Xiaoling even came to the auction house in Beijing to get a look at it, and to provide some cover for the thief. He made sure that the view of the box was blocked, and that Song was able to get away. Then Song decided to double-cross the man who had paid him to steal the box. It was a very bad decision on his part.

"What do you mean a large number of T'ang dynasty artifacts?" Zhang Anthony said, as if the information had finally sunk in.

"Fifty, fifty-five, at least. A friend and colleague of mine has been through ten years' worth of auction catalogs and noted a spike in T'ang dynasty artifacts beginning about five years ago."

Anthony turned toward his son. "You have been to Lingfei's tomb, perhaps?" Xiaoling shook his head. Anthony turned back to me. "Yes, there was a tomb, and yes, we took objects from it. It kept us from starving during the worst excesses of various regimes. My father may have been a confidant of Chairman Mao, and I may have been a red prince with privileges others did not enjoy, but during the Cultural Revolution, I, a U.S.-educated teacher, was sent to the countryside along with the rest of the so-called bourgeoisie. I worked in the fields, tending herbs used for medicine, actually. Fortunately for me, it was to Shaanxi Province that I was sent. My father had told me about the tomb, and exactly where it was. I found it. A discreet sale from time to time allowed me to return to Beijing and to this comfortable home. It helped me to send my son to law school in California, too, even if he failed his final examinations. Is that so terrible?"

"That's not for me to say. Your son, however, is far from starving. He is a criminal and a bully. Not only does he smuggle antiquities, but he gets off on intimidating people. No, wait, it goes well beyond intimidation. People both hate and fear him. There are very kind and brave individuals in a little village outside this city who are terrified of him. He is the Beijing end of a group that calls itself Golden Lotus, whose activities have expanded way beyond antiquities smuggling."

Anthony just looked at his son, a question in his eyes. Xiaoling spoke to him in Chinese. When he'd finished, Anthony turned to me. "My son has forgotten to respect his father. He tells me I am a fool to listen to you."

"Then, I'll stop talking and leave."

"You will not leave," Xiaoling said.

"Yes, she will," Anthony said in a warning tone. "Whenever she chooses to do so."

"The mistake you made," I said turning once again to Xiaoling, "was to have your goons threaten me in Xi'an. That told me there was a Toronto connection that I might not have known otherwise. No, I don't think Dory Matthews was part of the smuggling operation. I think she just thrust her beloved silver box out there in what might have been an ill-conceived gesture, more vain hope than any real certainty that it would lead her to her brother. That box sure made ripples in the pond, and yes, it attracted attention, most of it dubious.

"Without those threatening phone calls in Xi'an, I would have viewed all this as a strictly Chinese problem as opposed to an international one. Until you started me on that course of thought, I had just assumed it was an unfortunate coincidence that a box that had already been withdrawn from sale once was stolen in short order. It also put me on to Dr. Xie as the seller of at least one of the boxes offered through Molesworth and Cox auction house." Once again Dr. Xie declined to comment.

"But to summarize: Zhang Xiaoling has been systematically plundering at least one tomb and probably several more in Shaanxi province somewhere, I'd guess in the area around Hua Shan. To compound this, he has been smuggling the artifacts out of the country to places like Hong Kong and North America. Dr. Xie has been helping him do that using his distribution system for Xie Homeopathic."

"You will never prove anything of the sort," Dr. Xie said.

"Maybe not. You should know, however, that I have turned the teabags you gave me in to the police for analysis, and have pointed out that Burton Haldimand may also have received teabags from you. That latter fact may be hearsay, but my teabags aren't, and I believe they will pretty much speak for themselves. I think you killed Burton. It wouldn't have taken much, given his medical condition and all the stuff he was putting into his system knowingly, and I think you knew enough about his health to finish him off."

Anthony seemed to have reached a conclusion. "All of this activity of my son will now cease, I assure you," he said. "I would only ask that you leave it to me to deal with this matter. There was a point at which we needed the money, you understand. Even I, son of a friend of Chairman Mao, required cash. The T'ang artifacts were the debris of decadent imperialism, and I felt no qualms about selling them. I would not, however, sell Lingfei's boxes. It seemed a sacrilege, if I may be permitted a modestly religious term. My son has no such hesitation, apparently. He will be dealt with. Now leave me to do so."

"I think maybe it's a little late for that," Rob said, speaking for the first time. "Wouldn't you say?"

It was at that moment that Xiaoling lunged at me. Rob had moved over toward Dr. Xie, who appeared to be edging toward the door. In an instant Xiaoling was holding me with a knife at my throat. I knew how proficient Golden Lotus was with that weapon. Dr. Xie tried to edge his way behind Xiaoling, but there was no room to do so.

"Don't move a muscle, Lara," Rob said.

"I won't," I croaked. That was easier said than done, of course. My legs had turned to mush. The only thing holding me up was Zhang's grip. The room was absolutely silent for a moment except for the chirp of crickets.

"I have nothing to do with any of this," Dr. Xie said. Xiaoling gave him a look of pure contempt.

In a louder tone, Rob spoke out. "Do you have the shot?"

"I do," said a voice not that far away.

"Zhang Anthony," Rob said in a voice I hadn't heard from him before. "You see that red dot of light on your son's skull? It's a laser. The gun where the light originates is held by an extremely proficient marksman with the Ministry of Public Security by the name of Liu David. That red dot is exactly where the bullet will penetrate your son's brain.

There is no chance he will survive it, believe me. I suggest you exercise a little parental discipline and make your son drop that knife and release Ms. McClintoch."

I suppose Anthony did what he was told even if I couldn't understand what he said. He may even have spoken in English, but I was too terrified, trying so hard not to move, to know. One fact that did get through to me, though, was that his son wasn't for taking advice from his father. "The Ministry of Public Security?" he said in perfect English, a sneer on his face. Then he said something in a louder tone in Chinese. "In case you foreigners are wondering, I have offered a considerable sum of money to this person Liu to let me leave. Given that the ministry is corrupt, I expect he will accept. Now I am going. I am taking this woman with me."

Xiaoling took a step backward. I felt the knife pull against my neck. Then a shot rang out, and Zhang Xiaoling was no more. Rob caught me before I hit the floor.

A few hours later, Rob and I were sitting on a stone bench in the Zhang family's gorgeous garden. Even in winter, it was beautiful. The compound was awash in police, all directed by Liu David. While I was the one who had insisted upon getting out of the house, my teeth were chattering as much from nervous energy as the temperature. Rob had his arm around me very tightly. He kept clenching and unclenching his jaw.

"Stop that," I said. "You're going to crack your fillings. If you think today was bad, just wait for the root canal." It was a feeble attempt at levity to be sure, but you have to do something to take your mind off how close you have just come to oblivion.

He made a pathetically inadequate attempt to smile. "For some reason I never thought my work would endanger you and Jennifer. I knew I might be in danger because of my job, but you shouldn't have been. You will tell me that fondly held belief of mine was naive."

"Good grief, Rob," I said. "I got into this mess all by myself."

"But it started with those threats at your home. I should never have left you by yourself here. When I think what could have happened . . ."

"It didn't start with the threats at my home. It started when Dorothy Matthews asked me to try to buy her own silver box."

"You wouldn't have agreed if we hadn't been stuck in that hotel."

"You don't know that."

"Furthermore, it was Golden Lotus," he said. "And they were my responsibility."

There was obviously no arguing with him on this subject. "I think we need to adopt a lighter tone here," I said firmly. "Say something funny."

Rob pondered that for awhile. "I can't think of anything right this minute. Nothing about this strikes me as amusing yet. I have to tell you that I just didn't take to that guy, Xiaoling, or whatever his name is, was. Not only does he impugn the integrity of a fellow law enforcement officer, but he manhandles my girl."

"Girl?" I said. "Now that's funny."

Epilogue

I went to the tree in the peony garden that Number One Sister described and began to dig. After much effort, I still could not find Lingfei. I knew what I must do.

It was then that I had a tomb built for Number One Sister. I decorated it lavishly with paintings of her life. I had carved out of granite a coffin for her, and a tablet inscribed in her honor to remember her. Into the coffin I put robes suitable to her status in the Imperial Palace. The proper ritual, the summoning of the cloud soul, was observed so that her soul might rest, and an impressive funeral procession was arranged to accompany the hearse. I burned a great deal of paper money in the tomb to speed Lingfei on her way, and I put many beautiful objects of gold and silver, pearls, and jade in the tomb for her use. I left many terra-cotta servants and musicians, a veritable Pear Garden Orchestra, to sustain her. I also had three silver boxes made by the finest silversmiths in Chang'an, each one made by a different artist to my specifications so that no one would know the whole story of Lingfei's work. Into the smallest I put the lock of Lingfei's hair I had taken so long ago. I left it with her. The ghost that was haunting the harem was seen no more.

I wrote a poem the day before I buried Lingfei. It was a poor effort, unworthy of her, but it expressed my heartbreak. It too is in the tomb with her.

> Tomorrow in the gray dawn I will lay you to rest.
> Peonies bloom, but there is no one to share them.
> Snow blankets the courtyard, but there is no one to savor it.
> The drifting scent of patchouli haunts me.
> The breeze tinkling through the jade speaks your name.

I am an old man now, infirm and lonely despite sons and grandchildren who treat me with respect. Number One Son is a mandarin, Number Two a eunuch. Number Two Son has perhaps even more influence than I ever had, as eunuchs have been put in charge of the workings of the Imperial Palace. I listen with interest to their stories of intrigue.

More often than not, I sit in the gazebo in my garden. Hanging there are several pieces of jade that tinkle in the wind, ling, ling, ling. The jade is there to remind me of my sister, beautiful Lingfei. I tell my grandsons that brigands lurk in the bamboo forest on the edge of our domain, and that a ghost, a woman with fiery eyes and disheveled hair, haunts the well. Sometimes when I hear the sound the wind makes as it rattles the bamboo, I think it is a message from Number One Sister. I miss her still.

* * *

Zhang Xiaoling paid poor farmers the equivalent of sixty-five dollars a night to rob the tomb of Lingfei, imperial concubine and alchemist. And not just Lingfei's. Where hers was located was a large burial area that contained at least a dozen tombs, almost all of them looted to some degree or another. Her tomb was not too far from Hua Shan, partway, in fact, between two T'ang capitals, Chang'an and Luoyang.

Sixty-five dollars could be pretty close to the annual net income of these extraordinarily poor people, so I guess it's hard to blame them. Still, there was a real cottage industry going for a while, with many people in the area participating. I'm not sure the powers that be care what motive drove these people to rob the tombs, because it is possible that several of them will be executed.

Authorities were taken to the tomb by Anthony. The portable objects were gone, and all that was left was the sarcophagus, a large stone plaque that tells a rather sad story, placed there by someone by the name of Wu Yuan, and some extraordinary frescoes that in all probability illustrate the life of Lingfei. They show her in the imperial gardens, playing in an orchestra, tending to the sick, and yes, up there hovering over a mountain with the Jade Women. It's hard to imagine what life in the imperial harem would be, even under a relatively benevolent ruler like Illustrious August. It was logical, I suppose, to build her tomb not far from Hua Shan, home to the Jade Women, guardians of alchemists. The sarcophagus was opened, but there was no skeleton inside, just a few scraps of silk cloth that may have been her robes. I'm told that there may never have been one, that her body was not found, but rather a ceremony called "summoning the dead" was performed in the absence of a body.

I think Burton had relatively little trouble uncovering the Xi'an part of the operation. I think, and in fact Liu David has confirmed, that there were all kinds of rumors circulating in the antique markets of Xi'an that there was a massive looting operation going on. It's hard to keep that scale of operation secret, particularly outside the big cities where people keep track of their neighbors. A few strong young men are hired, they head out at night, and all of a sudden these young men, who spend a lot of time sitting idle during the day, have a lot more money than they used to, knockoff designer duds, a computer maybe, a big TV. Figure it out! Whatever they're doing, it is unlikely to be legal. That, in fact, is why Liu David was in Xi'an, to try to get a handle on the rumors, doing officially what Burton was doing for himself.

Unlike me, Burton spoke Chinese. He asked around, and eventually attracted attention, both from the people who had heard the rumors, and unfortunately the masterminds, Zhang Xiaoling and Xie Jinghe. I don't think that Burton had any clue that Dorothy had put the small box up for sale, nor do I think he realized just how far the tentacles of Golden Lotus reached or even that they existed until it was too late. I suspect that to him this was a simple case of locals looting tombs. He found someone who was prepared to talk about what he'd heard, the man in the mosque. We know what happened to him. Oblivious to the danger, at least right up until the last minute, Burton headed, not for Hua Shan exactly, but to that area to try to find the tomb.

In a way, the only mistake Burton made was going to see

Zhang Xiaoling. Burton overheard Zhang talking to the police the day the silver box was stolen in Beijing, when Zhang was arranging to absent himself from the investigation. It was actually Liu David who confirmed Zhang's name for Burton, and told who he was, not realizing that this information would get Burton killed. I don't think Xiaoling told Burton anything—although we'll never know, both parties to the conversation being deceased—but it did put Golden Lotus on the alert. When Burton went to Xi'an, possibly only on a hunch that if there was a T'ang tomb that was the place to look for it, some really evil people were waiting for him.

I suppose what bothers me more than anything about these events is the role I played in Burton's death. It was I who planted the idea in his head that Zhang Xiaoling, the man in black, was somehow involved in the robbery at Cherished Treasures House. If I hadn't told him that, perhaps he'd be alive now.

Rob disagrees, predictably I suppose. He says Burton would have attracted the wrong kind of attention all by himself, determined as he was to find the silver box. While I do know there is an element of truth in what Rob says, I wish I could believe it wholeheartedly. On the other hand, given all his health problems, and his attempts at self-medication, Burton wasn't really long for this world anyway.

Dr. Xie is in Canada, I regret to say. Somehow he managed to bribe his way out of China. China has asked that he be sent back. My home country does not usually extradite people to countries with the death penalty, so it will be interesting to see how Dr. Xie with all his money makes out in this regard. Due process in this kind of case takes a very long time in Canada, and so it will be some time before we know how this one will turn out. If he is forced to return to China, it will be equally interesting to see whether they will execute someone of his standing for smuggling. In China today, due process is still in short supply where crimes of this sort are concerned. No matter what happens, I rest easy knowing that his part of the smuggling will cease. It is people like Xie and their insatiable appetite for antiquities that fuel both the illegal trade and the looting of tombs.

While we were meeting with Zhang Anthony, police officers were raiding the Xie Homeopathic warehouse in Xi'an. Antiquities were indeed found. Xie used his legitimate business shipments to mask his illegal ones, and used his warehouses in Hong Kong, Vancouver, and Los Angeles to store the antiquities before passing them along to be sold, either through legitimate dealers or not-so-legitimate ones. Several auction houses are being investigated to see if they in fact knew the objects were looted.

My teabags are an important part of the case against Dr. Xie in the matter of the murder of Burton Haldimand, and the attempted murder of a certain antique dealer. Apparently there was arsenic in them. I'm glad I only used one, and that arsenic has to build up in the system to kill you. For whatever reason, Burton didn't realize until too late what he was getting himself in for. Most likely the man in the mosque told him that the rumors placed the tomb not far from Hua Shan. Burton went there to see what he could find, and already terribly ill, died in that dreary hotel.

I expect there would be arsenic in Burton's teabags, too, if they could be found, but they, like his tea kettle, have disappeared. David thinks that Xiaoling's goons were following Burton to Hua Shan, probably intending to kill him on the spot rather than waiting for the teabags to do their deadly work. They didn't have to kill him, at least there is no evidence they did so, but they did get rid of the evidence. It may be that Burton suddenly realized he was being followed, hence his panicky call to me. I will always remember his attempt to warn me of the danger that he suddenly realized existed.

Liu David of the Ministry of Public Security was investigating a corrupt official of the Beijing Cultural Relics bureau by the name of Song Liang, aka Mr. Knockoff. Burton conveniently afforded him entrèe into the world of art and those who buy it. David, too, was almost certain that it was Song who had stolen the silver box, and when Song turned up dead in Xi'an, David was sent there to investigate further.

Song had been sent to New York by his employers to try to purchase the silver box for China. While he was as unsuccessful as the rest of us, he did realize that others wanted this highly desirable object. Who knows what thoughts went through his mind? Maybe the bright lights and wealth of New York were just too much for him, and he wanted a piece of it. It was perhaps then that he had the idea of using the silver box as his entrèe into the smuggling racket. If so, he was decidedly out of his league. All it got him was dead. I may have some sympathy for the poor farmers who loot. I have none for someone like Song Liang. I think of Ting and Rong who saved me from Xiaoling at great personal risk, and the truly poor conditions under which they live. For all their poverty they had a dignity that few others in this saga share.

People to whom I have told this story ask me how I knew that Liu David was a policeman when I saw him in the market outside the Baxian Gong that day. I have a tendency to say it was feminine intuition. That's really not true. The answer is very simple. I more or less live with a plainclothes cop. Once, early in our relationship, I saw him at a restaurant. He was with two other men. I was about to go over to say hello to him, but he gave me this almost imperceptible shake of the head, and I kept going right past his table. I got the same look, an identical tiny shake of the head from David and I just knew. True, I saw him at a time when I was feeling relatively safe, having just heard the results of the toxicology tests on Burton. Under different circumstances, I might have seen him in an entirely different, and inaccurate, light.

David's investigation has broadened and caught a corrupt customs agent or three. Several people at Xie Homeopathic are being investigated as well. As for Zhang Anthony, he may well get off scot-free. He says he didn't know what his son was up to, and maybe he didn't. He wouldn't be the first parent to be surprised by an offspring's extracurricular activities. However, he did sell objects from Lingfei's tomb over the years. The question is whether it was so long ago that nobody will care. Dorothy's silver box was found in the trunk of Xiaoling's car. That would be his second car, after the white Lexus, in this case a red BMW. The wrecked white Lexus by the side of the road in the hills outside Bejing had no plates, but its serial number has been traced to Xiaoling.

Now that the head has been cut off, metaphorically speaking, Golden Lotus, Zhang Xiaoling's group of thugs, has more or less disbanded. In Toronto several were arrested for their involvement in Dr. Xie's antiquities smuggling operation. Good riddance is about all one can say.

That meant I could go back home. I love my little Victorian cottage even more than before. I have made one concession to the events of the past many months, which is that I have permitted Rob to put a gate in the fence between our two backyards, so that he can go out his back door and into mine. I tell him that the reason I agreed was so that I could stay in my own house if he managed to annoy some other scum, and that next time he's on his own in the hotel. Really, though, it's a small acknowledgment on my part of his importance in my life.

Before we left China, Jennifer came to Beijing and we had an early Christmas together. Rob had to stay for a few days to wrap things up with David, so we sent her a ticket. We went to the Forbidden Palace, the Great Wall, wandered through the hutongs, shopped in the markets, everything in fact that visitors to Beijing should do. Everywhere we went, people were lovely, everything we saw a jewel. I believe that despite all that happened, I fell in love with Beijing all over again.

One of the highlights of our time together was an invitation to dinner at Liu David's apartment, modest by Xie Jinghe standards, but attractive just the same. It is a real honor to be invited to a Chinese home. One of the other guests was a stylish woman by the name of Li Lily, a fellow officer of David's. At first I didn't recognize her without the shabby clothes and the fake scar on her cheek. David may not have returned my phone calls, but he made sure that someone was watching out for me nonetheless.

I did get to light some incense for Burton, too, at the

lovely Taoist temple called White Cloud, a serene and peaceful place in the bustle and noise of Beijing. Burton was an unusual man, but in his own way he was dedicated to art and history. I think of him every time I enter the doors of the Cottingham Museum where someone else now heads the Asian galleries, galleries named the Dorothy Matthews Asian galleries, thanks to a large donation from George. It's strange how things turn out sometimes.

I have no idea if Dorothy had any inkling of the danger to which she was exposing me, or whether if she did, she cared. If George knows the answer to that question, he is keeping that information to himself. I suppose she thought that by deciding she would donate Lingfei's boxes to the Shaanxi Museum, she was not only persuading me to do what she wanted, but was also mitigating her personal sense of guilt. George Matthews is donating the two boxes in his collection to the museum where the three boxes will be reunited for the first time in about sixty years.

Mao Zedong, a man Dorothy despised, often used a strategy that he called "luring snakes from their lair." He would encourage people to criticize his regime publicly, but when they did so, their words were turned against them. Thus exposed for their beliefs, they became objects of extreme vilification. Many of them died. I suppose that, in a way, was what Dorothy was trying to do, using the lure of the silver box to encourage a smuggler to identify himself. People died as a result of this ploy, too. Perhaps more than anything else, though, she wanted to find her long-lost brother. I try to have some sympathy for that. In a way, she sent the little silver box out as a message to him: I am here. Come and find me. Instead the message was received by people who understood it entirely differently, as a signal that their smuggling operation had been identified.

Regardless of Dorothy's intentions, I have not worn the pearls she left me. I don't expect I ever will. My plan is to donate them to a charity auction in exchange for a tax receipt. I'm thinking that an organization that helps women leave their abusive husbands might be just the thing. Every now and then I remember that Diesel, our shop guard cat, didn't take to Dorothy. I plan to pay more attention now when he sulks off to the back room when someone enters the store.

There was a poem in Lingfei's tomb, carved into a stone. David had a calligrapher and artist make an illustrated copy of its five lines for me, and had it framed. It's beautiful, the margins decorated with peonies, and at the bottom a winter scene with a lovely Chinese house with T'ang rooflines surrounded by snow. It has a place of honor in my home. The Chinese words sounded lovely when David read them to me, and he gave me a translation of it. He says the translation cannot capture the spirit of the original, only its words. It's a poem of love, I think, to someone precious who is gone. I value it more highly than any pearls.

I suppose, in wrapping up this story of a Chinese alchemist and her silver boxes, that in all fairness I should point out that if you are looking for the recipe for the elixir of immortality, I'm afraid I've told you all I know.